GRACE AND MERCY

GRACE AND MERCY

BRITTNEY HOLMES

Urban Books
1199 Straight Path
West Babylon, NY 11704

IBSN: 978-1-61523-047-1

Printed in the United States of America

Dedication

This is for all of the individuals who have been or are currently victims of abuse within close relationships. Whether the abuse is/was mental, emotional, or physical, I pray that God grants you complete deliverance so that your spirit may be renewed.

Acknowledgments

As always, I'd like to give honor and praise to God—my Savior and keeper—for all He has done for me. Lord, I can't thank you enough for all of the blessings and lessons you've allowed me to experience. I pray that as I continue on into adulthood, I will remember everything you've instilled into me through others, so that I will not stray. I pray that you will keep me covered in your blood and I will continue to use my gifts to acknowledge you.

To my parents, Jonathan Bellamy and Kendra Norman-Bellamy: I appreciate you both for the way you raised me. Through all of the love, support, reprimands, and encouragement, I turned out to be a pretty great young lady (smile). I promise I'll continue to make you proud as I evolve into the blessed woman God has created me to be. To Jimmy Lee Holmes: Daddy, I'm looking at your picture right now and your smile is the mirror image of mine. I know you are in heaven with the same look upon your face. I pray I've made you proud as well.

To Crystal, my baby sister: we've put up with each other for sixteen years and we argue quite a bit, but it's all in love. I hope that you do well in school and go on to do even greater things in life thereafter. I may think about letting you move in with me once you graduate, but don't bug me about it!

To my grandparents, Bishop and Mrs. Harold H. Norman, Mr. Jesse and Mrs. Dorothy Holmes, and the late Elder Clinton and Mrs. Willie Mae Bellamy, and the rest of my extended family (uncles, aunts, and cousins): thank you for always praying for me even when I may think I don't need or deserve it. For always being in my corner when it comes to my desires in life, I love you.

Terrance, my cousin and publicist ... chauffeur, photographer, advisor ... you wear many hats and you wear them well. Thank you for being there for me whenever I needed you.

To all of my friends from the great Redan High School— you know I wish I could name you all—thank you, thank you, thank you for supporting, loving, and encouraging me. To all of my close girlfriends (you know who you are), I hope we'll forever be friends, no matter where life takes us. May God bless you all in your future endeavors ... because I know we'll all be successful! To the great Redan High School— faculty, staff, and students—thank you all for your continuous support and for seeing me as a member of the Raider family even though I'm no longer a student there. To my new family of friends at the University of Georgia (Go, Dawgs!): thank you for bonds that I hope will last a lifetime.

All of my love to my spiritual family at my home church, Revival Church Ministries (Bishop Harold H. Norman a.k.a. Granddaddy), and my home away from home church, Church of God by Faith Ministries (Pastor Wayne Mack)—I thank you for your prayers, support, and the guidance I've received while participating in both ministries. You all have been by my side from the very beginning and I plan on taking you all the way to the end.

Kendra Norman-Bellamy (a.k.a. Mommy), Victoria Christopher Murray, Jacquelin Thomas, Stephanie Perry Moore, Tia McCollors, Sherri Lewis, Tanya Finney, Toschia Moffett, Vivi Monroe Congress, Michelle Stimpson, Vanessa Miller, Shewanda Riley, and Norma (Jarrett) York—thank you for being great role models in work and in life that I can look up to as I mature. Your literary works have inspired me beyond comprehension and I pray that my work is continuously blessed through your words.

To my publisher, Urban Books (Urban Christian imprint), my experience with you has been one that I will cherish for a lifetime. Thank you for making all my literary dreams come true. Special appreciation goes out to my editor, Joy-lynn Jossel. Thank you for your constructive criticism, and for challenging my creativity. I know that I am a better writer because of you.

And finally, to my readers, this book deals with an issue that is widely known across the universe. Though you may experience a variety of emotions while turning the pages, I hope this novel touches you in a way that none of my previous works have. I pray that by the time you read the last word of this book, you come to realize that there is a blessing and a lesson in every negative situation you may go through in life. So while weathering the storm, just remember that God is carrying you through. And in the end, you will be victorious! God bless and enjoy!

Chapter 1

The alarm clock was much too loud for Kenda's taste as she rolled over and hit the snooze button. Rolling back over, she hid under her pillow to block the sun's rays that had invaded the darkness that had surrounded her the night before. As soon as she felt like she was falling back into her deep sleep, her mother barged in and interrupted.

"Wake up, sunshine," Maxine Tyson sang joyfully as she pulled back the curtains to allow more sunlight into the room.

Kenda rolled over and groaned, not bothering to unbury herself. "Mom, please. Can't I sleep in on the last day of summer? Tomorrow we go back to school and I'm dreading it." She was surprised her mother was even home. Usually, her parents worked on Sundays.

"But you're about to be a senior," her mother said.

"Who cares? I'll be a senior . . . and still in school," Kenda moaned.

"Well, if you are going to sleep all day, I guess I'd better call Chantal back and tell her that you don't feel like going shopping." Kenda continued to lie motionless under the covers. "And I guess I'd better tell your dad that he can put his wallet away, too." Maxine laughed out loud when Kenda's sheets flew onto the floor as she jumped out of bed.

"I'm up, I'm up!"

"All right," Maxine said, catching her breath, "but Chantal and Roslyn aren't going to be here until one, so I guess that gives you two hours to get ready and eat a little breakfast."

"That's all the time I need," Kenda said as she watched her mother walk out of the room.

She wiped the sleep from her eyes and headed to her closet, scanning the many garments that lined the walls. Kenda pulled out a blue denim skirt and an orange halter top and threw them onto her bed before she walked out of her room and into the bathroom. She flicked on the light and stepped out of her pajamas, and then stared at her reflection in the mirror.

At the tender age of twelve, Kenda had been prematurely blessed with womanly curves. Now seventeen, she used them to her advantage every chance she got. Many guys had tried any and everything to get her attention, but very few had accomplished that mission. Kenda never let those who were lucky enough to impress her think that they had the upper hand. If she wasn't able to use a man to get what she wanted, then the relationship would be over before it could start. She used guys all the time and to her, the game never got old.

Kenda turned the shower on full blast, and stepped under the hot water. As she washed her body, she thought about the last guy she'd been in a relationship with: Raymond Shepherd. He was tall, dark, and handsome, but he wasn't the typical high school guy. He never felt the need to downplay his feelings for Kenda, telling her on more than one occasion that she was a beautiful, priceless gem that he'd never want to lose. But he wasn't down with Kenda's golddigging ways. Although he had the cash, he had not been too pleased with spending it all on her. He worked hard for his money, and felt she didn't deserve all that she had been taking.

When Raymond broke up with her, Kenda was surprised that she was actually hurt. It wasn't until after he was out of her life, that she realized that she had actually developed real feelings for him. Seeing him around school was difficult. He was so good-looking and genuinely nice, and he always spoke to her and even compliantly worked with her on various school projects. Although they weren't the best of friends anymore, they were friends, nonetheless.

Kenda stepped out of the shower and wrapped herself in a large towel. After brushing her teeth, she removed the shower cap from her head and let her kinky, nearly jet black hair fall against her shoulders. Some days she hated her wavy mane, but on days like today, when she felt like doing nothing to her hair, she loved to let it flow freely. Kenda quickly washed her hands before putting in her contact lenses, and then she moved into her bedroom to towel dry and moisturize her body. When she was done, she slipped into her clothes and ran a wide-tooth comb through her hair to tame those strands that never stayed in place. She looked into her mirror and decided to enhance her natural beauty with eyeliner, mascara, and lip gloss.

Kenda pranced downstairs and into the kitchen where her parents and her younger brother were enjoying their Sunday morning brunch.

"Morning," she said to father.

"Good morning, sweetheart," Xavier said as his daughter sat down. He eyed her outfit for a moment, but said nothing.

"Wassup, snot face." That was the greeting her brother, Aundrey, gave.

She smirked. "Nothing much, big head."

"Must you guys start this early in the day?" Maxine asked, placing a plate of eggs, bacon, and fruit in front of Kenda.

"He started it." Kenda tattled as if she were a child in grade school.

"Baby girl?" her father called.

"Yes, Daddy?"

"Don't you think that skirt is a little too short?" As he spoke, he looked at the jean skirt that stopped mid-thigh.

"Daddy, you bought me this skirt," Kenda said while shoving a fork full of eggs in her mouth.

"I did?" Xavier looked at it again. "Well, where's the receipt? I need to take it back."

Kenda laughed at her father's memory loss. He'd just purchased her the Apple Bottoms skirt a few weeks earlier. Maybe he didn't remember because he'd been on his cell phone at the time she'd asked him for it, but it didn't matter because there was no return on sale items. Kenda pulled at the shirt as she continued to eat. She was happy he hadn't said anything about the sleeveless top she was wearing. It had been a gift from one of her many male admirers, and she didn't feel like answering any questions about the guy who her father had never met.

Xavier's cell phone rang almost simultaneously with his wife's. "Tyson, Tyson, & Baker. Tyson speaking. How may I assist you?" They're voices echoed in harmony as both spoke into their Bluetooth devices in natural business tones.

Kenda's parents always had some type of communication device attached to their ears or to their hips, and it usually had something to do with their law firm. Tyson, Tyson & Baker was a very successful, seven-year-old law firm that her parents owned. They ran the company as tight as they could. For a small business, their demand was pretty high, usually requiring a lot of their time.

"We're going to have to go into the office today." Xavier had ended his call and was placing his empty plate in the sink. "That was Patricia. Lawrence needs to see us about his case."

"Apparently so. That was Lawrence on my end," Maxine informed him. She looked at her children. "Guys, we're going to be gone for most of the day, so if you go out, please remember to lock up the house."

"Yes, ma'am," they said.

Kenda wasn't surprised at all. Her parents practically lived at their office. She used to feel neglected when she was younger, but now she had become settled in the lifestyle. Deep down, though, she still wished that they spent more time with her and her brother. With their work schedules, just the simple ability to talk to them when she need to was wishful thinking.

"Kenda, I'm leaving my Visa for you to go shopping." Xavier pulled out his wallet as he spoke. "Don't get carried away," he added as he handed her the card.

"I won't," Kenda replied. When Xavier hesitated releasing the card, she added, "I promise."

"All right, we're gone." Maxine was practically already out the door when she made the announcement.

When she finished eating, Kenda retired in her room to wait on her friends' arrival. She turned on her stereo and replaced Beyoncé with her favorite artist, Alicia Keys, immediately turning it to her favorite song. She glanced at the clock at her bedside and wondered what time her friends would arrive.

Her best friends, Chantal Black and Roslyn Jones, were two totally different people, and that was probably why she loved them so much. Chantal was outgoing, while Roslyn, who they called Lyn, was more of an introvert. Chantal never had a problem with telling someone how she felt about them, whether good or bad, and she loved to cause a scene. Roslyn hardly ever spoke her mind unless she was trying to resolve a conflict or give advice. If Kenda had to label her best friends, she'd give Chantal the title of Drama Queen, while Roslyn would be dubbed the Peacemaker.

Chantal was the tallest of the three; she was also the darkest. At five foot nine, she had the stereotypical figure of a model: tall and lean. Her smooth dark skin and slim curves made up for her personality, which wasn't as tough as she tried to portray it to be.

Roslyn was the shortest and the prettiest, in a girl-next-door kind of way. She was five-five and thick in all the right places. Her shoulder-length, reddish-brown hair, and doe-like eyes added to her look of innocence, and her quiet personality caused people to label her as mysterious, wondering what was behind the good-girl masquerade. But once they got to know her, they found that it was no cover up; it was truly who she was.

Kenda, who seemed to be in between the two personalities of her friends, had the fairest skin. At five foot seven, her glowing, honey-brown skin and womanly figure got her most of the attention, and she didn't mind one bit. When first meeting someone, Kenda appear to be very shy. Then after getting to know her, people would find that she was actually outgoing and had no reservations when it came to speaking her mind.

When the three were together, they were known as the Terrific Trio. They loved the attention that they received, especially from guys. But the only one who really took advantage of it was Kenda. Her friends often told her that if she didn't quit while she was ahead, she would have to pay a price for her greed.

Kenda sat up in her bed when she heard someone burst into her room. "Boy, don't you know how to knock?" she yelled at her sixteen-year-old brother.

"No, not really." Aundrey laughed. "Anyway, your *fine* friends are downstairs."

Kenda glanced at her clock; she couldn't believe she'd fallen asleep. She hopped out of bed, looked in her closet, and grabbed her purse, a pair of sandals, and the short sleeved jean jacket that matched her outfit. While examining herself in the mirror, Kenda ran her fingers through her hair, and then smoothed down her shirt before going downstairs. She smiled at her friends who sat on the sofa in the living room.

"Hey, chicks," she said as she joined them with Aundrey following close behind. Chantal had on less clothing than she did, and it seemed as if Aundrey couldn't stop staring at the endlessness of her legs.

Chantal chuckled as Aundrey continued to drool. "Wassup, girl?" she said, pulling at the material that was supposed to be a skirt as she stood. "Are you ready to go?"

"Yeah, 'cause we need to hit the mall before it gets crowded." Roslyn stood and straightened out the straps on her spaghetti strapped shirt, and pulled at the bottom of her denim shorts so that they would rest smoothly over her hips.

"So," Aundrey said, finally finding his voice, "do you lovely ladies need an escort this afternoon?" He stood three inches taller than Chantal, making him an even six feet.

Chantal and Roslyn exchanged glances, then they both looked at Kenda before all three girls burst into laughter.

"Drey, we don't need *you* to escort us anywhere," Kenda said over the continued laughter.

Aundrey sat on the sofa and kept his eyes on his sister's friends. "I wouldn't be too sure about that," he replied, still looking them up and down.

Kenda sucked her teeth as she and her friends walked out of the house. "Whatever, Drey. Lock the door," she called over her shoulder.

They got into Chantal's black Chrysler Sebring convertible and rode down Interstate 285 toward Northlake Mall. The parking lot was already packed, and the girls laughed when Chantal almost hit another car just to get an available space.

"Girl, you better be careful," Kenda said as she got out of the car. "You just got this for your birthday."

"And you know your daddy will kill you if he finds out that you done got into an accident after having the car for just three months," Roslyn added.

As the friends walked inside, the mall was bustling with shoppers. Most were teens who were taking advantage of last minute back-to-school sales. As they made their way through the crowd, the three girls waved at a few people they recognized. As they strolled past several stores, Kenda and her friends were talking and laughing so much that Kenda was hardly paying attention to where she was going and ran right into her ex-boyfriend. Raymond Shepherd's strong hands gripped her forearms in an effort to keep her from falling into his chest. Immediately, Kenda's face flushed as he graced her with the gorgeous smile that first caught her attention a year ago.

"Hey, Ray," she said, backing up, trying to regain her composure.

"Wassup, Kenda?" he replied and then nodded toward Roslyn and Chantal.

The girls smiled their greeting before he turned his attention back to Kenda as she spoke again.

"I see where you've been spending your money," she said, noticing the Footlocker bag in his hand.

Raymond laughed. "Yeah. You know I had to get the new Jordans. I may not be able to be like Mike, but I might as well wear his shoes while I'm tryin', right?"

Kenda giggled. "Yeah. Might as well."

They stared at each other for a moment, neither knowing what else to say.

Raymond broke the tense silence. "So . . . I guess I'll see you tomorrow."

"Uh, sure," she said, and then watched as he walked away.

Chantal looped her arm with Kenda's and stared as Raymond's long, confident strides led him out of the mall's doors. "Girl, I don't know how you let a man that fine get away." She smiled. "Well, actually, I do."

Kenda rolled her eyes as they walked together into a department store. "Please. Don't even remind me."

"You know he still likes you," Roslyn said quietly, like it was some big secret. Her unexpected words caused Kenda to drop the dress she'd been looking at. Roslyn grinned and added, "I'm serious, girl. You didn't see the way he was smiling at you?"

"Not really," Kenda mumbled as she picked up the dress, placed it back on the rack, and picked up another in a smaller size.

Kenda continued to scope out the store as her friends talked about how Raymond was a one-of-a-kind guy and other things she didn't really feel like discussing. There was no need to indulge herself in the harsh reality of her breakup with the only guy she'd ever really cared for. She walked to the junior/misses section of the store and looked through the skirts, pants, and dresses that were on display. A few caught her eyes, and she decided to try them on. When she turned around, she bumped into a tall, handsome stranger dressed as if he were on his way to take part in a GQ fashion show.

"Oh," Kenda said as she kneeled to pick up the items she'd dropped. "I'm sorry."

The GQ guy helped her pick up her things. "No need to apologize. I should have been more careful," he said as he returned to his full height and handed her the clothes. He seemed to become speechless as he looked into her face.

Kenda's brown skin instantly turned red under the man's intense gaze. She fingered a strand of her hair as she looked down to hide her blushing. She wanted to continue making her way toward the dressing room, but her feet seemed to be fixed in their position. Finally the man extended his hand, and Kenda got a quick glimpse of professionally manicured nails and a wrist decorated with a sleek Rolex watch.

"Jerome Smith," he said.

Kenda took his strong hand and shook it softly. "Kenda. Kenda Tyson."

Jerome smiled, showing two even rows of pearly white teeth. "A lovely name for a lovely woman." He continued to hold her hand.

Kenda was sure her face was about to crack from the wide smile that was plastered there. "Thank you." She could hear Chantal and Roslyn's voices nearing, but suddenly, all was silent. Peeking around Jerome's lean frame for verification, she saw that it was indeed her friends that she'd heard approaching. Kenda caught a glimpse of them standing in the distance and wanted to die when they burst into laughter. Jerome slowly turned toward them and smiled. The girls wiggled their fingers in a flirty wave.

"Those your friends?" he asked, turning his attention back toward Kenda.

"Unfortunately." She shrugged and reluctantly freed her hand from his. "Well, it was nice meeting you . . . Jerome, but I have to go now."

"Wait." His deep voice stopped her footsteps as she walked away from him. "What do you say about us getting together some time?"

Kenda looked back at her friends who were obviously straining to hear what Jerome was asking her. "Umm, I don't know. I don't even know you and—"

Jerome's smile was wide. "I'm not asking you to marry me. I'm not even asking for a date. I just wanna get to know you." His gaze was deep and intense.

Kenda's heart skipped a beat as she looked into his face. Even his light brown eyes seemed to be smiling at her.

"Sure. I guess that would be cool." She rattled off her number and he saved the digits in his cell phone.

"I'll give you a call," he promised as he backed away and walked out of the store.

Kenda stood in place as her friends rushed up to her, bombarding her with questions.

"Girl, who was that?" Roslyn asked.

Chantal placed her hands on her slender hips. "How come you didn't introduce us?"

"Did you just give him your number? You don't even know him," Roslyn scolded.

"Why didn't you introduce us?" Chantal asked again.

"He looks a little old, Kenda" Roslyn observed. "Did he tell you how old he was?"

"Hel-lo," Chantal waved her hands for attention. "Why didn't you introduce us?"

Kenda covered her ears and closed her eyes. "Will you two please back up off of me?" Her friends became silent and took a few steps back. "Dang." Kenda breathed deeply and prepared to satisfy her girls' curiosity. "His name is Jerome Smith, and yes, I gave him my number, and I did it so I *can* get to know him." She paused and thumbed through her mental catalog of questions, recalling the ones they'd asked. "No, I don't know how old he is, and I really don't care at this point." She looked at Chantal. "And I didn't introduce you because *he didn't ask me to.*"

Kenda's attitude made Chantal take a few more steps back. "Sorry if we have an interest in our best friend's life," she said as she continued to peruse through racks of clothing. "He wasn't *that* cute no how."

Roslyn shook her head and chucked. "*Anyway.*" She turned her attention toward Kenda. "For real girl, I don't think you should have given him your number."

"Why not?" Kenda asked.

Roslyn smacked her lips as if her friend should have better sense. "Because he could be a serial killer for all you know."

Kenda rolled her eyes and headed toward the dressing room. Jerome's smiling face popped into her head as she tried on the various merchandise. His pearly white smile, his dancing, brown eyes, and his masculine scent—it all lingered in her mind. His persona screamed money and she couldn't wait to spend it.

Chapter 2

Chantal pulled into the student parking area of Fairfield High School and cut off the engine. She, Roslyn, and Kenda stepped out of the convertible in style. Chantal's strapless dress swayed as she walked in her black heels, making her an even six feet, and the black half-jacket made the outfit look more chic. Roslyn's hip hugger jean Capri pants flattered the curves of her wide hips, and the orange off-the-shoulder top went extremely well with her orange, three-inch-heel sandals. Kenda's ruffled knee-length skirt showed off her toned legs, and the pink V-neck shirt set off her skin tone with her pink heels adding about three inches to her height.

As they walked toward the school, several students who knew them gave compliments and looks of approval. As soon as she stepped inside of the building, Kenda was stopped by an administrator. She placed her arms along her sides and showed the woman that her skirt was well past her fingertips, as per the school's dress code requirement.

"Dang, these teachers always sweatin' us about clothes," Chantal said, barely out of the administrator's earshot as they walked off. "They need to be glad we come to school at all."

Roslyn rolled her eyes and Kenda let out a small laugh as they continued to walk toward the cafeteria to see which homeroom they'd been assigned. They pushed their way through the crowd to see the lists of names. Chantal used one manicured finger to run through the names, seemingly at the speed of light. She pushed her way out of the crowd and grabbed her friends.

"Okay, we're all in different homerooms, but with the way we filled out our schedules, we should have at least two classes with each other. I'm in Mr. Brown's homeroom," Chantal said as she recalled the list from photographic memory. "Kenda, you're in Mrs. Hudson's, and Lyn, you have Mr. Heralds."

"Yes!" Roslyn exclaimed as her friends looked at her in surprise. "I . . . I mean . . . that's cool." It was a terrible comeback, and they laughed, knowing that Roslyn was excited because she'd been assigned to their most handsome instructor's class.

"I guess I'll see you guys whenever," Kenda said as she headed toward Mrs. Hudson's room.

She walked down the hall and made a right turn to enter her classroom. Then she found a seat toward the back. She smiled at a few guys that were sitting up front talking, and then turned her attention inward, to the thoughts that clouded her head.

Jerome hadn't called like she'd expected him to last night, but Kenda wasn't worried. He'd call; they always did. Once he did, she'd be back in action. She knew he wouldn't mind spending a few dollars on her, and if he did, he'd just have to get over it; especially if he wanted to have a relationship with her. Kenda doesn't come cheap, she thought to herself.

"This seat taken?" a deep, mellow voice asked from behind.

Kenda looked up into Raymond's smiling face and her heart fluttered. "No. Help yourself." She motioned for him to sit.

He did and stretched his long legs out in front of him. "So how was your summer?" He seemed more comfortable talking to her today than he had been yesterday.

Kenda smiled. "It was good. I worked practically all summer at a day camp, but it was fun helping out with the kids. What about you?"

"Ah, you know me. Practically lived on the courts when I wasn't working my nine-to-five. And I attended a Christian seminar for two weeks in July."

Kenda raised an elegantly arched eyebrow. "A Christian seminar?" He nodded. She knew Raymond was a Christian, but hadn't realized that he was so into his faith that he'd actually spend two weeks in an environment where God would be the topic of conversation for the majority of the time. "I would have never guessed."

"Well, if you had been interested in getting to know me instead of my wallet, then you'd know." Kenda's face reddened in embarrassment. He leaned toward her and whispered in her ear, "I was just kidding."

She smiled as his fresh breath permeated the air. She looked at him and he winked before he focused his attention on Mrs. Hudson, who was now bringing the class to order.

Kenda tried to concentrate on what her teacher was saying, but Raymond's side profile, in her peripheral view, was distracting her greatly. She let her eyes wander from the top of his neatly faded haircut all the way down to the brand new Jordans he was sporting.

At six foot three and with a lean muscular build, Raymond looked as if he belonged on an All-American basketball team. She loved his dark complexion and his dark brown eyes. Although his preferred sport was basketball, Raymond was no dumb jock. He was an active member of National Honor Society and Beta Club, and he was in the top ten percent of their senior class. Raymond had beauty and brains. The thought made Kenda smile.

She missed the six-month relationship that they shared. They'd started dating at the start of their junior year, and Raymond had been good to her from the very beginning. He had no problem with giving her gifts, but it was when she began asking for things that were extremely unnecessary that he got fed up. As Kenda looked at him now, she knew she'd messed things up with a good one.

Her mind found its way back to Jerome. When was he going to call? Kenda willed herself not to worry, but she prayed that she would hear from him today.

After homeroom, the day passed much faster than Kenda could have ever imagined. Before she knew it, she and Chantal were waiting outside for Roslyn. They sat in the car, making sure the eight-hour day had not done any major damage to their nearly impeccable appearances. When Roslyn finally emerged from the school, she was walking with a guy who seemed familiar to Chantal and Kenda. The guy accompanied Roslyn to the car, greeted Chantal and Kenda by name, took down Roslyn's number and then left.

Roslyn climbed into the car with a grin the size of Texas on her face. The other girls stared at her. "What?" Roslyn asked as she put on her seatbelt.

"Who was that?" Kenda asked.

Roslyn rolled her eyes. "Y'all act like y'all don't know that boy." The blank stares on her friends' faces remained. "That was Damon. Damon Ellis."

Chantal's eyes bulged. "*Damon Ellis*? The little short boy who, just last year, had pimples all on his face and braces in his mouth that looked like a messed up grill? What happened to him over the summer?"

Roslyn smiled. "Girl, he had a *great* summer. Growth

spurt, face cleared, braces off, *and* his voice got deeper. Chantal, he's taller than you," she said, still smiling.

"Well, gon' girl," Kenda said as she turned around in her seat. "Look at you. *Miss Peace and Quiet*, pullin' digits on the first day back."

They laughed as Chantal drove the car out of the parking lot and headed toward Roslyn's house. Once they dropped her off, Chantal jumped into conversation about Jerome; something Kenda had hoped to avoid.

"No, he hasn't called," Kenda answered, holding to hope that the subject would drop right there. But she had no such luck.

"So if he does call, and y'all hit it off, are you gonna use his money like you did Ray's?" Although Chantal was just being her usual blunt self at the moment, her question triggered Kenda's attitude.

"Why you even got to go there?" Kenda asked. "What I do in my relationships is *my* business. I don't need you throwing mess like that in my face."

"My bad," Chantal said, looking briefly in Kenda's direction. But the tightness in her friend's jaw didn't stop her from continuing the conversation. "I was just saying because I know how much you liked Ray, and I didn't want you to have to go through something like that with this one. Jerome looks like the type who can really hurt you if you mess over him like you did all the others."

"I can handle myself," Kenda said, glad that Chantal was now pulling in her driveway.

"Look, I'm sorry if I ticked you off, but I'm just worried 'cause you're like a sister to me." Chantal sounded like she was trying to calm Kenda's fiery attitude.

Kenda took a deep breath. "I know that you were just trying to help, but I can handle myself," she repeated. "I know that I can come to you if I need to, and you'll do nothing but tell me the truth. And if I have to come to you, I will. But trust me, if me and Jerome get together our relationship will not end like the one with Ray did."

"Okay." Chantal shrugged. "If you say so."

Kenda smiled. "I do." When she got out of the car, she added, "Thanks for the ride," and ran up to her door as Chantal backed out of the driveway. While Kenda was in the process of walking upstairs, her phone began to ring. Using one hand to blindly search her book bag, she recovered the phone, removed it from the protective case, and flipped it open without bothering to check the caller ID.

"Hello?" A deep voice returned her greeting. "Kenda?"

"Yes," she confirmed, hoping it was who she thought it was.

"This is Jerome." He paused. "Jerome Smith . . . we met at Northlake yesterday."

Kenda laughed. "I know who you are."

His chuckle was velvety smooth. "I guess so." He was quiet for a moment. "I was just calling to see if you'd like to hang out this weekend."

Play hard to get. "Umm. I don't really know if I'm available this weekend. Let me check my calendar." She paused for a moment, as if she were actually looking through her planner. "Oh . . . I'm sorry. I have plans with—"

"Listen, Kenda," Jerome's silky voice cut her off, "I like your style and I was hoping to get to know you better, but if you're not with it, then I can take a hint." His bluntness caught her off guard. "So would you like to go out with me Saturday night or not?"

Why was she trippin'? She'd been waiting for this phone call ever since he'd walked out of the store yesterday. Kenda put a smile in her voice. "Sure, Jerome; I'd love to hang out with you this Saturday."

"Good," he said. "I promise you'll have a great time. I'll call you later with details."

"Okay, bye," she said, and then waited for him to hang up. It seemed like minutes passed before Kenda heard the line disconnect. She placed the closed cell phone on her bed and exhaled. For some reason, she knew that if she got involved with this guy, it would be nothing like her other relationships. And as far as she was concerned, that was a good thing.

Chapter 3

The first week of school had been a rough one. Getting used to her schedule hadn't been the hardest part. Kenda had two courses with her best friends and somehow, Raymond ended up in half of her classes; so she was at ease in knowing she had good friends in all of her classes. The workload was what had worn Kenda out. The week had been filled with plenty of work and too many pretests for her to count. She was glad the weekend was finally here.

Kenda stood at her locker, pulling out the necessary materials she needed in order to complete her weekend assignments. She would start her work tonight so she'd be able to spend most of Saturday preparing for her date.

The popular teenager had been preparing for her date all week, but she hadn't heard a word from Jerome since Monday afternoon. If she didn't speak to him, he'd be in for a surprise when he came to pick her up. Xavier wanted to meet him before they went out, and she figured that she needed to prepare him for the third degree that her father was sure to give him. Every day that she didn't hear from him, Kenda grew more anxious. Jerome had called her from a private number, and she didn't know how to get in contact with him. She never thought to ask for his number, so she'd just have to wait and hope that he would call her tonight.

She shut her locker and headed for Chantal's car. For the third time this week, Kenda was standing alone at the car while she waited for her friends. Chantal was most likely hugged up with her football-playing boyfriend, Wesley. She'd definitely be a minute. Roslyn was probably with Damon. The couple had been hanging out all week, and Kenda wouldn't be surprised if he was asking Roslyn out for the weekend.

As Kenda stood by the car, she noticed the tall, muscular guy coming her way and without realizing it, she quickly ran her fingers through her candy curls and smoothed down her jean dress.

"Hi." She smiled as he approached her.

"Hey," Raymond said, taking out his keys to unlock his car door.

Kenda was embarrassed to find that he wasn't coming to see her. She hadn't realized that his blue Honda was parked right next to Chantal's car. Kenda turned away to hide her disappointment.

Raymond threw his book bag in the backseat, climbed into the car, and shut the door. When he started the engine, Kirk Franklin's "Declaration" blasted through the speakers. He lowered the volume of the music and let his window down. "Hey," he called, gaining Kenda's attention again, "do you need a ride home, 'cause I saw Chantal and Roslyn inside." He chuckled. "It don't look like they comin' out any time soon."

Kenda sighed as she looked toward the school building. Most of the students that were outside were getting on buses, and there were a few others that were just standing around, but none of them were Chantal or Roslyn. She needed to get home so she could start on her homework and get prepared for tomorrow night.

She looked at Raymond's wide, deep-dimpled smile and couldn't help but give in. "Sure," Kenda said. "But let me let them know that I'm gone." She pulled out her cell phone to call Chantal. She knew her friend wouldn't answer if she were with her boyfriend.

"Hey, Chantal," Kenda said after the voicemail greeted her. "Ray is taking me home since y'all takin' so long. Call me later." She hung up and walked around to the passenger side of Raymond's car. She wasn't surprised when he got out and helped her get situated. He'd always been the perfect gentleman when they dated.

Raymond pulled out of the parking lot and turned the music back up. She watched him as he bobbed his head and sang off-key. Turning away, Kenda stifled her laughter.

"What?" Raymond asked when she covered her face. When she continued to suppress her amusement, he repeated, "What?"

Kenda faced him and burst into full-fledge laughter. "Ray, you are definitely a save-it-for-the-shower singer," she said, still laughing.

He laughed with her. "You know you wrong for that." Turning serious, he said, "But if you'd sing sometimes, I'd have a reason not to."

Kenda turned and looked out of the window. She could feel Raymond periodically glancing in her direction. It had been awhile since he'd said something about her hidden talent, and for some reason, he always made her slightly uncomfortable when he brought up the subject. Kenda knew she could sing, but doing so in public had never been on her agenda, and she wished she could get that through Raymond's head.

He turned on her street and soon pulled into the driveway of her family's lavish, split-level home. Shifting the gear to park, he turned and faced Kenda. When he touched her arm, shivers rippled throughout her body. She gave him her attention.

"Kenda, you should really acknowledge your talent," he said, looking into her eyes. "You can really sing and you should use the gift God has given you."

Kenda smiled slightly at his compliment. "I . . . I'm not really that good."

In overdramatic fashion, Raymond placed his right hand over his chest and gasped while Kenda laughed. "You? Not that good? You know I used to catch you singing a lil' when we were together. You're better than good. You're terrific. You could give Chanté, Beyoncé, or even Yolanda or CeCe, a run for their money."

She blushed. "I . . . I don't really know about all of that."

Raymond shook his head. "Well, I guess I'll keep on singin' then."

Kenda covered her mouth to restrain the amusement that tempted to erupt at the sound of his high-pitched squealing.

He stopped singing and smiled. "But for real; all you need is a little practice so you can come on out of that shell." He thought for a moment. "Maybe you could come to the youth service at my church tomorrow night? We have an open mic session that would be perfect for you to show off that beautiful voice of yours." Raymond's eyes were hopeful.

"Don't you think that's a little short notice?" Kenda cocked her head to the side.

He shrugged. "Well, you don't have to sing, but you could still come."

Kenda realized the former suggestion had just been a subtle attempt to get her to join him for a church service. It was an offer he hadn't made in a while and one Kenda had never taken him up on. But in spite of the past, she allowed the suggestion to tempt her. "Youth service?" she asked just for clarification.

Raymond nodded.

"Sorry, I can't. I have plans tomorrow night."

He shrugged again. "Well, whenever you're free, you should come to a service." He pulled a card with the church's information on it from his glove compartment and handed it to her.

Kenda took it and nodded her response as she grabbed her things. Raymond got out and jogged around the car to open her door. He helped her out and closed the door behind her exit.

"Thanks for the ride," Kenda said as she adjusted her shoulder bag against her side.

"No problem." Raymond walked back to the driver's side of the car.

Kenda took her time walking to the porch, hoping that Raymond was watching her. She felt like Loretta Devine in the movie, *Waiting to Exhale.* Kenda unlocked the front door and turned to look at Raymond before entering the house. Like Gregory Hines in the movie, Raymond was watching with a pleasant smile. Once she was safely inside, he waved and began backing out of the driveway. Just before closing the door, Kenda waved back.

As she walked up the stairs toward her room, she wondered why she wanted to recapture Raymond's affections so badly. Kenda knew she still had feelings for him, but he had nothing to offer her. Sure, he'd win a gold medal in the categories of good looks, winning smile, and great personality, but where would that leave her in the long run? She needed someone who'd be capable and willing to support the lifestyle she wanted to live. Raymond was just not that type of guy. It was way past time for her to get him out of her mind and out of her heart.

"Hey, Drey," she said as she passed her brother's room.

"Was that Ray who just backed out of the driveway?" Aundrey asked from his bed. He eyed her. "Did you ride home with him?"

Kenda frowned. The least her kid brother could have done was return her greeting before grilling her. "I'm just fine, thank you," she said sarcastically before going into her room and shutting the door.

She plopped down on her bed, kicked off her sandals, then rummaged through her purse in search of her phone. She looked to see if Chantal had called her back, and hardly to her surprise, there had been two missed calls. Kenda had forgotten to turn up the volume to her ringer after leaving school, but she was sure that she hadn't missed much in missing the calls of her best friend. She dialed her voicemail number, and listened for the message. Kenda shook her head when she heard Chantal's voice.

"Girl, why you ain't answerin' your phone? Ain't nobody told your fast tail to ride home with Ray. You act like you can't wait a few minutes for your girls. Anyway, I just dropped Lyn off, so I should be home in a few. Call me when you get home. That is *if* you get home." Chantal's laugh was heard before her message ended.

Kenda erased the message and listened as the next one, thinking it was Chantal again, asking why Kenda had yet to call her back. But she was wrong, and this time the caller's voice made her smile.

"Hey, Kenda, this is Jerome. Uh . . . I was just callin' to fill you in on what's goin' down tomorrow night. I'll call you later. Peace."

She deleted his message as well, and then looked back through her missed calls. There it was again. PRIVATE NUMBER. She wondered why Jerome didn't just leave a number where he could be reached. As soon as she tossed the phone onto her bed, it rang. She waited for it to ring again before picking it back up.

"Hello?"

"Girl, didn't you get my message?" Chantal said into the phone without a greeting.

"Yes, I did."

"Then why haven't you called me back yet?" Chantal demanded to know.

Kenda suppressed her sarcastic comment and answered honestly, "My phone was on vibrate, if you must know."

"Yeah, you probably didn't want to be interrupted. I understand." Chantal laughed. "But seriously, you just left me and Roslyn hanging for a guy."

"I did not. You guys were the ones who left me out to dry while y'all were hookin' up with your men," Kenda defended. "And if you and Lyn hadn't taken so long, I wouldn't have had to take Ray up on his offer for a ride home."

"So, *he* offered to drive you?" Roslyn spoke up, letting Kenda know they'd called her on three-way. "I knew he was still feelin' you."

Kenda rolled her eyes. She should have known that they'd try to double-team her. "Whatever." She was tired of her friends trying to put in their two cents about her relationships. "It was just a ride; we are *just friends*."

"Sure." Chantal and Roslyn said in chorus. Then they both broke into laughter.

Kenda took a deep breath. This was really starting to anger her, but she wasn't sure whether it was because they were teasing her, or if it had to do with her lingering feelings for Raymond. "Look, I don't have time for this," she said as her other line beeped. "I have another call. I'll talk to y'all later." She clicked over before either could protest. "Hello?" she greeted her new caller.

"Hey." Jerome's now recognizable voice, once again, brought a smile to her face.

Kenda sat on her bed and folded her legs beneath her. "So

what's the plan for tomorrow?" she asked with unfamiliar anticipation.

"You tell me," he said. "We can do dinner and a movie, or movie and then dinner, or skating, or bowling, or—"

"*Bowling*?" Kenda asked in disbelief.

Jerome laughed. "Yes, bowling. It's real fun."

"I have never bowled a day in my life," Kenda told him. "Wearing rented shoes never seemed appealing to me."

"Then that's what we'll do."

"You can't be serious."

He chuckled. "As a heart attack." His voice became soft and smooth. "Look. I'm the type of person who'll try anything once, and when you're with me, you're liable to do the same." He paused. "So are you with me?"

Kenda was rendered speechless. She wasn't accustomed to not being in charge; this was very new to her. She silently nodded her head in reply.

As if Jerome could sense her movement, he said, "Good. I'll pick you up at seven."

"Okay," she said softly.

"But in order to do that . . ." he spoke slowly, ". . . I would need your address."

"Oh," Kenda said, coming out of her shock. She quickly gave him her address and sketchy directions to her house from the nearest connecting interstate.

"No problem; I'll find it. I'll see you tomorrow," Jerome said as he prepared to end the call.

"Wait."

"Yeah?"

Kenda took a deep breath. "My dad wants to meet you before we go out." She paused, hoping she wouldn't seem like one of those girls who had to have her father inspect every guy she went out with.

"Okay." There was no hesitation in Jerome's reply.

"For real? 'Cause my dad can get a little overprotective and—"

Jerome's laugh cut her off. "Kenda, don't worry about it. I can handle anything your dad throws my way." He sounded quite sure of himself.

"Okay, well I guess I'll see you tomorrow." She was still a little apprehensive.

He said, "All right; bye," and then hung up

Kenda placed the phone on her nightstand and pulled her shoulder bag up on her bed. Retrieving her U.S. History book, she began to study; all the while, daydreaming of what tomorrow would be like.

"I can't believe he liked you," Kenda said as Jerome opened the door to the bowling alley.

"Why not?" Jerome seemed slightly insulted. "I'm a likeable person."

Kenda almost laughed at the offended look on his face. "I didn't mean it like that. I just meant that he was extremely easy on you," she said as they approached the counter.

When Jerome came to pick her up, Kenda had been so nervous that she'd changed her outfit several times, and still ended up wearing the Roca Wear jean short jumpsuit she'd picked out the night Jerome asked her out. Her dad had come home early from work for the sole purpose of meeting Jerome, and he answered the door when Jerome rang the doorbell. To Kenda's surprise, the interrogation she'd dreaded wasn't bad at all. Xavier had only asked the basic questions: where Jerome was from, how old he was, was he in school or did he have a job, and what were his plans for the evening. Jerome seemed genuine in telling Xavier that he was originally from Florida, but moved to Atlanta with his family when he was thirteen. Kenda was slightly surprised when Jerome said that he was twenty-one, but her father didn't seem bothered, and she was content if Xavier was. When Jerome told her father that he was a junior at studying business at Morehouse College, Xavier smiled and bid them a pleasant evening of dinner and bowling. Kenda wondered if the wine, which her dad only drank after long, stressful days at work, had some type of effect on his cross-examination skills. If so, she was glad he'd had the extra glass.

Jerome paid for two games and two pairs of bowling shoes. As he took the cash out of his wallet, Kenda caught a glimpse of a few hundred-dollar bills and several major credit cards. *Jackpot, baby.* She smiled as she took the size sevens that the man behind the counter handed her. Jerome took his shoes and led her to lane five.

She sat in one of the empty chairs and took a small bottle of disinfectant spray out of her purse. Jerome laughed as she sprayed each shoe—hers and his—forcing them to wait for them to dry before putting them on. After stepping into his shoes, Jerome sat at the score machine and set up the score sheet.

"Oh my goodness!" Kenda suddenly shrieked.

"What?" Jerome looked up and laughed when he saw Kenda being pulled to the floor by the ball she was holding.

He got up and took the eighteen-pound ball out of her hands with no exerted effort. Placing it back on the rack, he handed her a much lighter one.

Kenda smiled and accepted. "Thanks."

"You go first," Jerome said as he walked back to the chair he'd vacated earlier.

Kenda walked forward and used both hands to pull the ball back between her legs before thrusting it down the lane. It ended up in the gutter before it got halfway to the pins. She turned and faced Jerome, who concealed his desire to laugh by clearing his throat. She rolled her eyes and waited for her ball to return to her. The same method afforded her the same results. She looked around and noticed a few other people looking at her as if she were from some other planet. Surely she wasn't their introduction to a first-time player.

Jerome got up and picked up a heavier ball. He placed his fingers in the holes and took a few steps back, then one step forward before releasing the ball; landing himself a strike. He turned and smiled at Kenda. Her arms were crossed over her chest in playful jealousy. Jerome took his ball for a second turn, once again, bowling perfectly.

"Wait a minute," Kenda said, jumping out of her seat when Jerome finished his turn. "How did you do that?"

Jerome smiled, and without saying a word, he grabbed her ball and took her hand. He gently and patiently told her how to hold the ball. Then he stood behind her and showed her how to roll it down the lane. He made it a purpose to hold her waist and her hand as she released the ball. Chills ran up and down Kenda's spine at the feel of his touch. They stood in that position as they watched the ball go down the center of the lane. All ten pins came crashing down from the impact.

"Strike!" Kenda screamed. "I got a strike." She jumped up and down before turning to hug Jerome. When she realized what she was doing, she pulled back. She was so close to him that she could feel his heart beating.

Jerome smiled as she inhaled deeply and took a step back. "I'm glad you're not regretting coming here," he said.

Kenda returned his smile. "Me too." She grabbed her ball to take her second turn.

After winning both games, Jerome took Kenda to CeCe's Pizza, much to her surprise. She figured that with all of his big bills, they'd be spending them at some upscale restaurant. She wasn't worried though. She'd have plenty of time to work her way up from the all-you-can-eat eatery to a four-star gourmet restaurant.

"So this is your last year of school?" Jerome asked as he bit into a slice of supreme pizza.

Kenda nodded. "My last year of high school, but after graduation, I would like to go to Emory University, or maybe even Duke . . . or Harvard to study law." She shrugged as she bit a slice of pepperoni pizza. After swallowing, she continued, "I've already applied to all three schools, and now I'm waiting to hear from them. My grades are good so I should be able to get into at least one of them."

Jerome seemed impressed. "That's good. I see you're following in your parents' footsteps."

Kenda smiled. "Yeah. Mama and Daddy are great lawyers, but they never pressured me to be like them. I've always been very good at proving points and winning arguments, so I thought that would make me very successful in the courtroom. Plus I want to take over the firm one day." Kenda had always wanted to be a lawyer. Not only was it a lucrative career, but she'd always been very argumentative and figured it was a trait destined for the courtroom. Though Kenda planned to have her dream career, she would make it a purpose to be around for her family. She looked up at Jerome. "So tell me something about you."

"Like?" Jerome stuffed more pizza into his mouth.

"Like . . . what type of business do you plan to go into once you graduate?" Kenda watched him closely as he slowly wiped his mouth with a napkin. He seemed to be in deep thought as if he were contemplating answering her question.

"Can I be honest with you?" he asked softly.

Kenda suddenly became guarded. "That would be nice."

He smiled apologetically. "I lied to your father."

She tried not to choke on her pizza. "Why would you do that?"

" 'Cause when you told me your parents were lawyers, I

got a little intimidated. When your dad asked me about school, I made up the most believable lie I could to get on his good side."

Kenda glared at him. "So you're not studying business?"

"I'm not even in college," he admitted.

"Are you serious?" Her attitude began to flare. "I'm sorry, Jerome, but if I wanted to date some kind of wannabe, I would've hit up one of the little boys at my high school. You're a grown man. Why would you feel the need to lie?" She noticed that his eyes had glazed over and wondered if he were upset, but she almost didn't care.

He shrugged. "Like I said, I was intimidated. But make no mistake about it; I'm not a wannabe anything." Jerome's voice was firm, but he smiled a little when he added, "And I'm not some loser without goals, either. I happen to be an entrepreneur."

"Really?" Kenda asked with some measure of disbelief. "What's your line of business?"

Jerome made eye contact so that she could see he was telling the truth. "It's not really my business. It belongs to a friend of mine. I work with him and a few other guys that live down in Miami. We work with an importing company."

Kenda raised an eyebrow. "What do you import?"

Jerome smiled. "Just some goods from the coast."

"Oh . . . that seems interesting . . . I guess."

Jerome laughed. "It's better than it sounds and it pays a lot," he revealed, causing her interest to return and a smile to grace her lips.

As Kenda smiled, he seemed to study her appearance. Her heart-shaped face set off her facial features. Her small, dainty nose, her slightly slanted eyes, and her full lips made her face look absolutely unique and even more beautiful.

Kenda held her head down when she noticed Jerome looking at her. She didn't know what was wrong with her. She never blushed when she knew someone was looking at her in the manner that Jerome was. She usually would display more confidence. Until now, Raymond had been the only guy whose gaze she couldn't hold.

Jerome lifted her chin with his index finger. "You're very beautiful." He gazed into her brown eyes.

Kenda smiled bashfully. "Thank you."

As they continued to help themselves to the all-you-can-eat pizza and salad bar, they talked and got to know each other better. An hour and a half later, they were standing on Kenda's front porch.

"I really hope you had a good time," Jerome said.

"I did." Kenda fiddled with her house keys. "Bowling turned out to be better than I expected."

Jerome smiled. "So you wouldn't mind doing this again?" He stooped down to catch her eyes.

Kenda looked up at him and noticed how the porch light made his eyes glow. She smiled. "Sure. I'd like that."

"Great. I'll give you a call." He looked at her intently before leaning in to deliver a brief, soft kiss to her lips.

Kenda smiled as she unlocked the door. She watched as Jerome got into his car and pulled off before floating into the house as if she were on cloud nine.

Chapter 4

Kenda hadn't stopped smiling since Jerome asked her to be his girlfriend two weeks ago. Her happiness was apparent to anyone who came in contact with her. Friends teased her about the permanent smile she wore; looking as if she were posing for a never-ending photo shoot.

"There's Mrs. Jerome Smith," they'd say, laughing.

Even Raymond had known something was up when she walked into their second period English class. He caught her admiring the gold ID bracelet Jerome had just bought her and remarked, "Looks like somebody's got a new sugar daddy." His voice was full of sarcasm with a hint of disappointment.

Kenda let his statement go in one ear and right out the other. Lately, she hadn't even been thinking about Raymond. The only person on her mind was Jerome. He had been so attentive over the past two weeks; taking her out to dinner on the weekends, and driving her to and from school. He'd even started using his big bucks to buy her nice gifts.

She'd received the bracelet with their initials engraved in it this morning; a gift to mark their two-week anniversary,

Jerome had told her. She sat at her usual lunch table as she studied the piece of jewelry on her wrist and smiled as she remembered the words Jerome had said when he presented her with the bracelet.

"A jewel for my jewel," he'd said, lightly touching her chin.

Now that Kenda thought about it, it seemed extremely corny, and if it had been anyone else, she probably would have laughed. But coming from Jerome it sounded lyrical. Kenda could feel herself falling hard for this guy, and although it felt weird to her, she didn't want to stop herself.

"Nice piece of jewelry," Raymond said over Kenda's shoulder.

She mumbled, "Thanks" without looking up.

He helped himself to the empty chair next to her and bowed his head to bless his food. When he finished, he turned toward Kenda and asked, "Who's the new guy?" before biting into his sub sandwich.

Kenda pushed a mouthful of salad into her mouth so she wouldn't have to answer right away. She wondered if she should tell him about Jerome. She knew Raymond still had some feelings for her, but if they were as deep as Roslyn and Chantal thought, she didn't want to hurt him. She looked at him as he took another bite of the sandwich. Then he looked at her, obviously awaiting her reply.

"His name is Jerome Smith," Kenda said, twisting the bracelet around her wrist.

Raymond rubbed his chin. "Jerome Smith?" he repeated as he tried to place a face.

"You don't know him," Kenda said, knowing what he was thinking. "He doesn't go to this school."

Raymond looked at his food. "Oh. What school does he go to?" he asked before eating more of his sandwich and sipping his soda.

Kenda looked at Raymond who seemed to be asking a lot

of questions for someone who appeared to be totally unin-
terested. "He's not in school," she simply stated.

He gave her a sidelong glance that asked for an explana-
tion.

Kenda rolled her eyes. "He's graduated already," she said,
although she was just assuming since Jerome hadn't told her
much about his educational experiences.

"Really?" he asked. She knew what was coming next.
"How old is he?"

"Ray, why do you care?" Kenda tilted her head to the side.

Raymond held up his hands in surrender. "Dang, I'm sorry.
Forget I asked."

She watched him bite off another piece of his sandwich
and dig into his potato chips. She hated snapping at him, but
sometimes he acted as overprotective as her own brother.
However, she knew Raymond always had her best interest
at heart, and she felt like she could share anything with him.

"Look, I'm sorry," Kenda said as he continued to eat. She
sighed. "He's twenty-one."

Raymond glanced in her direction, but continued eating.

She breathed loudly. "Aren't you gonna say something?"

"Nope. I don't want to give you the impression that I
care," he said without looking up from his food.

"I said I was sorry," she moaned.

Raymond looked up at her and smiled. "I know. I just like
messin' with you." He nudged her as she playfully rolled her
eyes. "Twenty-one, huh?"

She nodded.

"And you'll be what? Seventeen in February, right?"

She hit his arm and he rubbed it, pretending that it really
hurt him. Kenda smiled. "Boy, you know I'm not sixteen. You
forgot that I'm five months *older* than *you*." They laughed. "I
will be *eighteen* on February nineteenth," she reminded
him.

"I know." Raymond laughed again. "So I guess he's not too much older than you. If he's not in school, what does he do?"

"He's an entrepreneur." Kenda shrugged. "I think he told me that he and a few of his friends work for an importing company in Miami."

Raymond gave her a suspicious look. "What do they import?"

She shrugged again. "Jerome says that they import goods from the coast."

"*Goods . . . from the coast?*" Skepticism dragged out the sentence. "That's what he told you?"

She looked up at him and saw the disbelief on his face. "Yeah. Why?"

"And you believe that?"

Kenda nodded. "Why shouldn't I?"

Raymond turned away from her and shook his head. He ate the last of his chips before crumpling the bag, and stuffing it in the sandwich tray. He turned his attention back toward Kenda, who was still looking at him. "Look, I'm not trying to ruin your relationship before it even gets started good," Raymond began, "but you shouldn't get caught up with this guy. He might be bad news."

"Bad news how?" Kenda challenged, her tone showing signs of brewing anger.

He touched her arm. "Kenda, you're a smart girl. Just use your common sense." Raymond got up and threw away his trash, and then he made his way down the hall.

Kenda watched him walk away, mumbling insults that she didn't have the guts to say to him while he was sitting beside her. She couldn't believe he had the nerve to tell her how to conduct her relationship with her boyfriend. Who did he think he was? He was almost as bad as Chantal and Lyn. She didn't need anyone telling her how to live or who to love. Thoughts ran through Kenda's head. She wondered if Raymond was just trying to scare her, or if he were sending her a warning. Either way, it didn't matter. Jerome wouldn't lie to her.

The bell rang, signaling the end to her lunch period. Kenda gathered her trash and discarded it. She walked leisurely toward her class, knowing as soon as she got there, Raymond would give her a look that would make her think about what he'd said. That was the last thing she needed. Kenda walked into the classroom and avoided contact with Raymond for the rest of the period.

Raymond's unvoiced accusation about Jerome's job had been on Kenda's mind all day. She wanted to ask Jerome about it, but she wasn't going to take the chance of losing him over something as measly as a job. It wasn't her business anyway. As long as the job paid well enough to keep gifts coming like the gold glistening on her wrist, Kenda was happy.

She walked out of the school building with Chantal and Roslyn. They had been okay with Kenda riding with Jerome as long as they were able to get the 411 about their best friend's blossoming relationship. When they walked outside, Jerome's Mercedes was parked in front of the building.

Chantal smiled. "Look at him, leaning up against the car like he all cool," she teased.

"My baby is cool," Kenda said as they approached the car.

"Hey," Jerome greeted as he slipped his arm around Kenda's waist and kissed her in front of her friends and everyone else who was standing near them.

Kenda didn't mind one bit. When he released her, she was grinning from ear to ear. Chantal cleared her throat and placed her hand on her hips.

"Oh . . . hey, Chantal." Jerome smiled. "Wassup, Roslyn?"

"Hey," they sang in unison.

Roslyn pulled Kenda's arm to gain her attention. "Don't

look now, but Mr. Shepherd is comin' this way and he looks a little jealous."

Kenda turned around to see Raymond walking toward them. She wished . . . hoped . . . prayed that he'd keep walking. She didn't need more of his assumptions to put a damper on her day. Much to her dismay, he approached them.

"Hey, Ray," Chantal and Roslyn sang collectively.

Raymond nodded in their direction, and then focused his attention on Jerome, whose arm was still around Kenda's waist. "Hey." He stuck out his hand. "Raymond."

Extending his free hand, Jerome simply said, "Jerome."

"Kenda's told me a lot about you," Raymond said, glancing at Kenda.

Jerome looked at her too, but he directed his words toward Raymond. "Really? Well, I feel slighted because I haven't heard a thing about you." Kenda winced when he gave her waist a reprimanding squeeze.

Raymond noticed the exchange, but didn't address it. "Kenda tells me you're a businessman. She says you import from the coast of Florida." He noticed Jerome's jaw line tighten up.

"Yeah," Jerome forcefully spoke. "Me and a few guys import some goods."

"And other things?" Raymond added. He smiled mischievously. "I'm sure it pays well."

The tightening in Jerome's jaws increased, and Kenda winced once again at the pain searing through her side.

Raymond glanced at Kenda again; her eyes were drilling, angrily, into his.

Noticing the look on her friend's face, Roslyn grabbed Raymond's arm. "Ray, why don't you walk me and Chantal to her car?"

"Yes," Kenda interjected, a little too quickly. "That's a good idea." The smile on her face was tight.

Raymond shrugged. "Sure." He nodded his goodbye to Jerome.

"Call us, girl," Chantal said as they walked off.

Jerome barely waited for them to be out of earshot before he glared crossly at Kenda and asked, "Why you tellin' him all my business?"

Kenda winced again as Jerome tightened his hold around her waist. "Ouch." No one had ever glared at her like that before. His jaws were so tight that she wondered if his teeth hurt. "All I told him was that you work for an importing company. I . . . I didn't think anything was wrong with it." She looked at him with pain in her eyes. "Jerome, you're really hurting me."

He loosened his grip. "I'm sorry." He rubbed the spot where he'd caused her pain.

She placed her hand on top of his. "No, I'm sorry. I shouldn't have told him anything; especially since you don't even know him. I just didn't see the big deal, but I'll know better next time." Kenda kissed him and offered him a sweet smile.

She knew she definitely couldn't ask him anything about his job now. Especially after seeing how angry he got just from her mentioning it to someone else. She wanted to keep everything tranquil between them. If that meant keeping her mouth shut . . . so be it.

Chapter 5

"Where'd you get the gold?" Aundrey asked his sister as she looked at herself in the mirror positioned in the corner of her bedroom.

Kenda glanced at her brother's reflection before resuming the task of making sure every strand of her straightened hair was in place and that her outfit was perfect. She'd gotten the bracelet two weeks ago, and hadn't shown anyone in her family. Being that her parents were always working, they never took notice of it. She was glad that her brother was the first one to see it.

Kenda continued to fix her clothes. "Jerome," she answered as Aundrey came in the room and sat on her bed.

"Girl, it ain't been but a month." He looked at her in the mirror. "He's buying stuff like that already?"

Kenda turned around and looked at him. "What's wrong with that?"

"Nothin', I don't guess. As long as he ain't lookin' to get somethin' out of it," he warned with his tone and his eyes. Aundrey allowed his eyes to roam over his sister's attire and then laughed.

"What's so funny?" She was ready to throw her brother out of her room.

"The fact that you actually think it's cool for you to walk out the house lookin' like that. Dad would have a fit."

"News flash: Dad's not here. He and Mama are working late like they do every night," she said. "It's not like he'd notice anyway." She turned back around to face the mirror before asking, "What's wrong with what I have on?" The body-hugging blue halter dress stopped just above her knees. "I got this from . . ." She tried to think of the guy who'd bought her the dress. "What's his name? The guy that was on the football team who graduated and went to FAMU."

Aundrey looked at Kenda and then said, "Leon?" He scrunched his nose. "You went out with Leon?"

She laughed. "I know he wasn't cute, but he had money." She went into her closet to find a pair of shoes to match her dress.

"Is that all you think about?" he asked. "*Money*? What happened to personality?"

Kenda came out of the closet with a pair of silver heels in her hand. "Well, personality is a must, but I need to feel secure in my relationship. I need to know that if something happens to my husband, I will be well taken care of." She slipped her feet in the shoes and admired them in the full length mirror.

"Girl, you're only seventeen. Who you 'bout to marry?" He laughed as she rolled her eyes.

"You know what I mean. I need someone who's gonna take care of me like I deserve."

Aundrey looked at her. "So what you're saying is that every girl should care about money more than anything else because they should feel secure in their relationship."

"Exactly," Kenda said.

"But why can't they feel secure with the love that they share with that special person in their life?"

She looked at her brother as if he had no wisdom at all on

the subject of relationships. "Drey, love's not going to help you survive if your mate dies and leaves you with nothing in your pockets." She smiled as she daydreamed. "I need a man who's gonna take care of me as if I'm the most valuable piece of jewelry in the world; as if nothing else in this world is going to compensate for me if he ever loses me. I need someone who's gonna love me, yes, but love comes secondary to financial security. I refuse to be left in debt because my husband decided that he didn't need money because he had *love*." She paused. "If a guy wants me he has to have his pockets full, and when they become empty it's time to bounce." She laughed as she dipped slightly and snapped her fingers before returning to a standing position.

"So that means, you wouldn't mind it if some girl started going out with me for my money. Using me just to get all the clothes and the jewelry she wants, and then dumping me just because she's done using my money, or because I refuse to continue doing what she wants me to do?"

Kenda looked at him. "Of course I'd mind, but . . . but it's different because you're my brother."

"But it's the same theory. Boy has money . . . girl gets with boy . . . boy buys girl everything she wants . . . girl dumps boy when he stops throwin' out the big bills."

"You make it sound so harsh."

Aundrey chuckled. "It is."

"Baby bro, that's life." Kenda took a thoughtful pause. "Do you think that it has a big effect on the guy?"

"Depends on the guy. If he's arrogant and thinks he can pick up another chick just like that," he snapped his fingers, "then probably not. But if the guy really liked the girl, and thought she really liked him; then most likely, yes."

Kenda sighed before sitting next to her brother on her bed. "Drey, do you think Ray really liked me?"

He nodded. "Wasn't it obvious? Shoot, that boy is *still* feelin' you."

She sighed. The last thing she wanted was for Raymond to think that she never genuinely cared about him. He had been a good boyfriend and an even better friend. Kenda just couldn't bear the thought of him holding what she did during their relationship against her. She got up and faced the mirror. "I hope I didn't hurt him."

Aundrey looked at her reflection in surprise. "You actually care about his feelings?"

"Well, yeah," Kenda said, not sure of how she really felt. "I guess I do. I mean, he *is* my friend."

He thought for a moment before saying, "I just realized something. He's the only one you're still cool with."

"What?" she asked, turning away from the mirror.

"Ray. He's the only one of your exes that you still talk to. You don't talk to Leon, or Gilbert, or Victor, or—"

"Okay, okay I get it. But what's your point?"

Aundrey's smile was cunning. "You still like Ray. Don't even deny it," he added when she opened her mouth to protest. "I know you do. You don't even have to admit it 'cause I know I'm right."

Kenda giggled and placed her hands on her hips. "Get out."

"Okay, but let me leave you with this," he said as she pushed him toward the door. "You're never gonna find anyone like Raymond Shepherd. Not even that Jerome guy can measure up to my homeboy, Ray. So you might want to get your stuff together and grab him before someone else does."

Kenda stood in her doorway as she watched her brother walk up the hall to his bedroom and shut the door. She stood immobile for a few more minutes before walking back into her room to finish getting ready for her one month anniversary date with Jerome.

"You're never gonna find anyone like Raymond Shepherd . . ."

Her brother's words stuck with her as she grabbed her

purse and walked down stairs to wait for Jerome. Kenda hated to admit it, but she didn't know if she'd ever find anyone like Raymond again. She wondered if even Jerome, with all of his money and gifts, could measure up.

Raymond was handsome and caring. He had great conversational skills and had much respect for her. He took her feelings into consideration and even asked for her input on matters. But Jerome was handsome and caring too. Like Raymond, he held good conversation. But there was more about Jerome. He made Kenda feel like a woman, not a young girl. He didn't get too many points in the respect category, however. Jerome had the tendency to let his hands wander a little too much, and he hardly ever asked for her opinion. He was usually the one deciding what they'd be doing when they were together.

Kenda was sitting on the sofa, pondering over the two guys and their similarities and differences when the sound of the doorbell intruded her thoughts. She got up and straightened out her clothes and her hair. When she answered the door, Jerome immediately pulled her into his arms and delivered and unexpected, passionate kiss.

Kenda pulled back and looked at him in surprise. She was thankful that her parents weren't home. Xavier would have been in total outrage at what he would have seen as Jerome's lack of respect for him, his house, and his daughter.

"Nice to see you too," she said as he continued to hold on to her.

Jerome laughed and kissed her again. "Girl, you look good," he complimented while admiring her dress.

"Thanks," Kenda said once she pulled away again. "You look very handsome yourself."

He grabbed her hand and led her out to the car, climbing into the driver's seat without first showing her to the passenger's side. Kenda hadn't realized until now that Jerome never helped her into the car before getting in himself. Again she found herself comparing him to Raymond, a gentleman who had religiously opened any door she had to walk through when she was with him.

"*. . . not even that Jerome guy can measure up to my homeboy, Ray . . .*"

She tried to shut out her brother's words as she opened the door herself and climbed into the vehicle. Jerome pulled out of her driveway and sped down the street. When they arrived at Canoe Restaurant, Jerome got out of the car and started toward the front door of the eatery. Kenda let out a deep sigh before getting out of the car and following. Jerome went into the restaurant with Kenda trailing behind him. She watched as he candidly flirted with the hostess while they waited to be seated. Kenda cocked her head to the side and looked at him as he continued to rub his mustache and grin at the woman, who was average-looking, at best.

When Jerome caught her stare, he faced her. "What?" he asked as if he didn't understand why Kenda seemed to have an attitude.

She rolled her eyes before glancing at the woman who was now busying herself with new patrons that had just entered the restaurant. Kenda refocused her attention on Jerome who'd obviously thought she'd grown a third eye by the way he was looking at her. She didn't say anything; she simply pushed herself further into her seat before making a loud, unladylike grunt.

Minutes later, the hostess led them to a table that sat outside, giving them the perfect view of the Chattahoochee River. The hostess's tone and body language was sending out negative vibes and Kenda didn't like it one bit. She became especially irked when the woman talked only to Jerome as she told him that their waiter should be out momentarily. Jerome let his eyes follow the sway of her hips as she walked away. Kenda sat back and folded her arms across her chest before clearing her throat noisily.

"What is it, girl?" Jerome's tone caused her eyes to widen, but it didn't soften her fiery attitude.

Girl? She couldn't even believe he went there. "I can't even believe that you are going to sit here and act like you weren't just drooling over that . . . that . . . *thing*," she said, "and while I'm sitting here, nonetheless."

Jerome dismissed her accusation with a wave of his hand. "Ain't nobody droolin' over that girl. She was the one sweatin' me," he claimed, pulling at the lapels of his suit jacket.

"Well, you weren't trying to let her know that your *girlfriend* was sitting right here." Kenda was rolling her eyes and neck at the same time.

"Look," he spoke, grabbing her hand and looking into her eyes as if he could see right through her, "I'm here with you. I'm not trying to get with nobody but you, girl. You got me open, and that's for real." He smiled.

Kenda's expression softened and she smiled back. She leaned in to kiss him as the waiter approached their table. When they looked up, the server held a grim expression on his face. After taking their drink orders and their dinner choices, he left them to continue their public display of affection.

Very little conversation was exchanged between the pair as they sat. Their body language was doing enough talking for both of them, and neither had to say a word to know what was on the other's mind.

Although no one would be able to tell through her actions, Kenda prided herself in being a virgin. She'd never made any obvious plans to remain chaste until marriage. It was just that no guy she'd met, in her opinion, had been good enough to receive her most precious gift. Kenda knew exactly what Jerome was thinking. He wanted to get with her, but it wasn't going to happen. Not any time soon, anyway. She could tell he definitely had the potential to be a great candidate, but until he showed himself worthy, he'd have to continue to fantasize about what it would be like to be with her.

Jerome gazed at her as he continued to hold her hand. "Can I ask my girl to do me a huge favor?" he spoke, finally breaking the silence between them.

Kenda crossed her legs at the knee, causing her already short dress to rise even higher. "Sure."

Jerome smiled at the sexy side of her personality. "Could you drop by my place tomorrow and wait for this guy I work with? He's supposed to be dropping off a package for me, and I have to give him something to take back to Miami."

Kenda's face became pale. "Why . . . why can't you do it?"

Jerome's smile never left his face, though his voice became a tad bit firm. "Because I have to go out of town on business, and I won't be back until Monday afternoon. I just need for you to make sure that this guy leaves that package." His voice became soft again. "Can you do that for me?"

Kenda's mind traveled back to her lunch conversation with Raymond. *"He might be bad news."* Could Raymond have been right about Jerome's importing company? *". . . you're a smart girl. Just use your common sense."* Maybe his job wasn't as legal as he'd tried to make it seem.

But her heart spoke louder than the echo of Raymond's voice in her head. She needed to stop trippin'. Jerome would never put her in a position where she'd end up doing something illegal.

Her head interjected. *Girl, don't be so naïve. Think about it . . . Miami . . . packages. That screams trouble.*

Her heart rebutted. *You got him open, remember? He'd never use you like that.*

"Sure," Kenda answered, hoping her heart wasn't moving faster than her head.

Jerome grinned and handed her a key to his apartment. "I need for you to be there by six o'clock, and make sure that he gives you that package. The envelope that he needs is in a cabinet under the table in the den." He spoke slow, as if trying to make sure she clearly understood his directions. "*Please* don't forget."

Kenda's smile was reassuring, but she'd never been so unsure of this herself. "I promise I won't. Your girl's got ya back," she vowed as their food arrived.

Chapter 6

Chantal's car made a sharp right turn as Kenda did her best to direct her toward Jerome's apartment complex. Kenda hadn't wanted to make the trip by herself and had asked if her best friends would come along. They readily agreed, wanting to see what type of living arrangements Jerome had. When they pulled into the gated community, Kenda told Chantal the code to put into the machine. They watched the gate slowly open and then drove in. As they rode toward the building, they were amazed. The apartment buildings were enormous, and not one car parked in the area seemed to be worth less than fifty grand. Mercedes Benzes, Jaguars, BMW's, and other expensive cars lined the lot.

Chantal pulled her car into an empty parking space. The neighborhood was quiet; only a few people stood outside. They were thirty minutes early for the appointment because Kenda had insisted that they leave early just in case they got lost. The girls got out of the car, their eyes still filled with excitement and curiosity.

Kenda led them into the apartment building and toward

an elevator that would take them to the second floor. She pulled out the key once they stopped in front of apartment 206 and saw a young man, about Jerome's age, approaching them just as she was about to unlock the door. He looked like a wannabe thug, though his boyish face made him easy on the eyes.

"Hey. What you fine ladies doin' tryna get up in J-Man's apartment?" The guy leaned against the wall. "I ain't never seen y'all before, and I know J-Man don't let just anybody up in his crib. Shoot. I can hardly get up in there, and me and him been cool for years."

Kenda glanced back at her friends before responding. "I'm *Jerome's* girlfriend; these are my friends."

"Hey," Chantal and Roslyn mumbled.

He nodded toward them. "So whatchu doin' tryna get in his apartment?"

Kenda placed her hands on her hips. "He needed me to do him a favor, as if it's any of your business."

"A *favor*, huh?" The guy smiled. "He must got you trappin'," he mumbled to himself.

"What was that?" Kenda inquired, thinking the guy had said something derogatory.

The guy looked at them and shook his head. "Nothin'. Y'all gon' 'head and do what you do," he said before walking down the hall and getting on the elevator.

Chantal laughed once he was out of sight. "Okay, let's see what *J-Man* has in this apartment of his."

Kenda unlocked the door and they stepped inside. "Definitely not your typical bachelor's pad," she said as she looked around.

The inside of the apartment was absolutely luxurious. The living room was adorned in black and white décor. A black leather sofa was positioned in front of the far wall, and a matching loveseat and chair sat on either side of it. A small crystal clear glass table was in the center of the furniture with a crystal chess game set up on top. Two glass end tables were on each side of the sofa, and both had black lamps standing on them. African American art that Kenda had seen in Underground Atlanta many times, decorated Jerome's walls. As they made their way to the den, the plush, white, carpet softened the sound of their heels. The den held a big flat screen television that sat facing one long couch. A large coffee table with cabinets was positioned in the center, just like the table in the living room.

"This must be the cabinet he was talking about," Kenda said as she kneeled before the table.

"No." Chantal grabbed Kenda by the arm before she could open the cabinet. "Let's look at the rest of the house."

"This is an apartment," Roslyn stated, "and we don't have no business all up in his stuff."

Chantal looked at Roslyn as if she were more than naïve. "First of all, it should be a house as big as it is, and in the second place, a brotha with a place this nice wants to have people admiring his stuff. So let's go." She strutted out of the den and into the kitchen.

Black marble countertops, white tiled floors, and black cabinets with silver handles welcomed them. The kitchen looked like it belonged on the cover of *Better Homes & Gardens*.

"Dang. His kitchen is almost as big as mine," Kenda said.

"His kitchen is *bigger* than mine," Roslyn spoke up as she admired the detailing of the cabinet doors.

Chantal opened the refrigerator. "He must have spent all his money on this place 'cause he sho' don't have no food."

Kenda shut the refrigerator and scolded her friend. "Girl, you don't go in nobody's stuff like that."

Chantal shrugged as she walked around the island that sat in the middle of the kitchen and through double swinging doors that led to the dining room.

"He must not eat here very often." Roslyn noted that the

table and its place settings looked as if they hadn't been touched since being purchased.

Kenda walked down a hall and saw that Jerome had only one bedroom (besides his master suit), and one bathroom. The room she peeked inside of looked as if he used it for a guestroom. Its queen bed was covered in black cotton sheets, but it had very little furnishings. And the bathroom's decorations continued to illustrate the black and white color scheme.

"I found paradise," she heard Chantal say from down the hall.

Kenda left the bathroom and walked briskly in the direction of where her friend's loud shout had come from. As soon as she saw the room, she felt as if they really had found paradise. This one had to be Jerome's room. They admired the king, four-poster bed that was covered in black silk sheets. A black chair sat in the corner across from the bed, a full length mirror was positioned parallel to the bed, and a smaller flat screen TV was mounted high up on the wall. A black nightstand held a digital clock, and a photo of Jerome and Kenda standing outside the Georgia Aquarium they'd visited only a week before. Kenda picked up the photo and smiled. Chantal looked at Roslyn and they both rolled their eyes. Kenda placed the photo back on the nightstand and strolled over to the walk-in closet. The doors were already open so she peeked inside. Designer suits and other expensive clothing lined the walls; shoes from various designers around the world, sat in boxes on the floor.

She walked back out toward the room and saw Chantal about to open a drawer.

"Girl, what are you doing?" Kenda's voice was frantic.

Chantal looked like a child who'd been caught sneaking a cookie before dinner. "Nothing. I was just 'bout to see what type of underwear he had?"

Kenda laughed at the statement that Chantel posed as a

question, and the accompanying innocent expression on her
face. She turned and looked at Roslyn, surprised that she
wasn't having a hissy fit over Chantal's nosiness. "Lyn, I can't
believe you were about to let her do that," Kenda said.

Roslyn's face held a guilty look. "I wanted to see too."

They all laughed before Kenda said, "I guess it wouldn't
hurt." She walked over to the dresser and opened the drawer.
She was amazed to find that, though Jerome had a few pairs
of boxers, he was more of a briefs man. Definitely a plus.

Chantal immediately picked up a fire-red thong she'd
found under the other underwear, and held it in the air.
Kenda snatched it from her as if afraid someone would see
them. Chantal laughed. "I didn't know guys wore thongs."

Roslyn reached in, pulled out an animal print pair, and
they all laughed when she held them out.

"Does he actually wear these?" Chantal asked, examining
both pairs.

Kenda's face was red from laughter. "I don't know, but do
you think he'd model them for me?"

They laughed again, but jolted into quietness when they
heard someone knocking on the front door. They quickly
tried to place the items back in the drawer just as they had
been before they took them out. Kenda led them out of the
room and toward the front of the apartment. The knocking
came again, just before Kenda opened the door. A man
dressed in a black suit stood before them.

"Hello," Kenda greeted him cautiously.

"I got somethin' for J-Man," the man stated as his eyes did
a quick scan of the apartment. "Is he here?"

Because he was so tall, Kenda had to strain her neck to
see the man's face. He had to be at least a foot taller than she
was. "Umm . . . no, he isn't here, but he told me to take whatever you had for him and to give you a package for it." She
motioned for Chantal to retrieve the package from the cabi-

net in the den. "Would you like to come in?" she asked, hoping he chose to remain outside.

"Naw, I got more business on this block," he said to her relief.

Chantal returned with a large envelope that felt as if it was packed with something. Maybe money. Kenda took it and handed it to the man.

"'Preciate it." He took the envelope, opened the flap, and looked through it before reaching inside his oversized jacket and handing Kenda a square package wrapped in brown paper. He looked at the three girls. "How y'all know J-Man anyway?"

Kenda replied, "Oh . . . I'm Jerome's girlfriend, and these are my friends."

"Mmm . . . and he got y'all doin' his biz while he gone?" His stare made Kenda uneasy. "Ain't y'all a lil' prissy to be trappin'?"

They looked at each other.

"Excuse me?" Kenda said, knowing she hadn't heard the man correctly.

"I don't mean no harm," he said as if he thought he had offended them. "But y'all just look a lil' too girly to be dealin' drugs."

Kenda looked back at Chantal and Roslyn. They all had their mouths wide open. The man placed the package inside of his suit and left. Immediately, unshed tears filled Kenda's eyes. Roslyn pulled her into a hug as Chantal took the package out of her hand and placed it in the cabinet. Afterward, she and Roslyn helped a weary Kenda out of the apartment.

Chapter 7

Kenda had been unusually quiet at school and it was start-ing to weigh on Raymond's heart. He'd never seen her look so despondent before. It was worrying him. When he walked into class this morning, she muttered a quiet greeting and hadn't said anything to him since. He could tell some-thing was wrong when he saw Kenda get out of Chantal's car this morning, and hoped that her sadness had nothing to do with Jerome.

Raymond had gotten a bad feeling when Kenda told him about Jerome a couple of weeks ago, and the feeling grew worse after actually meeting him in person. Although he'd apologized to Kenda for his childish behavior in dealing with Jerome, the day after the encounter, Raymond couldn't deny that he had gotten the impression that Jerome had the ten-dency to become very aggressive if he were pushed to his limits. And the last thing Raymond wanted was for someone he cared for so dearly to be trapped in an abusive relation-ship.

Raymond had passed Kenda a note during their Human Anatomy class, asking that she meet him in the library during lunch, and she'd hesitantly agreed. Now that he was sitting at one of the back tables in the library, he wasn't sure if she was going to show up. Ten of their allotted thirty minutes had already passed. He prayed that she'd show up soon. And she did.

Kenda walked through the doors of the library looking incredibly fashionable. Her summer dress danced across her legs as she walked, searching for Raymond. One of the things he loved about her was the fact that she always looked good, regardless of the situation. Raymond waved her over and Kenda forced a faint smile onto her lips. When he pulled out her chair, she sat, placing her Gucci bag on the table.

"So how are you?" Raymond asked, watching her fiddle with her manicured nails.

"Fine. What about you?"

"Not too good," he responded, gaining her full attention.

"What's wrong?" Concern etched her face.

"A dear friend of mine looks like she's had a bad weekend," he said, causing her to lower her head.

"I . . . I'm fine." Kenda played with the sleeves of her dress. "I . . . I just don't feel too good, that's all."

Raymond lifted her head. "Are you sure that's all?" he asked, his eyes pleading with her to tell him the real problem. "Are you sure that there's not more to it than that?"

Kenda blinked back tears, and hesitated before blurting, "I . . . I just don't know what to do. I should have known that he was dealing. I was just too blinded by love, I guess. I don't wanna lose him, but I don't want to be a part of it either. I . . . I just feel like he used me. He could have told me the truth. I wouldn't have gone along with it, but at least he would have been honest with me. I just can't believe he did this." She cried softly.

Raymond placed his arm around her and began to pray. "Father God, I come to you right now, giving you honor and praise. I ask that you heal my friend, your child, Lord.

Kenda's hurting as I know you can see. Lord, show her that you love her and that you'll never leave or forsake her. Let her know that it is you who placed her here for a specific reason. I ask that whatever thorn it is that is pricking at her heart be removed right now, in the name of Jesus. Lord, I love you, and I thank you in advance for this healing. In Jesus Christ's name I pray. Amen."

When Raymond finished his prayer, Kenda's soft cries had become sniffles, and she used her hands to wipe her face.

"Now," he said, pushing a few stray hairs away from her face. "Tell me what happened."

Kenda turned to face him. "You weren't wrong in being suspicious about Jerome's job. He's a drug dealer."

Neither Raymond's face, nor his tone, showed any surprise at the news. "How'd you find out?"

New tears fell as Kenda told him the story of what had happed over the weekend at Jerome's apartment. "I just can't believe he used me like that. And then I brought Chantal and Roslyn into it with me. What if that man got caught with that money on his way back to Florida? Or what if the police get suspicious and search Jerome's apartment and they find that stuff? All of our finger prints are on it." Her eyes were soaked. "I . . . I don't wanna go to jail for something I didn't even know about. Chantal and Roslyn didn't know either. I just thought I was doing him a favor. I shouldn't have brought them; he didn't even tell me to take anyone else. I should have just gone by myself." She shook her head. "I shouldn't have gone at all."

Raymond rubbed her back gently while he listened to her troubles. He wished he had voiced his thoughts more when they'd talked about Jerome's job. He just didn't want to interfere, but now he wished he had. "Kenda, I really don't know what to say." He looked out of the window across the room. "Jerome's not the guy for you. He's too much trouble."

"But Ray, I love him," she confessed. "It's not even about the money; he cares for me and he's a genuinely nice guy . . . well, as long as he isn't mad or something."

Raymond tried not to let the dissatisfaction show on his face. "I know, and I understand how you feel. It's hard loving someone, and then they turn around and disappoint you." He gazed deep into her eyes.

She knew he was talking about her. "Ray, did I hurt you?"

He grinned sheepishly. "We're not talking about me right now."

Kenda sat up and wiped her eyes. Pushing her untamed mane away from her face, she asked him again. "I really want to know."

Raymond looked across the room, reminiscing, and allowing a brief silence to envelop them. "When I first saw you, I thought you were the most beautiful woman on earth. You had this confidence about you that was really attractive to me," he commented, causing her face to redden. "I never thought you'd give me the time of day, but when I got the chance to be with you, I felt like the most blessed man alive." He looked back at her. "I wanted to treat you like the queen I thought you were, but I didn't know that you felt it was my *duty* to do so. When you started to use me for my money, I just couldn't handle it."

Kenda's eyes spoke the apology that she knew was long overdue. "I'm sorry. I promise I never meant to hurt you."

"It's okay now, but when we were together, I wanted to be so mad at you." He chuckled. "But I couldn't because I loved you so much."

She blushed when he tenderly traced her jaw with his finger.

Raymond's stare deepened. "So what do you plan to do about Jerome?"

Kenda shrugged her shoulders. "I don't know, but I can't

break up with him. It really is just a job and as long as I'm not participating in it, I guess it's . . . kinda, sorta . . . okay," she said, sounding totally unsure of herself.

"Kenda, you know it's not okay."

"I know, but I can't lose him." She looked at Raymond. "I really do love him, Ray, and I'm not just saying that."

Raymond put his arms around Kenda and pulled her in for a hug. "I know," he said, knowing she was telling the truth by the look in her eyes. "I'm not going to force you to do something you don't wanna do. You have to make this decision on your own." He pulled back and their eyes connected once more. "I just hope you make the right one." *God, please help her. Guide her, Lord. Let her make the right choices and let her see Jerome Smith for who he truly is.*

Chapter 8

As Kenda, Chantal, and Roslyn walked out of the school building, Raymond followed close behind. Kenda knew he just wanted to see how she was going to handle Jerome, and while Chantal and Roslyn walked ahead, Kenda lingered with Raymond as he continued to assure her that everything was going to be okay. When they neared the Mercedes, her heartbeat quickened. She saw Jerome standing against the car, but instead of his usual causal demeanor, he looked rather upset.

When Chantal and Roslyn saw Jerome give them a malicious look, they quickly said their goodbyes to Kenda and walked away. Raymond wasn't affected at all by Jerome's attitude. He continued to stand behind Kenda just in case she needed his assistance or an alternate ride home.

Jerome looked from Raymond to Kenda, then back at Raymond. He didn't know what Raymond was trying to prove, but he carried a nine millimeter in his pants that could set him straight better than any words could. He mused at the thought of putting a bullet into Raymond's head just for even thinking he could stand up to him. Jerome turned his heated gaze toward Kenda. "Let's go." He opened the car door for her for the first time in their relationship.

"Jerome, I—"

"I said let's go." He was clearly irritated. "I have an errand to run." He glared at Raymond.

Kenda turned to face Raymond once Jerome had moved toward the driver's side of the car. She looked as if she were afraid to leave, but said, "Bye."

"Take care of yourself," Raymond whispered before walking to his car.

As soon as Kenda got into the car and closed the door, Jerome sped out of the parking lot.

"When I got back this afternoon, I got a call from my boy down in Miami," he suddenly said after a few moments of silence. "Said I shouldn't have such young, prissy girls handlin' my business for me when I'm away." He glanced in Kenda's direction. "Tell me, what did he mean by *girls*? I thought I only told you to go."

Kenda looked out of the window as if the answer would appear on the street signs. When she didn't respond right away, Jerome banged his fist on the steering wheel, causing the horn to blast.

She jumped into full confession. "I . . . I asked Chantal and Lyn to come . . . to come with me because I didn't wanna go alone, and because I didn't have a way to get there. I . . . I didn't think—"

"Apparently not," he interjected. "If you had been *thinking*, you would have known that you could have taken MARTA, or even a cab. I didn't need for you to bring two people who don't need to know nothin' about my business into *my business*. Nor did I need them to be all up in my underwear drawer."

Kenda looked at him to see whether or not that last statement was said in order to lighten the mood. The familiar vein in his neck and tightness in his jaw said it wasn't. How could he possibly know that they went through his drawers? Kenda swallowed and said, "Well, what was I supposed to do? I didn't have a clue as to what *your business* was, yet you pulled me into it without telling me anything. For all you know, a cop could have been in that neighborhood, and if he had suspicions, he could have searched that house. *I* could have gone to jail," she said, getting angrier by the moment. "I would have never brought my friends into this if I'd had known. Shoot, I wouldn't have put myself in this mess if I'd known." She looked at him, anger and hurt seething through her clenched teeth. "I can't believe you used me like that. Why didn't you just tell me?"

"What for?" he asked, his tone less harsh. "For you to get all scared and leave just like everybody else? That's what usually happens." He glanced at her. "I don't have no friends, Kenda. All I have are acquaintances that I do business with. That's it. You're the first person to even give me a chance. Most people see my money; they never see me."

The hurt in his eyes caught her off guard and softened her heart. "Why can't you just get a regular job?" she asked, not wanting to talk about what was apparently, a painful part of his life.

Jerome looked as if he didn't know how to answer her question, but he gave a response anyway. "I didn't finish school," he simply stated.

"You mean college?" she asked, hoping that's what he meant.

He shook his head. "I dropped out in the eleventh grade," he admitted quietly.

Eleventh grade? Kenda's eyes opened in shock. "Eleventh grade?" she blurted aloud. "Why? I mean, what happened?"

Jerome continued to keep his eyes on the road. "I guess life just happened." He shrugged. "My parents for one. My dad was so abusive and my mom . . . well, she was just naïve. He beat her like she had stole something, and she never even thought about leaving him. He'd get sloppy drunk and drag her all around the house with my sister and me screaming for him to stop. He never did, though." Jerome paused. "But the day my mom finally saw the light and decided that enough was enough, it was too late. When he found out we were trying to leave, he beat her to death."

Kenda gasped in shock.

"So my dad ended up in jail, and with my mom gone, it was just me and my sister. We really didn't have no other family, so we were put in a foster home until this family decided to take us in. They took my sister, that is. They didn't want me, and since I was turning eighteen in a few months, I just kissed my sister goodbye and went back to our old neighborhood. I was staying with one of my friends and his family, but me and my sister kept in touch. I guess she finally showed her ugly side to her foster parents and told them more than once that she wanted to be back with me, 'cause the next thing I knew, they were droppin' her on my homie's doorstep. Never understood why they didn't take her back to the foster home, but regardless, we were glad to be together.

"With us both still being in the system, we were afraid that the cops would come after us and put her in another home. So unless I was going to the store with the little bit of money I found in our parents' room before we were taken from our home, we hardly ever left the house. We couldn't keep up in school 'cause we were missin' so many days. I was already a grade behind, and my sister was only a letter grade away from being kept back too; so we just dropped out. My sister was only in the ninth grade at the time. It was just a crazy time all the way around. My friend's parents were so knocked up on dope that they couldn't care less if we missed school or not. I tried finding a job, but any job worth having required at least a high school diploma. So I did the next best thing to get some food on our table."

"What about your sister?" Kenda asked. "Did she get a job?"

Jerome was quiet for a few moments. He rubbed his chin before letting out a dry chuckle. "Yeah, she finally stopped being scared of the outside world and got one. She worked the street corners for some abusive pimp who had her strippin', trappin', and prostitutin'. I couldn't even help myself, so I knew I couldn't help her. After sleeping with so many Johns, she eventually got HIV. But a drug overdose is what killed her. She was only sixteen. She's been gone for 'bout two years now."

Kenda sighed. She really didn't know what to say to her boyfriend. She'd never experienced such a hard life. And he was only twenty-one. She couldn't even imagine the affect it was having on him. As he pulled into her driveway, she began to tenderly massage his neck and could feel the tension leaving his body.

"Jerome, do you actually use drugs?" she asked.

He shook his head. "Naw, I just buy it from the guys in Florida and sell it up here for a larger profit. I've never even thought about using it, seeing what it did to my sister." Jerome looked at her. "Baby, I owe you an apology. I shouldn't have brought you into this mess. I really do love you, and I love spending time with you, but this is me. It's who I am, and if you don't want to get with that then I'ma have to let you go."

Kenda looked at him wide-eyed. She saw his lips moving, but hadn't heard anything after "I really do love you." A grin spread her lips. "You love me?" She was trying to make sure she'd heard correctly.

Jerome put a finger to his chin. "Did I say that?" He feigned ignorance.

"I believe you did." She was still smiling.

"I believe I did too." He looked deep into her eyes. "I love you, Kenda," he repeated.

She kissed him and replied, "I love you too," before finding his lips once more.

"I had a feeling you'd say that," Jerome smiled, showing off his pearly whites.

"Can I ask you a question?" Kenda inquired.

"Sure."

She smiled. She'd never rest until she knew the answer. "How in the world did you know we went through your underwear drawer?"

Jerome's smile widened. "I have a particular system for my underwear. I keep all my boxers and boxer briefs on top and the more risqué items toward the bottom."

Kenda's face turned red. "And we didn't put them back where we found them?"

"Exactly."

"Do you actually wear those?" she asked, almost laughing at the memory of her and her friends playing with the underwear.

"Only on special occasions." His answer sounded suggestive.

"Mmm, maybe we should plan one sometime soon," Kenda flirted. She had no intentions of sleeping with Jerome just yet, but a little teasing never hurt.

"Maybe we should," Jerome agreed through lust-filled eyes.

Kenda's smile hid her sudden uneasiness. "I have to go." She kissed him once more.

Kenda could feel Jerome watching her as she climbed out of the car and walked toward her front door. When she turned back toward him, she could see the simmering lust in his eyes and she wondered what was on his mind. Part of her honestly knew what had the wheels of his mind turning and she hoped one day she'd be able to satisfy his curiosity.

Chapter 9

Jerome pulled up to his apartment, and he and Kenda got out of the Mercedes.

"What are we doing here?" she asked as she followed him into the building.

"You'll see."

Dating Jerome for the past two months hadn't been anything like Kenda would have expected. Everything that happened in their relationship had been a spontaneous decision. Jerome would take her to parts of Atlanta she'd never been. Fancy restaurants, concerts, and several jewelry stores, where he let her get something special "just because he loved her." She'd never had so much fun in a relationship, and she'd never felt so much love *from* a relationship. At this point, Kenda couldn't envision living without Jerome Smith. He was everything she'd ever wanted in a man, and she could definitely see herself spending the rest of her life with him.

As they got off of the elevator, they came across a familiar face. Kenda recognized him as the guy who'd questioned her and her friends the day they'd stopped by Jerome's apartment. Though the men seemed to be around the same age,

Jerome looked much more mature than his friend, who sported a head full of messy twists and a pair of saggy jeans that covered everything except for his behind.

"Wassup, J-Man," the guy said, giving Jerome some type of complicated handshake.

"Nothin' much, G-Dawg," Jerome said. "Just 'bout to hang with my girl at the crib." He put his arm around Kenda. "This is Kenda. Kenda, this is G-Dawg, one of my business partners."

G-Dawg . . . J-Man? Why couldn't they just call each other by their real names? Kenda shook G-Dawg's hand.

G-Dawg looked her up and down and grinned. "Yeah, we met."

Kenda eased her hand out of his and clandestinely wiped it on the back of her dress, like she thought he carried a virus transmittable through a casual touch.

"Well, I'll holla, man." G-Dawg headed toward the elevator. "I got to take care of some bi'ness."

"All right," Jerome said as he led Kenda toward his apartment.

When he unlocked the door and opened it to let Kenda inside, her mouth dropped open in astonishment. The lights were romantically dimmed, soft music came from the stereo that sat in the den, and red rose petals were scattered on the white carpet, leading down the hall toward Jerome's bedroom.

Although Kenda loved the surprise and had thought about being with Jerome on many occasions, she wasn't sure if she was ready to allow this type of intimacy into their relationship. She loved Jerome so much, and she could see herself giving her virginity to him, but she knew that now wasn't the right time.

She turned to face him. "Jerome, this is so beautiful, but—"

His mouth caressing hers interrupted her statement.

"Jerome . . ." she muttered between kisses. "Jerome . . . I . . . need—"

"I know," he said gutturally as he unzipped her dress.

She pushed away from him. "Jerome, wait a minute." She pulled up her zipper.

"What is it?" Agitation saturated his voice.

She looked at him and hoped that she could make him understand. "Baby, I want this just as much as you do, but I . . . I just don't think I'm ready."

He rubbed his mustache and sighed. "It's cool."

She was surprised. She'd expected an all-out argument. "Really? You're not mad?"

Jerome shook his head and pulled her closer to him. "A little disappointed, but I can wait for you."

Kenda felt like pinching herself to see if she was dreaming. "I love you so much." She gazed into his eyes, adoring every ounce of him.

"I love you too." He kissed her lightly on the lips, then led her to the dining room and told her to sit. He then went into the kitchen to bring out the food, which he had apparently hoped to share with her after showering her with his love, but he improvised brilliantly.

"You made dinner?" Kenda asked. "It looks great."

Jerome set the plates of salmon and garlic mashed potatoes with mixed vegetables on the table. "Thank you, but I can't take all the credit," he said as he sat next to her. "G-Dawg's girl helped me out a little. She can burn in the kitchen."

Kenda noticed a slight twinkle in his eye as he spoke of his business partner's girlfriend, and her mind began to wonder. But she pulled her negative thoughts together when she realized that Jerome was too into her to get caught up with any other girl.

"Well, this looks so delicious." She cut into her salmon and placed a piece into her mouth. "Mmm, it *is* delicious."

They ate dinner as Kenda chatted about school and the project she had to complete on Old British writers, given to her by her Literature teacher.

"Me and Ray have to do a report and presentation on Christopher Marlowe, whoever that is," she said as she ate a forkful of her vegetables.

"You and *who*?" Jerome's forehead creased.

Kenda looked up at him. "Me and Ray. You remember my friend, Raymond."

"Yeah, I know who he is, and I don't want you working with him," Jerome said as he sipped his sweet tea.

Kenda stared at him as if he'd lost his mind. "Why not?"

"Because I don't like him."

"Baby, you barely know him," she stated with a chuckle. "How can you even say that?"

Jerome's jaw tightened. "Because, Kenda, he's always around you and I *know* that I *don't* like that."

"What do you mean he's always around me? I know he's in most of my classes, but it's not like I can help it."

"Oh, so y'all have classes *after* school now?" He placed his fork on his plate. "Because I didn't know that you needed an escort to my car everyday."

Kenda looked down at her plate. "He's just looking out for me . . . kinda like a brother."

He shook his head. "I don't think so, Kenda. And I don't think that y'all have always been *just* friends."

She averted her eyes away from Jerome's piercing stare. "I never said that we've always been just friends," she mumbled.

Jerome hit his fist on the table and Kenda jumped along with the dinnerware. The impact almost overturned his tea. "Don't get smart with me, Kenda."

"I wasn't gettin' smart." She watched as his fist tightened. "Look, we did go out last year, but it only lasted for like six months, then it was over."

"*Six months?*" he seethed. "Seems like a long time to me."

"Why are you getting so upset?" Kenda asked him. "I'm not with Ray, I'm with you."

"I know that, you know that, but homeboy can't seem to get that through his big head."

"Ray knows how much I love you, and he knows that there's nothing between me and him anymore. So you have nothing to worry about." She tried to put out the fire behind his eyes by massaging his tightened fist.

"I still don't want you working with him," Jerome stated.

Kenda sighed. "There's not much I can do about that, Jerome. The teacher assigned us partners and there's no switching."

"Well, tell her you can't work with him." His anger was flaring.

"I can't do that," she spoke softly. "It's not fair to the other students."

Jerome's voice became sharp. "I don't care what's *fair* to the other students, Kenda. I'm *telling* you to get a new partner."

Kenda shook her head. "I won't do that, Jerome; it's not fair."

Suddenly, the back of his hand flew across her face, causing her to fall out of her chair and onto the floor.

Jerome got up and stood over her. "I told you not to talk back to me, girl. I don't care what's fair. I don't want you working with Raymond!" He watched her lie on the floor with both her hands covering her face.

Kenda rocked back and forth as the pain continued to singe her skin. That, accompanied by her cries, afforded her a massive headache. She tried to process what was going on, but it all seemed so unreal. Her breathing became unsteady as she gasped for breath between sobs.

Jerome ignored her tears as he finished his orders. "Monday morning, you go to your teacher and tell her that you need a new partner. I don't care what excuse you have to give her, but you are not to be working with that boy on this project. Is that understood?" He sounded more like an overbearing father than a loving boyfriend.

She continued to lie on the floor rocking back and forth, but managed to nod her head slowly.

"Good." Jerome seemed satisfied. "Now get up so we can finish having dinner."

Slowly, Kenda rose to her feet. The thought of running from the apartment passed through her mind, but with nowhere to go and miles away from the safety of her home, she sat back down at the table with her right hand still covering the right side of her face. She watched as Jerome continued to eat as if nothing had just happened. She rubbed the sore spot on her face, praying that she didn't have a bruise in the morning.

Kenda looked in the mirror and saw the small, light mark on her cheek, and could only hope that people would mistake it for a blemish. She still couldn't believe Jerome had hit her. She hadn't even seen it coming, nor did she understand why he'd gotten so angry over her friendship with Raymond. He'd apologized when he dropped her off at home, and he said it would never happen again. Kenda couldn't help but to forgive him, but the memory of the situation still stung in her heart, and she felt she needed to talk to someone before she broke down into tears once again. She picked up her phone and dialed Chantal's number.

"Hello."

"Hey, it's me," Kenda said. "Can you get Lyn on three-way, please? I really need to talk to y'all."

"Okay, just hold on a second."

Kenda heard Chantal click over to the other line. When she clicked again, Roslyn's phone was ringing in the background.

"Hey, y'all," Roslyn spoke after being told that both her girlfriends were on the line. "I was just about to call you guys. I have something to tell you."

"What?" Chantal asked.

"Damon is taking me to see the Falcons game this coming Sunday. He has some extra tickets and wanted to know if you guys wanted to come. He only has two, so y'all can't bring your boyfriends," Roslyn explained.

Chantal laughed. "Lyn, do you even like football?"

"Yeah . . . well, not as much as Damon, but it's cool," she said. "So do y'all wanna go or not."

"Sure," Chantal said. "Ain't nothin' like watching a bunch of muscle-bound men slam into each other."

"Good." Roslyn sounded excited. "You're mighty quiet, Kenda. What about you? I know how much you love the Falcons." She laughed.

"Yeah, when Michael Vick was playin'; right, Kenda?" Chantal interjected.

Kenda touched her bruised cheek. "I would like to go, but I'll have to see if it's okay with Jerome."

There was silence on the phone before Chantal laughed. "Why do you have to see if it's okay with Jerome? He's not your daddy. You don't have to ask him . . . just tell him you're gonna hang with us."

Kenda sighed. "He might have something planned."

"Well, that's okay," Roslyn said. "Just see if he does, and if he doesn't then you can roll with us."

"Okay." Warm tears rolled down her cheeks, burning the spot where she'd been hit. She whimpered and wiped her eyes.

"Kenda, girl, are you crying?" Roslyn asked. "It's not that important. It's not like the world's gonna end if you can't make it."

"It's not that," Kenda assured her. "It's just that . . . that . . ."

"Kenda, does your crying have anything to do with the reason that you called us?" Chantal asked.

Kenda's sniffle was all the answer they needed.

"Girl, what's wrong?" Roslyn asked.

"Did you and—*J-Man* break up?" Chantal asked.

"No," Kenda cried. "But . . . but . . . I don't know how much longer our relationship is gonna last if he hits me again."

"What!" Both her friends virtually screamed into the phone.

"Oh no!" Chantal said. "He hit you, Kenda? You better be joking."

Kenda cried harder. "I'm not. It happened last night. He just slapped me across my face. Knocked me dead out on the floor."

"What'd he do that for?" Roslyn asked softly.

"Does it really matter?" Chantal asked. Her voice wasn't nearly as soft. "He shouldn't have done it at all, no matter what happened."

"I told him that me and Ray were working together on Ms. Jones's project for Lit. And he told me that he didn't want me to work with Ray 'cause he thought Ray still had feelings for me. He said that I needed to tell Ms. Jones to assign me a new partner, and I told him that I wasn't going to do that 'cause it wasn't fair to everybody else. Then he got mad and slapped me across my face," she whined.

"And what did you do?" Chantal asked. Kenda could tell from her voice that Chantal fully expected to hear that she'd put Jerome back in his place.

"He told me to get up off the floor and finish eating dinner," Kenda said, ashamed of her own self. "So I did."

"That doesn't sound like the Kenda I know."

"Lyn is right," Chantal said. "I can't believe you didn't, at least, curse that boy out. I've seen you do that in a hot second."

"I was too stunned, I couldn't say anything." Kenda

sighed. "He apologized when he brought me home. Said he didn't mean it and that he would never do it again."

Roslyn spoke up. "I don't know, Kenda. You might wanna cut things off with him before they get out of hand."

"I can't. I've already fallen for him and he says he loves me too. I . . . I just don't know." She wiped her eyes.

"Girl, give him another chance," Chantal said to Kenda's surprise. "If he says he won't do it again, you have to trust what he says. I've seen the way that boy looks at you, and I can tell he loves you. He just may have had a bad day, lost his temper or something, and had a lapse of judgment."

"Chantal, please," Roslyn snapped. "If he did it once, he'll do it again . . . and *again*, and *again*," she stressed. "Girl, you need to get out of it now before you're trapped later," she advised Kenda.

Kenda cried as her friends argued over the situation. She thought that by calling them she'd lose all of the confusion that was crowding her head, but now she just had an even bigger headache. "Look," Kenda spoke up, "I'll just talk to y'all later."

"All right," Chantal said. "I have to go anyway 'cause Wesley's coming to take me to the movies tonight."

"Don't forget about the tickets," Roslyn said. "It seems you could use a break from Jerome anyway."

When they hung up, Kenda sighed. She had no clue as to what to do about the situation. When her phone rang, she jumped, praying that it wasn't Jerome. She wasn't ready to talk to him just yet, and figured he felt the same way after she hadn't heard from him all day. Her muscles relaxed when she noticed Roslyn's number on the caller ID.

"Hello?" she answered.

"Hey, girl," Roslyn started. "I just wanted to let you know that I'm here for you if you need anything. A policeman, a hit man, anything you need, I can get it," she offered.

Kenda laughed softly. "Thanks, girl, and I promise I'll be careful."

When they ended the call, Kenda lay back on her bed with a heavy sigh. "God, please help me," she whispered as a new stream of warm tears soaked her pillow.

Chapter 10

"I'm sorry, Ms. Jones, but I'm going to need another partner for this project. I can't work with Raymond," Kenda said to her teacher as Raymond walked up behind her to place his class work on the desk.

"What?" Raymond asked. "Why not?"

"Why can't you, Ms. Tyson?" Ms. Jones asked, a concerned look on her face.

Kenda avoided looking back at Raymond. Tears threatened to reveal themselves as she tried to think up a liable excuse. "I . . . uh . . ." Coming up with nothing, she said, "I just can't."

Seeing the tears in her eyes, Ms. Jones relented, "Okay then, you can work with Marla, and Raymond, you work with Joseph." She searched Kenda's eyes. "I hope that everything is okay."

Kenda nodded. "Thank you so much." She walked out of the room and headed toward her next class.

Raymond followed behind her. "What was that all about, Kenda?" he asked as he tried to keep up with her fast paced walk.

"Nothing," she said, wiping tears from her eyes. "I just can't work with you on this project."

Raymond used his long legs to jump in front of her. "Why not?"

Kenda looked up at him. Her eyes were red and her head was pounding. "I . . . I just can't, okay?" She tried to move past him, but he continued to block her path. "Ray, I'm going to be late for class." She lowered her gaze.

"Kenda." Raymond lifted her chin so that her eyes would meet his. "What is going on?"

Her eyes filled with tears. "I can't talk to you anymore, Raymond. I'm sorry."

Raymond's face became a mixture of confusion and sadness. "Why?"

Kenda averted her eyes, not wanting to have to answer his question, but when she turned her head, he caught a glimpse of the bruise on her cheek. Suddenly, she wished she would've used concealer to hide the mark. She had been determined not to wear any makeup, other than the eyeliner, mascara and lip gloss that usually decorated her face.

Raymond gently rubbed his hand across the bruise. "Kenda, what happened?"

She covered her cheek with her hand before turning away. "Nothing. I have to go."

He stopped her again, and his eyes bore into hers. "Kenda, what happened to your face?"

She looked away. "Nothing happened to my face. I . . . I just . . ." She tried her best to invent an excuse, but failed once again. She wanted to jump for joy when the warning bell rang. "I have to go." She walked past Raymond and headed down the hall.

Kenda watched as each class period went by at the speed of light. Usually, the day seemed much too long. She wished the dismissal bell would never sound so she wouldn't have to go outside and see that silver Mercedes parked in the parking lot. She prayed that for some reason, Jerome wouldn't be able to pick her up today, so she could ride home with Chantal and Roslyn. But she knew he wouldn't just not show up. The one thing he was, was dependable.

Kenda watched the clock as it ticked away the last few minutes of the day. When the bell rang, she took her time gathering her things. She walked as slow as she could, and spoke to every familiar person she came in contact with on her way out. When she neared the hall where she usually exited, she saw Chantal, Roslyn, and Raymond waiting for her. She smiled slightly. She had such wonderful friends, but she hoped to God that Chantal and Roslyn hadn't told Raymond about the incident. Kenda knew that Raymond wasn't stupid, and that he could clearly see that something wasn't right with her and Jerome's relationship. She just hoped, for her sake, that he'd stay out of it.

When she joined her friends, Chantal looped her arm with Kenda's as they walked toward the parking lot. "Would you like to ride home with us today?" Chantal offered.

Kenda shook her head. "I can't," she spoke softly. "I—"

"Kenda, you cannot let him rule your life like this," Roslyn spoke up. "He's not your guardian and he doesn't have a say-so in everything you do."

"Wait a minute," Raymond said, stepping in front of Kenda. "Did Jerome put that bruise on your face?" His question sounded more like an accusation.

Kenda looked at him. "Ray, please; I have a headache, and I don't have time for this."

"That didn't answer my question." He pulled her away from her friends. "Now you know you can tell me. Did he do this?" he asked again, pointing to the bruise on her cheek.

Kenda breathed deeply. "Ray, I can handle myself."

"That still doesn't answer the question," Raymond stated.

She looked toward the parking lot and saw Jerome standing in the usual spot with his arms folded and his jaw tight. She looked up at Raymond and said, "I have to go." She walked off, saying a quick goodbye to her friends, and made her way toward Jerome's vehicle. She winced as Jerome gripped her arm and shoved her into the car. She avoided looking back, afraid of seeing the disappointment in her friends' eyes.

"Jerome, I told you that we were just talking," Kenda said as Jerome pulled into her driveway.

Jerome put the car in park. "I don't care what you were doing, I told you not to associate yourself with him anymore."

She lowered her head. "I'm not. That's what I was telling him today."

He looked at her and softened his tone. "Look, Kenda. I know you think I'm being a real jerk about this, but I just don't like that guy. He still has feelings for you. I can tell just by the way he acts around you. I just don't want to lose you to some high school boy who could never love you like I do."

Kenda smiled and looked him in his eyes. "Jerome, I promise you that there is nothing between me and Ray. I told him today that I can't hang with him anymore and you never have to worry about someone taking me from you because I won't let it happen."

He touched her wounded cheek. "Baby, I'm so sorry about this. I really didn't mean to do it."

"I know you didn't, and I apologize for upsetting you." She looked toward her house, her eyes focused on her brother's bedroom window. "Jerome . . . would you mind if I go to a Falcons game with Chantal and Roslyn on Sunday?"

Jerome looked upset. "Well, I thought we'd go to Lake Lanier this weekend and spend some time together."

"Isn't it kind of chilly to be going there?" she asked. Spending so much time with Jerome over the last couple of months had caused her to miss out on social activities with her friends, and she really missed them.

"We're not going to participate in any water activities," Jerome explained. "They have this spa that I want to take you to." He smiled.

"Oh . . . well, I'll just tell them I can't go." She was disappointed, but Jerome didn't notice.

He smiled. "Good." He kissed her. "Well, I have to run an errand, so I'll see you tomorrow."

"Okay." Kenda grabbed her things and got out of the car. She turned around when she heard him call her name.

Jerome gazed at her tenderly. "I love you."

Kenda smiled as her eyes glazed over with bittersweet tears. "I love you too," she said before he backed out onto the street.

She walked into the house, surprised to find her parents at home. She hardly ever saw them unless she happened to stay up past midnight. They were sitting on the couch comparing notes for a new case.

"Hey, Mama. Hi, Daddy." Kenda closed the front door behind her.

"Hey," they said without looking up from their work.

"What are you guys doing home?" she asked.

"Had to get away from the office," her mother answered, highlighting something on the papers they were looking at.

"Oh. Well, I'll be upstairs. I have a ton of homework." Not that they cared, but she told them anyway. Kenda sighed as she trudged up the stairs.

Her brother was blasting his music and her head began to pound even harder. It amazed her that her parents could work through the noise. Kenda banged on the door of her brother's room with one hand, and massaged her left temple with the other.

"What is it?" he yelled. The music got even louder once he opened the door.

"Do you think Mr. Tupac would mind keeping it down? Some of us have homework to do," she said sarcastically.

Aundrey used the remote to lower the volume. "What's wrong?" he asked, watching her rub her temples.

"Nothing, I just have a headache, that's all." Kenda walked to her room, shutting the door behind her before crawling into her bed with a heavy sigh.

The day had been long and painful. She rubbed her arm—the one Jerome used to force her into the car. He must not have realized his own strength. She wanted to be mad at him, but couldn't find the anger inside. All she felt was love, and she hated that she felt so inferior to him. Usually, Kenda had the authority in a relationship, but in all of two months, she'd basically given her soul to this man. She didn't even know who she was anymore. Kenda held her head as she reached into her bag for her ringing cell phone.

"Kenda, it's me," Raymond's voice came in loud and clear.

She wished she'd check her caller ID before answering, but tried her best to sound normal. "Ray, I told you I can't talk to you anymore."

"Why not?" Raymond seemed upset. "Just because Jerome says you can't? Don't deny it because Chantal and Roslyn already told me that's what's up. I know he's the one who told you to get a new partner too." He sighed. "Kenda, why are you letting this jerk run your life? He's not God, you know. You don't have to answer to him."

Kenda's head began to pulsate with more vigor, and tears clouded her vision. "Ray, I don't need this right now. I'm sorry, but—"

"No buts, Kenda," he interrupted. "Are you gonna let him ruin our relationship? That's exactly what's gonna happen. He's pulling you away from your friends . . . the people who *actually* care about you. Is that what you want?"

"No," Kenda said. "But I can't lose him, Ray. Don't you get that? I'm trying to tell you that I love him and he loves me, and things are going to get better instead of getting worse. He's only hit me once and we've already talked about it. He's sorry; he didn't mean it. I don't need anyone telling me that he's no good because *none* of you guys know him like I do. He comes from a dark past, and he has no one *except* me. I can't leave him just because he couldn't control his anger *one time*."

"Why not? Why can't you leave him, Kenda?" Raymond continued before she could answer. "I understand that you love him. But if a relationship is not going where you want it to go, then you have to get out of it before it's too late. Trust me, it was the hardest thing I ever had to do when I broke up with you, but I did it for me. And you can do this for you. You say he loves you. You say he'll never do it again. But what happens if he gets upset with you again? Kenda, I don't want to see you get hurt." He paused as if giving her time to process all he'd said. "I promise that I'll stay out of the way for now and *only* for your safety, but I need you to promise me that you are going to end this soon." There was silence on the phone. "Promise me, Kenda," he pressed.

"I can't do that, Ray," she replied softly.

Raymond sighed heavily. "Okay, fine. But after everything is said and done, and you end up with a broken heart, and maybe even a broken body part, don't expect for me to be there to pick up the pieces." He abruptly ended the call.

Kenda's face fell at his words. She'd always been able to count on Raymond, but now he was telling her that he wouldn't be there if she ever needed him. That made the tears, which she'd tried to hold back during their conversation, burst forth. She rolled over and looked out of her window. The skies had been cloudy all day and the predicted rain soon began to fall. She closed her eyes and wondered if it was all worth it. To lose, just to be loved.

Kenda and Jerome were just alike in one way. They only had themselves. Sure, she had friends, but it wasn't what she was yearning for. She wanted to be loved. By her friends and her parents, who would never know her neediness as long as they had their heads stuck in legal documents. Kenda had tried denying it for too long, but today, when she walked in the house and neither of her parents got up to welcome her home, she realized that she felt neglected and unloved by the people who were supposed to care for her the most. Now she wondered if she was going to lose her friends, too.

She cried herself to sleep, praying that things would get better.

Chapter 11

Friday afternoon, Kenda walked to Jerome's car alone. She watched as Chantal and Roslyn barely wave their goodbyes, and almost cried when Raymond refused to look her way. Going against Jerome's wishes, she'd tried to talk to Raymond, but he'd avoided her all day as he'd done all week. Tired of the rejection, she finally decided that maybe it was best that they dissolve their friendship.

When she arrived home, Kenda tried to give Chantal a call. The phone rang and rang until she heard, "Hi, you've reached Chantal. Sorry you missed me, but if you leave a message, I'll try my best to fit you into my busy schedule."

When she heard the beep, Kenda said, "Hi, Chantal; it's me. I was just calling to talk. Call me back. Bye."

Maybe she was paranoid, but she'd never known a time when Chantal wasn't available, for her at least. Kenda thought about calling Roslyn, but remembered that she had caught a ride home with Damon. She didn't want to interrupt them if they were spending time together.

Kenda sighed. There was no one to talk to and she felt Raymond's words down in her soul. *"He's pulling you away from your friends . . . the people who actually care about you.*" Kenda hoped beyond hope that that wasn't what was happening. They were just busy, that's all. She tried to convince herself that was the case, but Raymond's words wouldn't leave her heart.

When her phone rang, hope sprang back into her spirit, but she was a little disappointed when PRIVATE NUMBER showed up on the caller ID.

"How would you like to spend the weekend with me?" Jerome said as soon as she greeted him.

Kenda was thrown. "What are you talking about? I thought we were going to Lake Lanier this weekend."

He laughed. "We are, but since we're goin' out tomorrow and Sunday, I thought you could spend the weekend at my crib and we go from here."

"Jerome, I . . . I don't know about that. I mean—"

"Look, I just want you to spend the weekend with me. I ain't say nothing about us doing anything."

She chuckled. "Jerome, do you really expect me to believe that you are inviting me to stay at your place for the *entire* weekend without any benefits included?"

Jerome laughed with her. "Actually, the thought crossed my mind, but only if you'd agree to it."

Kenda smiled. Maybe spending the weekend with Jerome wouldn't be so bad. She could use some undivided attention since she seemed to be practically invisible to everyone else she knew. Plus, her parents were away on business, and wouldn't be back until Monday night. Her brother would definitely be fine by himself. Nothing was holding her back.

"Sure," she said to his delight. "But only on one condition."

"What's that?" Jerome asked.

Her tone became soft and enticing. "I would like to see those animal print underwear on display."

He laughed before saying. "I think I can arrange that for

you. But this little fashion show needs a female model too, so pack something real sexy."

"Okay." She smiled.

"Great. I'll pick you up tonight at nine."

She frowned. "Why so late?"

"I got some business to take care of," he stated.

Kenda wasn't surprised. "Oh. Well, just make sure that your business won't interfere with *our* business," she flirted.

"Trust me, baby. It won't." Jerome's voice was husky.

Once she ended the call, Kenda began to pack her clothes for the weekend, making sure she packed her most tantalizing pieces of lingerie. As she placed a red silk teddy into her bag, Aundrey barged into her room.

"Boy, I swear, if you don't stop bustin' in my room, I'm gonna beat your tail," she said, her hands on her hips. "I could be doing anything up in here."

"Whatever." He dismissed her threat with a wave of his hand and looked down at her bag. "Where you goin'?"

"I'm staying at a friend's for the weekend," she replied, packing a long jean skirt. "Do you think you'll be okay until Sunday night?"

"I ain't a baby, you know," he retorted. "So you, Chantal, and Roslyn having one of them girl nights or something?"

She shook her head. "Nope." She placed another silk teddy and a negligee into her bag.

Her brother raised an eyebrow. "What you need those for?" he asked. "Where'd you even get them?"

"They were gifts from guys who *thought* they were going to get with me." She laughed.

Aundrey looked at her. "I don't even wanna know who those guys were." He shook his head. "But that doesn't answer my first question. What do you need them for?"

Kenda looked up at him and almost laughed when he folded his arms across his chest. He looked and acted so much like her father that Kenda felt as if Xavier was the one interrogating her. "Not that it's any of your business, but I'm spending the weekend with Jerome."

Aundrey's mouth dropped in surprise. "With *who*?" he asked, knowing full well that he didn't need or want her to repeat the answer. "Oh no you're not. I know Daddy and Mama don't know about this."

Kenda looked at her brother and sucked her teeth. "Drey, it's not like they are going to notice. Besides, they won't be back until Monday night. You'll have the whole house to yourself. You can do as you please. You can even bring that lil' Patrice girl over here," she spoke of the girl Aundrey had been seeing for the last few months. "But you're not gonna tell me I can't go to my boyfriend's house."

"I'm not against you going to his house, but for the *weekend*?" he stressed. "You know that something is going to happen."

Kenda smiled. "I know." She added a shrug. "I'm ready for this, Drey, and I'm going to do it."

Aundrey covered his ears. "I don't wanna hear that."

She laughed. "Why not? It's not like you're the Virgin Mary."

"It's different though. You're my sister."

"Doesn't Patrice have a *couple* of brothers?" she asked. He nodded. "Well then how would you think they'd feel about their sister sleeping with you?"

Aundrey shrugged. "We've only done it a few times, but that's beside the point."

"Look," Kenda said, placing more items in her bag, "I'm going. End of discussion."

"Fine, but what if Mom or Dad calls? What do you want me to tell them?"

"Drey, how many times must I tell you? They don't care so they're not going to call. They are going to be too wrapped up in their little work junk to even think about how their children are doing." Kenda sighed when he gave her a skeptical look. "*But* if they do, by some miracle, call to check up on us, tell them that I'm at Roslyn's house and if they need to call me, they can reach me on my cell." She placed her cell phone in her bag before she forgot.

"Okay." Aundrey walked toward the door, but then turned back. "Sis, make sure you use protection."

Kenda smiled. "Drey, don't worry, I'm covered." She held up a box of condoms she had purchased a while back, just so she'd have them on hand. Finally, she'd be able to use them. She laughed as he shook his head on his way out of her room.

Once Kenda finished packing, she went through her bag to make sure she had everything she needed. Satisfied, she decided to take a shower, using her scented soaps and moisturizers. When she decided to use the Vanilla Mango bath set, she realized that she hadn't used this particular scent since her last date with Raymond. *No, I'm not even going to start thinking about him. Not tonight . . . or ever. It's all about Jerome now.* She washed herself and tried to occupy her thoughts with something worth thinking about. Like this weekend. She couldn't wait to engage in her first sexual experience with the man she loved. She felt like it was time, and she was glad she'd waited. Kenda knew Jerome was not a virgin, but what man was in this day and time?

Raymond.

Kenda smiled at the thought. Raymond wasn't actually a virgin, but he'd been celibate for some time, and that was about as close to a virgin as Kenda knew any guy to be. Raymond's vow to be celibate was also a trait Kenda found very appealing about him. When she'd asked him about it, he told her that he'd experienced sex outside of marriage and it was completely overrated, so in order to receive full gratification from the interaction, he had decided to do things God's way and wait until he was married so that the union would be blessed.

"You see, God created sex to be shared between a man and a woman who have committed themselves to each other through holy matrimony," he'd told her on their second date. "And I believe in waiting."

"How long do you expect to wait?" she'd asked him.

He'd shrugged. "How ever long it takes me to find the wife God has for me. It's all in His timing."

All in God's timing. The words did a rerun through Kenda's head as she turned off the shower, and wrapped a towel around her body. Well tonight was going to be all about *her* timing. She walked out of the bathroom and proceeded to prepare herself for Jerome.

"Baby, how long does it take to change?" Jerome yelled from his bedroom.

"I . . . I'm almost . . . I think I'm almost ready," Kenda stuttered. She was so nervous about tonight that she could hardly think straight. She looked at herself in the mirror and knew she looked great in the red silk teddy, but she didn't know if she'd look good to Jerome. Pulling at the material, she took a deep breath before stepping out of the bathroom and walking up the hallway. Although no one was in the house except the two of them, she felt as if she were on display for the whole world to see. She peeked into the room and saw Jerome waiting impatiently on his bed. Clearing her throat, she gained his attention.

"I'm . . . ready," she said, still standing outside of the room.

Jerome's stare made her even more nervous. She didn't know if it was a stare of disappointment or of satisfaction. His face was void of reaction and that made her want to run back into the bathroom and hide. He got up and rubbed his mustache as he walked toward her. Finally, he cracked a smile, which made Kenda's stomach settle a little. Jerome reached for her hand and she, timidly, gave it to him.

"You look so . . . good." He smiled as he pulled her close to him.

Kenda looked down at his boxers. "I thought you were going to wear the underwear," she pouted.

Jerome laughed. "We've got all weekend, baby," he said before leaning in for a kiss.

He led her to his bed and laid her down gingerly as he continued to caress her with his lips. The silk sheets felt wonderful against her soft skin. The goose bumps on her arms rose at his touch. When she looked into his eyes as he whispered how much he loved her, Kenda knew this was where she wanted to be.

Chapter 12

Saturday morning sunlight peeked through the black blinds, stirring Kenda out of her sleep. She smiled, remembering last night, and turned to awake her sleeping prince. A frown replaced her smile when all she felt were the cold sheets beside her. She pulled back the covers, and then, realizing she had on no clothes, she quickly pulled them back up to hide herself. Searching the area around the bed for her overnight bag, Kenda remembered that it was in the closet. She wrapped the comforter around her body, put on an oversized T-shirt that she retrieved from her bag, and then walked back into the room.

"Jerome," Kenda called out, not wanting to walk out of the room to get him. "Jerome!"

With no answer, she figured he'd gone out. The least he could have done was left a note. As soon as the thought ran through her mind, a white sheet of paper, on his nightstand, caught her eye.

Baby thanks for taking care of me last night. It was wonderful. I had to run a couple of errands this morn-

*ing, but I should be back by twelve so we can go to
Lake Lanier. Oh yeah, and I promise we'll have that
fashion show today.*

   I love you,
   Jerome

Kenda smiled as she placed the note back on the table
and headed toward the bathroom to take a shower. Last
night had been the most wonderful night of her life. Jerome,
fully aware of her innocence, had handled her in the most
delicate manner. Kenda's body was a little sore, but last
night's experience had been worth this morning's discomfort.

Twenty minutes later, she came out of the bathroom, fully
dressed in a long wrap skirt, and a baby blue, long-sleeved,
V-neck top. She went into the room and pulled out her matching blue pumps, but decided against putting them on when
she looked down at Jerome's spotless white carpet. She was
glad that she'd thought to press her hair before coming to
Jerome's because all she had to do was pull it back into a
bun at the nape of her neck, and just like that, she was ready
for their trip.

At twelve forty-five, Jerome came waltzing through the
door. Kenda sat in the den watching television. She looked
up when he walked into the room.

"What took so long?" she asked as he kissed the top of her
head.

"Had a little delivery trouble." Jerome shrugged. "The guy
decided he didn't want to pay, so I had to take care of him."

"What did you do?" She looked up at him. "You didn't kill
him, did you?"

Jerome laughed. "Of course not. But he is going to be
wearing a cast on his leg for the next three months."

Kenda shook her head. She wanted to tell Jerome that his
job was much too dangerous. She wondered if he ever

thought about going to get his GED so he could at least go to a community college to get a decent job. She didn't want to wake up one day and hear about a drug deal gone bad on the news, and then see Jerome's picture on the screen because he was either in jail or dead. Just thinking about it made her shudder with fear.

"Did you eat anything?" Jerome asked from the kitchen.

"No. I'm not hungry," she said, staring at the television. Thoughts of Jerome lying in a grave haunted her mind.

"Baby, what's wrong?" he asked as he walked up behind her, eating a slice of toast.

Kenda turned to face him, settling her knees into the cushions of the sofa. "Jerome, do you ever think about going back to school?"

His laugh caught her off guard. "At the age of twenty-one? Not really."

"I'm serious," she said. "You could get your GED and go to Georgia Perimeter or something like that."

Jerome rolled his eyes. "Kenda, didn't we already discuss this? I'm not quittin' dealin'. It's what I do. It's who I am."

"But, baby, it's not who you *can be*. You can be so much more than that. It's too dangerous." She pleaded with her eyes for him to realize that she was only thinking of him. "I . . . I just think you can do so much better than . . . *selling drugs*." She saw the vein in his neck pop and she sank down in the couch.

"Kenda, I'm not going to quit. End of discussion." He picked up his car keys. "Let's go 'fore I change my mind."

Kenda got up and pulled her purse over her shoulder as she followed him out of the apartment.

Lake Lanier had been nothing like she'd expected. She'd thought it was just a big water park with rides, but she'd been wrong. Although they did have water rides, Kenda and Jerome spent most of their time at Great Restoration Day Spa, where they received couple's body massages, facials, and hand and foot massages. Afterward, they stopped by the mall and visited a Victoria Secret department store. Jerome picked out a few lingerie items for Kenda to sport in their fashion show, but Kenda couldn't fully enjoy any part of the day because her mind stayed on Jerome and the potential dangers of his job. Her failure to thank him for his purchases yielded her a good scolding when they returned to his apartment.

"I'm sorry," Kenda said as they sat on the couch. "My mind was just preoccupied."

Jerome rolled his eyes. "What was so heavy on your mind that you couldn't enjoy an afternoon out with me? Kenda, I spent well over a thousand dollars today, and you didn't appreciate one penny of it."

He acted like she'd asked him to spend that kind of money on her. She hadn't and was tempted to tell him so. Instead, she said, "Baby, I do appreciate it. Every cent. I was just kinda worried about some things, that's all." She leaned into him.

"Do you really appreciate it?" he asked, apparently still not convinced that he wasn't being taken for granted.

"Yes, I promise." She delivered a tender kiss, and then allowed his hands to explore freely as she deepened their kiss. When she moved to help him out of his shirt, his cell phone began to beep loudly. "Oh please don't answer it," Kenda whined as she lay on his chest.

"I got to," Jerome said. "It's an urgent page." He picked up his cell and dialed the number on the screen. All of his words and responses were short. "Wassup? Right now? No, I can get it there in five. I'll get someone else to drop the other one. A'ight. Cool. Peace." He hung up the phone and looked up at Kenda with an I-need-a-favor grin stretched across his face.

She had already begun shaking her head. "No, Jerome. I won't do it."

"Baby, please," he begged.

"No! Why can't you just handle your business and come back."

" 'Cause two different people need it. One in this building and another down the block," he explained. "I can handle the one down the block, but I don't have time to stop and drop off the one downstairs. When these people need their stuff, they need it at that moment. All you have to do is take it down to apartment 110 and make sure he gives you the money. Please, baby, please. I swear, I won't ask you to do it again."

Kenda pulled herself out of his embrace. "No, Jerome! You must be out your mind. I'm not getting caught up in your mess. Unlike you, I do want a better life for myself." As soon as she'd said the words, she wished she could take them back.

The back of Jerome's hand sailed across her face in a fury, and just as before, the impact knocked her to the floor. But this time, he repeatedly hit and stomped on her. Kenda lay on the floor in fetal position, pleading for him to stop as she tried her best to protect her body with her small arms. Ironically, the only thing on her mind was that she wished he had taken off his shoes if he were going to kick her.

"Who you think you are, huh?" Jerome demanded as he pulled Kenda up by her arms. "You think you better than me 'cause you go to school and you gon' be some stankin' lawyer?" He slapped her again, sending her crashing back on the floor. She covered her face in agony. Unsympathetic, he kicked her again, and then screamed, "Get up!"

In painful, slow movements, Kenda climbed back to her feet and coiled in fear as he took a small packet out of his pocket and threw it at her. He reached into the cabinet under the table and pulled out a spare key to his apartment and tossed it on the sofa.

"Lock the door when you leave, and you better be here

when I get back." He grabbed his car keys. "And that stuff better be sold too," he warned as he walked out the front door.

Kenda felt a trickle of blood on her lips and gently wiped it away. She waited a couple of minutes before making her way toward the door. As she walked down the hall, she wiped her face and tried to appear normal, but the tears wouldn't leave her. She was sure she looked as if she'd been through a road war. Her legs were killing her, and her head was pounding so hard that she thought her brain would soon plop out into her hands. She sighed once she reached the elevator, wishing she wouldn't have said a word. If she would have just taken the drugs and made the delivery, none of this would have happened.

When she reached apartment 110, she knocked on the door. Seconds later, a large, white male appeared in the doorway. He looked down at Kenda, and without words, he handed her a roll of money that she stuck into her pocket. She handed him the small bag of drugs just before he shut the door in her face.

As Kenda dragged her sore body back to the elevator, she thought about running. But she knew Jerome would come looking for her, so without a second thought, she got onto the elevator and pushed the button for the second floor. Once she got back into the apartment, she locked the doors. Just as she'd been told.

Looking into a mirror that hung above the mantle piece in the living room, Kenda cried at her reflection. Blood leaked from her top and bottom lips. Her hair was mangled as if she'd just awaken from a restless sleep. Her face was swollen. Her arms and legs were sore. She looked down at the carpet and knew that Jerome would have to have it professionally cleaned in order to get the bloodstains out.

Bit by aching bit, Kenda made her way to the bathroom to take a hot shower before Jerome got back. She wanted to go home, but knew he wouldn't take her back before Sunday. She peeled off her clothes, careful not to cause any more agony to her sore body. She climbed into the shower and sank to the floor of the stall, cringing as the hot water pelted against her skin, stinging the bruises in the process.

As she wept, Kenda wondered why she wasn't even contemplating leaving Jerome. They'd only been in the relationship for a little less than three months, and she already felt trapped. She loved Jerome, but wondered if he really loved her as he said he did. She also wondered if karma was coming back around to haunt her. For the last few years, she'd been using guys for selfish desires, never once giving a thought to their feelings. She would use up their time and money, and then dismiss them once she became bored. She wondered if she were living the saying, "What goes around comes around." Was this her punishment for all of her own abuse? Physical abuse in return for the emotional torment she'd caused others?

The sound of the shower door opening startled Kenda. She looked up at Jerome as he joined her under the steaming water. He gently pulled her to her feet and into his arms. He ran his fingers through her curly hair, which had returned to its natural state as the steam moistened her once-straightened locks.

"Baby, I'm so sorry," Jerome said as she cried on his bare chest. "I really am sorry. I didn't mean to do it. I promise, I didn't."

"Why do you do it, Jerome?" she cried. "What did I do? Why do I make you so angry?"

He gently touched her swollen face. "It's not you; it really is me. I have a problem, but I promise I won't do it again. I'll go get some help. I swear."

"Promise?" Kenda asked, feeling a new surge of hopefulness.

"Promise," Jerome said as he kissed her, pulling her body closer to his.

Her legs weakened at his gentle touch and he proceeded to position her against the shower wall for support as he showed her that he did love her, and that he didn't want her to leave him alone.

Chapter 13

The rest of the weekend went by much too slow for Kenda, and she was happy to be back in her own home. As she'd predicted, her parents hadn't called. Her brother went out for most of the weekend, staying out late with his friends, but had been home when Kenda walked through the door Sunday night. She tried to keep her distance so he wouldn't be able to see the bruises on her face, arms, and legs. The make-up, that Jerome had taken her to buy, was doing a pretty good job of masking her wounds. She knew Aundrey would ask questions about her weekend and she gave him a brief synopsis of her time spent with Jerome, leaving out the parts about the drugs and the abuse.

Kenda didn't know if her friends would be as easily persuaded that things had gone well, but as she prepared for school, she hoped they would. She pulled the gold Apple Bottoms shirt over her head and slipped into the matching boot cut blue jeans she'd bought last year, but had only worn once. She almost cried at the fact that she had to wear jeans. Although it was the middle of November, Atlanta's weather had proven year after year, that mild fall temperatures never really faded until mid-December. During this transitional time, Kenda usually sported her more conservative fall fashions until the winter temperatures fully revealed themselves. But now, because of Jerome's anger management issues, she was being forced to hide inside of a pair of Apple Bottoms jeans what she considered to be one of the most appealing parts of her body.

Hearing a car honk outside, Kenda took one final look in the mirror and shook her head before walking out to Jerome's car. While Jerome carried on a conversation as if nothing had happened over the past weekend, Kenda sat silently, nodding her head and making short comments as if she were listening. Once he pulled up to the school, she kissed him, and got out of the car.

She watched as Chantal and Roslyn pulled up and got out of her convertible, looking as if they'd just left a photo shoot for a teen magazine in their casual, but stylish wear. Kenda wanted to walk with them, but it seemed as if they'd been avoiding her, so she continued to make her way toward the entrance.

"Kenda," she heard Chantal yell.

Kenda stopped and smiled as she waited for the two girls to catch up with her. "Hey, guys," she said, putting on a cheery front.

"I've been trying to call you back all weekend, but all I got was your voicemail," Chantal said, gazing at Kenda as if she looked foreign to her. "What happened to your face?"

Kenda self-consciously touched her face. "Nothing. I think I'm allergic to some of this makeup."

Chantal laughed. "Or maybe you just put on a little too much." Kenda turned away, but Chantal continued with her questions. "Where were you all weekend?"

Kenda smiled, remembering that the time with her boyfriend wasn't *all* bad. "At Jerome's."

"All weekend?" Chantal's voice showed her surprise.

When Kenda nodded, Roslyn's eyes bulged out of her eye sockets. "You mean you . . . ?"

Kenda nodded again. She gave them full details about her weekend, once again, leaving out the drugs and the abuse. "He even modeled *the underwear* for me."

Chantal laughed. Well, go 'head girl!" she said, slapping hands with Kenda.

Roslyn smiled slightly. "I never would have thought . . . I mean . . . oh my." She couldn't find the words to express her shock.

Kenda and Chantal laughed. As they walked inside of the school, Kenda was glad she didn't look too out of place with her fashionable friends. Chantal's skirt stopped just above her ankles and her short-sleeved, orange shirt set off her dark skin tone. Roslyn's black Capri pants and red top went well with her black Reeboks. When they sat down in the commons, Chantal noticed that Kenda had grown uncharacteristically quiet.

"What's up, girl? Why are you so quiet?" Chantal asked.

Kenda shrugged her shoulders. "No reason. I'm fine."

Roslyn looked down at her clothes. "Girl, I like that out-fit," she commented, trying to lighten up Kenda's mood.

"Thanks." Kenda's reply was barely a mumble.

Roslyn glanced at Chantal and they both knew something was wrong with their friend. "Kenda, what's wrong with you?"

"Lyn, I just don't feel good today," she said, nearing tears.

Chantal laughed. "With the weekend you had, I would think you'd be around here hoppin', skippin', and jumpin' like a love sick puppy."

Kenda's first tear fell, and she got up quickly and headed for the nearest restroom. She prayed her friends wouldn't follow her, but she knew that prayer wouldn't be answered. They burst through the restroom doors within seconds of her entry.

"Kenda, why are you crying?" Chantal asked, grabbing a

few paper towels and wetting them for Kenda to clean her face of the tears.

Without thinking, Kenda took them and wiped her tears. She soon regretted the action when Roslyn screamed, "Oh my God!" at the sight of the bruise that marked a large portion of Kenda's cheek.

Kenda turned away and let all of her tears out. Roslyn pulled her into her arms and consoled her as Chantal looked on in total disbelief.

"Kenda, what happened?" Roslyn asked in a nurturing tone.

Kenda shook her head. "I never even saw it coming," she said through her tears. "He wanted me to do it, but I didn't and he got so mad."

"Wait a minute," Chantal barked angrily. "Did Jerome force you to have sex with him by beating you up?"

Kenda's eyes opened wide. "Oh no. No, we had consensual sex. He wanted me to take some drugs to one of his customers, but I didn't want to. So he beat me into doing it. Kicked me and punched me all over my body. It hurt so bad," she cried.

Roslyn kneeled and lifted up Kenda's pants leg. The material was harsh against her irritated skin. Her friends gasped at the sight of the light red bruises that decorated her legs like ill-placed tattoos.

"After I sold his stuff, I went back to the apartment and—"

"You went back there after he did this?" Roslyn asked while she pulled down Kenda's pants leg and stood up.

Kenda nodded. "But only because he had gone to make a sell down the street, and he told me that I'd better be there when he got back. I knew if I didn't do as he said, he'd come after me. So I went back and got in the shower. Then when he came home, he got in with me and told me he was sorry and that he was going to go get help. Then we had sex again."

"Let me get this straight," Chantal said, motioning with her hands that she wanted to review the conversation. "Jerome wanted you to sell his drugs, but you said no. He beats the mess out of you and tells you to make the sell. He also tells you to be back at the apartment when he gets back, and you do as you're told because you're afraid." She paused as if digesting it all. After a moment, she said, "Okay. I understand all that. Most of it anyway. But then you actually let him get in the shower with you *and* touch you after he had kicked . . . literally *kicked* your tail?" Kenda nodded and Chantal shook her head. "Okay, Kenda, I know before I said you should give him another chance," she said, lifting Kenda's chin, "but look at your face." She turned Kenda toward the mirror.

Her face looked even worse than it had last night when she'd examined herself after icing down her wounds. Though Kenda's lips went from being twice their normal size to being half as swollen, there was still a reddish bruise that ran from the corner of her eye down to her jaw. She looked down at her hands. "But he said he'd get help. Things are going to get better, I just know it." She tried to convince her friends, but she was having a hard time believing her own words.

"Kenda, I know you're not buying that. He's just saying that so he won't lose you," Roslyn said, wiping her own tears. "And honestly, he doesn't even deserve you."

"Kenda, he's turning you into someone you're not," Chantal said. "He has you running his drugs all over the place, and he's beatin' you like you're his slave. And if you don't be careful, that's exactly what you're gonna become. His own personal slave. He's already telling you who you can and can't hang out with. And just so you know, Raymond's acting like he don't care nothin' about what's going on, but trust me, he's been blowin' up my phone to see of you've kicked that dog to the curb yet."

"Really?" Kenda was surprised.

"Girl, he's been calling me too," Roslyn revealed. "I told you he cares. Now that's who you need to be with. Raymond loves you and he cares about you. Can you say that much about Jerome? He may say he loves you, but does he mean it? He definitely don't care about you with the way he's beatin' on you."

Kenda's tears wouldn't stop coming. She wanted to leave Jerome, but she couldn't. Not when he needed her the most. She could help him through the counseling and help him gain control of his anger. She knew if she just complied with everything he said, she'd be okay. *They'd* be okay. As soon as he started working with a counselor, she'd be able to stay with him and be happy. Kenda told her friends her idea, and her tears continued to flow when they solemnly stared at her and shook their heads. She knew they wouldn't agree, but she had to endure it. Seeing Jerome become a new person would be her reward.

When the bell rang, Kenda finished washing off her makeup so her face wouldn't look to be uneven in its tone. Then Chantal gave her a pair of designer sunglasses, and Roslyn gave Kenda her hooded jacket. Kenda placed the sunglasses on her face, and then put on the jacket. Once she got into her classroom, she pulled the hood over her head, slid into her seat at the back of the classroom, and hoped no one would notice her masquerade. Her heart stopped for a second when Raymond came and sat in the desk beside her, not even looking her way.

As Ms. Jones began the class, Kenda tried hard to focus on what she was saying about the projects that they were supposed to be working on. She watched as the students gathered with their partners and she did the same with Marla. Kenda listened as Marla told her about the information she'd looked up on Christopher Marlowe.

"Do you have the plays from the list?" Marla asked, giving Kenda a strange look.

Kenda silently reached into her backpack and pulled out the books that she'd gotten from the library last week. "These are some of the plays he's written," she said softly.

Kenda's teacher walked around the classroom, checking on each group's progress. When she came to where Kenda and Marla worked, she eyed Kenda's attire.

"Ms. Tyson," Ms. Jones said, "I do not believe that there's a sun in this room, so if your sunglasses are not accompanied by a doctor's note, I would suggest that you remove them."

"But Ms. Jones—"

The teacher shook her head, interrupting Kenda's excuse. "Do you have a doctor's note?"

"No, ma'am," Kenda said softly. She held her head down as she slowly took off the sunglasses.

"The hood also," Ms. Jones said.

Kenda silently did as she was told and tried to shield her face with her hands.

Ms. Jones gave Kenda a peculiar gaze. "Ms. Tyson, are you all right?"

Kenda nodded. "Yes, ma'am." Her head was still lowered.

"It would be nice to see that pretty face of yours when you say that," Ms. Jones said, lifting Kenda's head with her index finger.

Tears immediately flooded Kenda's eyes when she saw Ms. Jones's smile turn upside down. Gasps flew from the mouths of those who were close enough to get a glimpse of Kenda's battered face.

"Class, continue to do you work," Ms. Jones said as she pulled Kenda out of her seat and led her out of the classroom.

As they passed Raymond's desk, Kenda saw the anger on his face before turning away from his heated stare.

* * *

"Kenda, I can't help you if you won't tell me who did this to you." Mr. Zimmerman folded his hands on his desk and waited patiently for Kenda's response.

Kenda looked away without a word. She'd gone from being hysterical during the walk to the counseling center, to being upset at Ms. Jones for exposing her bruises, to being angry with Mr. Zimmerman for trying to pry information out of her for the past fifteen minutes. But she'd been strangely proud of herself for not bursting into confession.

"Kenda." Mr. Zimmerman had called her name a third time, and she finally faced him. "Kenda, if you don't tell me who did this to you, I am going to have to place a call to your parents and find out from them."

Kenda shrugged and turned away again. She could tell she'd thrown him off guard with her response. She knew that he'd expected for her to jump up with a start, and give him the abuser's full name, address, and telephone number, but she continued to look away from his prying gaze.

Kenda watched as the counselor looked up her information on the computer and called her parents' job. He held short pleasantries with her father and then asked Xavier if he and his wife were available to come down to the school. Kenda almost laughed as she heard Mr. Zimmerman plead with her father, telling him that it was an extreme emergency, and that he desperately needed to speak with them both. Once he ended the call, Mr. Zimmerman left the room, telling Kenda he'd be back momentarily.

As she sat in his spacious office, Kenda wondered if this would be the end of her relationship with Jerome. She prayed it wouldn't. She really wanted to help him make a change in his life, but couldn't help but wonder if he actually wanted to change. If he did, that was the second step in the recovery process. He'd already admitted to having a problem; that had been step one. Yeah, she could see it happening. She smiled slightly before touching her face in pain.

"Girl, you are out of your mind," her head started in on her again. *"That boy ain't changing nothin'. Just 'cause he say he is, don't mean a thing."* She held her head as it reprimanded her.

Soon, her heart jumped in on the action. *"Don't listen to that brain of yours. Jerome loves you. He just has a few problems. He needs you; you're all he has right now, remember? And as long as you stick around, he's gonna be motivated to change his lifestyle."*

"As long as you stick around," her head interrupted, *"he's gonna be motivated to keep placing the back of his hand upside your face. He's already told you that he wasn't gonna quit dealing drugs. That should be enough to get you up and walking, but no, you're gonna sit around and let him make you sell his mess and still come home to a butt whippin' every other day. I don't think so, Kenda. You are a smart girl . . . why not make a smart decision?"*

"Staying with Jerome is a smart decision," her heart stated. *"He loves you. He's the only person who loves you like you need to be loved. You don't get that affection from anyone else like you get it from him. Jerome loves you, and that's where you belong. All you have to do now is help him get himself together so y'all can be happy."*

Kenda tuned out her head and listened to her heart. It was right. All she had to do was help Jerome get himself together and they'd be happy. She was satisfied with her decision and there was nothing her friends, her counselor, or even her parents could say or do to change her mind.

Chapter 14

Kenda had defiantly positioned herself on the sofa across from the loveseat her parents were sitting on. She knew that the tears in her mother's eyes were a result of having to see her beat-up face. When her parents arrived at the school and were brought into Mr. Zimmerman's office, Kenda was sure that they were fully prepared to hear that she had been in an of altercation of some sort. Kenda was known for her smart mouth and quick rebuttals, so the notion wasn't a far-fetched one. But when her parents walked into the counselor's office and were confronted with Kenda's swollen face, Maxine burst into tears, and Xavier looked as if he were about to go on a rampage.

After checking Kenda out of school early, they'd had a quiet ride home. Now as they sat in the living room of their home, Kenda refused to talk. But she didn't have to because Xavier knew exactly what was going on. His protective, fatherly intuition had kicked in moments after his eyes had adjusted to seeing his daughter's face. When he'd asked Kenda who the culprit was, she had avoided eye contact with him and shrugged her shoulders indifferently. That was enough evidence for him. With fire in his eyes, he continued to mutter unfavorable words that would have been directed toward Jerome had he been in the room.

"I'll kill him," Xavier continued to repeat over and over as his wife tried to keep his emotions in tact, all the while having more trouble trying to keep hers under control.

"Xavier, we have to handle this rationally," Maxine said, wiping tears.

"Rationally?" Xavier spat. "Oh we passed rational a *long* time ago, the moment that boy put his hands on my daughter!"

Kenda continued to look out of the window, trying her best not to listen to her parents as they argued on what was good for her. But they soon gathered her attention when her father said, "Kenda, you are not to see him anymore!"

"What?" she exclaimed. "Daddy, no!"

"*No*?" Xavier seethed. "What do you mean no! This guy is abusing you, Kenda. Or did you not know that? Have you not looked at your face? You look as if you've been hit by a car or something," Xavier said as his wife tried her best to get him to downplay his words for their daughter's emotional sake.

"I know that, Daddy! I know what I look like and no, I don't like it, but I love Jerome and I know he can change," Kenda said with tears streaming down her face. "We've talked about it. We're going to get counseling and he's going to get some help."

"*Counseling*?" her father yelled. "You're not married to him, Kenda!"

"Kenda, you don't even know what love is," Maxine added in a gentler tone.

Kenda nodded. "Yes, I do."

"Girl, you're only seventeen," her father stated angrily. "Which not only means you're too young to know what true love is, but in my eyes it also makes you too young to even be dating this monster. I should've made you stop seeing him a long time ago."

"Well, the legal age of consent in Georgia is sixteen and since I'll be eighteen in a few months, I'm governed under the law," Kenda refuted. "Besides, you guys never cared about Jerome's age before. Mama, you said I was mature enough to handle it, and Daddy, you agreed because I'd be legally an adult in a few months." She gladly refreshed her parents' memory of the conversation they'd had after her first date with Jerome. "And just because I'm young doesn't mean that I don't know what love is. Jerome makes me feel wanted. He makes me feel needed. He needs me, and I can't leave him."

"Oh yes you can!" Xavier said, standing to his full height of six feet two. "And you will!"

Kenda's eyes became balls of fury as she stood up, for the first time, challenging her father. "Why do you even care?" she asked through clenched teeth. "Since when do you care about what's going on in my life? I've been going out with Jerome for three months and he's hit me once before." She showed her father the fading bruise. "You didn't even notice. I wonder why?" she asked sarcastically. "It might be because you and Mom are never here. And when you are, y'all are too busy doing work to even notice Drey and me. We don't even be here half the time, but you wouldn't know it because *y'all* are *never* here.

"You've never taken an interest in my personal life. You meet a guy once and then that's it. It's all in my hands. You guys have no clue as to what goes on in my life. You have missed important milestones that I should have been able to share with you, but I couldn't because you weren't around for me to. So why would you care now? Just because someone put their hands on me? Because I have bruises on my face? Are you going to wait until I'm lying half dead somewhere to even tell me that you love me and that you care about me?" Tears streamed down Kenda's face during her rant.

Maxine stepped up. "Kenda, we do love you."

Kenda chuckled dryly. "Funny. That's the first time I've heard it come from your mouth in years. I was starting to think that T, T, & B was your firstborn instead of me." She folded her arms across her chest.

Xavier softened his stance along with his tone of voice. "Baby girl, we do love you, and we're sorry if you've ever felt neglected because of our careers. But I promise you that I'll be dead and buried before I let you continue seeing someone who treats you like this."

"Well start digging that grave," Kenda spoke maliciously as she stomped up the stairs toward her bedroom, leaving her parents standing in the living room in shock.

She didn't care what anyone had to say; she was not going to leave Jerome. They needed each other. But the more she thought about it, the more she realized that she needed him more than he needed her. He was the only one to ever really show her how much she was loved. She didn't want to lose that. She refused to let anyone take that feeling from her.

Kenda was in an unfamiliar dark building. She crouched in the corner of the room, and continued to scream for help as the man came toward her with the weapon in his hand.

"God, please. Please, God, help!" she screamed. "Somebody, please help me!"

The man kept drawing closer, and her cries continued. She saw him draw back his fist before she felt blow after blow on various parts of her body. Nonstop, she screamed for help as the man punched her in the face and stomach. Then just like that, her cries came to a halt as she unconsciously protected her abdomen while the man physically abused her.

No longer worried about the abuse she was enduring,

Kenda began to whisper, "Everything's gonna be okay. Mama's got you. Mama's got you."

Kenda's eyes popped open and she sat upright in her bed. When she rubbed her stomach and realized she'd been dreaming, she breathed a sigh of relief. Hearing the front door open, she realized she'd been asleep for several hours. Her brother came barreling up the stairs and burst into her room.

"Kenda, what's going on? Everybody's saying that you got—" He stopped when she turned to face him, revealing her bruised face. "Who did it?" he asked, jaw tightened and visibly trembling.

Kenda had never seen her brother so angry. It brought tears to her eyes to know that he was ready to stand up for his big sister. When she didn't answer right away, he got even angrier.

"Who did this to you? I wanna know now!" Aundrey shouted with tears brimming in his eyes too as he looked past the bruises and into the depths of his sister's soul.

Kenda got up, tears falling from her eyes onto the carpet. She wrapped her arms around her brother's waist, resting her head on his chest. Aundrey returned the embrace and tried to keep his emotions intact as snapshots of his sister's bruised face entered his mind. He'd never seen her look so bad before, and he wanted to hunt Jerome down like a lion hunting for its prey. He knew something wasn't right the day he met the guy. His slick ways and smooth talk gave off a negative vibe about him that Aundrey never liked. He'd wanted to tell his sister, but knew that she wouldn't listen to anything bad he had to say about *the great* Jerome Smith.

"I'm sorry," Kenda said, wiping her face, wincing at the pain she felt when her palm brushed across her eye.

Aundrey stopped his tears before they fell. "Why are you apologizing?"

"Because I know you're gonna be like everybody else,

telling me to leave him, but I'm not and I know you're gonna be disappointed in me," she said. "I can't go because he needs me . . . I need him . . . Drey, we need each other. It's like we're all we have."

Aundrey wanted to shake some sense into his sister's head. "Kenda, you have family and friends. You got me, Chantal, Roslyn, Ray, Mama, Daddy—"

"I don't have love, Drey," she said, gently wiping more tears. "I don't have anyone to love me. I know all of y'all care about me, but it's not the same. I can count on one hand how many times all of you, put together, have told me you love me. But I need more than just my two hands to count the many times Jerome has confessed his love for me, and that makes me feel special. It makes me feel needed. I can't leave that. I'm sorry."

Aundrey was stunned into silence. He'd never known his sister had these feelings about her family and friends. Until now, he'd never even thought about the sad truth that they were in elementary school the last time he'd let her know that he loved her. Kenda sat on her bed and they let the silence envelop them.

"You remember when I was in the fourth grade and that guy was trying to beat me up?" Aundrey asked as he sat next to her.

Kenda nodded. "Yeah. And your friend, Janice, came and got me from lunch. She told me that you were about to get handled." She laughed softly.

He chuckled. "Yep, and just when he was about to hit me, you came outside yellin', 'Hey, leave my brother alone!' " He gave his best imitation of a young girl's voice.

"And he asked me what I was gonna do if he didn't." Kenda smiled at the memory. "So I showed him." She shrugged, remembering how she'd punched the boy in the jaw, knocking him to the ground.

"I'd never seen a girl hit a boy before," Aundrey recalled.

"You knocked him out good. Although you got suspended, and I was picked on because my sister had beat up a boy for me, I was amazed at you. I was so happy that you were my big sister. I knew no one would mess with me anymore."

Kenda laughed. "Yeah, and you kept telling me how much you loved me and you hoped that I would never stop being your big sister."

Aundrey looked at her. "And that was the last time you ever heard those words come from my mouth."

She nodded solemnly. "I guess as we got older, expressing our feelings wasn't as important."

He gazed into her eyes, so she'd know he was being sincere. "Sis, I do love you and I hope you know that. Love is not worth being beaten over if you can get it scar-free," he said as a tear rolled down her cheek.

"I love you too, Drey," she said, hugging him. "But I really want to work this out on my own." She pulled back. "So please don't get involved."

Aundrey saw her eyes begging him to comply with her plea, but he wanted so badly to beat Jerome into his grave. He resigned to the fact that his sister was old enough to make her own decisions, no matter how stupid. Nodding, he said, "Okay, but don't take too long to come to your senses." He stood up, kissed her on the top of her head, and left the room.

Kenda's phone rang shortly thereafter, and she looked at the caller ID before answering.

"Hey girl," Chantal said.

"How are you doing," Roslyn's voice followed.

"I'm fine," Kenda answered. "I went off on my parents though. They want me to stop seeing Jerome, but I told them I wasn't going to."

"Girl, are you out of your mind?" Chantal asked. "You know that fool came up to the school to pick you up and flipped out on us when he heard you went home early because of what he did to you. I almost cursed his behind out. Then he got the nerve to tell us that it wasn't his fault, that he just lost his temper. Girl, he better be glad Lyn was out there 'cause that's the only thing that kept me from going upside his head."

"I guess I need to talk to him just to let him know everything's fine," Kenda said softly.

Chantal snapped. "No, everything is *not* fine. Girl, have you lost your mind?" she repeated her earlier question. "What is going on in that head of yours?"

"Kenda, why are you doing this to yourself?" Roslyn asked like a concerned mother.

As seemed to have become a way of life for her lately, Kenda began to cry again. "I'm not doing anything to myself, Lyn. I'm doing this for Jerome . . . for our relationship. I know it's going to get better. All I have to do is stay with him and he'll do better, I know he will."

"Okay," Chantal said bitterly. "Do what you want, but don't expect for us to be around in the end when you're in the hospital somewhere." She hung up the phone.

Kenda sighed. "Lyn, are you mad at me too?"

"No. But I'm very disappointed because the Kenda I know has much better judgment than the one I'm talking to right now."

"I know things have been different since I got with Jerome, but I finally have something that I've always wanted."

"That being?"

"Love," Kenda replied quietly. "I've never experienced real love until I met Jerome."

"Kenda, real love is not painful, it is not abusive," Roslyn spoke the words softly so Kenda would not think she was being lectured. "Real love is kind and nurturing. It's caring and patient. Jerome is not showing you real love."

Kenda was silent. She was tired of hearing other people's opinion. She'd already made up her mind; she wasn't leaving.

"I talked to Ray," Roslyn stated casually. "He asked about you."

"Why didn't he just call *me*?" Kenda asked, tired of Raymond acting as if he cared. If he were really concerned, he would call her, not her friends.

"He said he was trying to stay out of the way. But Kenda, he's tired of watching you get hurt. I've never heard or seen him so angry. He was about to run up on Jerome after school today, but I talked him out of it so he wouldn't end up suspended. He wouldn't even walk outside 'cause he knew if he saw Jerome, he was gonna react."

"How noble of him," Kenda replied cynically.

The line was silent for several moments. If Roslyn hadn't heard Kenda breathing, she would have thought her friend had hung up. "Ray said he loves you," Roslyn spoke up, almost causing Kenda to fall off the side of her bed.

"Wha . . . what did you just say?" Surely, Kenda didn't hear what she thought she'd heard.

"I said that Raymond said that he loves you," Roslyn repeated. "We were talking and he got off on this rampage and his exact words were, 'Man, I love that girl too much to sit back and watch her go through this'." She became quiet, waiting for Kenda's response.

"He . . . he said that . . . really?" Kenda asked with more tears leaking down her face.

"Yeah, he did. I don't even think he realized that he'd said it, but he did and I brought it to his attention. He didn't even try denying it. He just said, 'Yeah, I guess I do'." She paused for a moment. "Kenda . . . Kenda, are you still there?"

"Yes." Kenda cried softly.

"Oh sweetie, it's okay." Roslyn knew her friend was wishing she could take back all the things she'd done in the past. "You love him too, don't you?"

"I never really got over him," she admitted.

"Girl, it's okay. That's a good thing."

Kenda shook her head. "No . . . no, it's not. I've always loved Ray, but I love Jerome too. I can't love two people like this. It's wrong. How can I love two people?"

"Kenda, you're heart is big enough for you to love the whole world. But right now, you have love for two completely different guys who love you in two completely different ways. While Jerome says he loves you, he shows his love by placing bruises all over that beautiful face of yours. He makes you do things you don't want to do. He bosses you around as if he has rule over you. He pulls you away from the people who he thinks will take you away from him. The people who really do love you with *real* love.

"Ray loves you from the depths of his soul. He cares for you so much that when you hurt, he hurts. He hates seeing you like this and he's really worried about you. He takes time out to pray for you everyday, even if nothing may be wrong. He calls me and Chantal *everyday*, checking up on you. He's being patient with you while you go through this mess with Jerome. He wants so badly to talk to you, but he's afraid that Jerome will find out and that will only add to the problem. He wants you to get out of this, so that you can go back to being the old Kenda. That's real love, girl. Somebody who cares about you and wants the best for you."

By now, Kenda was sobbing. She hated herself for all of this mess and wanted to go back to that day at Northlake Mall, tell Jerome that she wasn't available, that she wasn't interested; anything that would prevent her from being in this position months later.

"Kenda, it's going to be okay." Roslyn's maternal tone caressed her. "God will work it all out."

God? This was the first time Kenda had heard Roslyn say anything about God. As far as she knew, Roslyn was about as much of a Christian as she was. Not wanting to get into a religious conversation, Kenda told Roslyn how much she appreciated her and ended the call. She sat on her bed and wondered how she was going to get Jerome to change. She knew she could do it though; it was just a matter of putting her words into actions. She'd prove all of the naysayers wrong. She'd show them all.

Chapter 15

Kenda's face looked much better than it had a few weeks ago, but it hadn't completely healed. Although the swelling had fully disappeared and the bruise on her cheek was gradually fading, she still had a sizeable scar next to her right eye. She looked in the mirror and sighed.

The Thanksgiving break had done Kenda some good. She'd spent much of the time with Jerome because of her parents' uncooperative work schedule. Her refusal to spend the holiday with her grandparents out in Texas left her brother to spend the holiday with his girlfriend's family. For the most part, Jerome and Kenda had fun. She'd slipped up and talked back to him once, earning her a bruise to the arm when he grabbed it with too much force. Other than that, no new scars adorned her body. Jerome had been attentive and somewhat gentle. He made dinner and they shared it over candlelight. After he ran his errands, they spent the rest of the day in bed.

The strained relationships between Kenda and her friends were starting to have an emotional effect on her. She would find herself crying for no reason when she really wanted to be happy with the decision she'd made. Sometimes she would be angry with the wrong people in order to justify her choice to stay with Jerome. She had been so stressed out that she had actually missed her menstrual cycle this month. Initially, it frightened her, but she recalled several times when she'd missed it before due to stress, so she wasn't worried. She just hoped that she'd soon be able to rid herself of this anxiety.

She'd found out, through Roslyn, that Chantal was no longer speaking to her. Apparently, until Kenda came to her senses, her best friend of six years wouldn't be associating with her. Raymond continued to keep his distance too. And although it was required for the school to inform a social worker when an incident such as abuse occurred, Kenda had refused to file charges against Jerome. Her parents must have agreed that she was old enough to make her own decisions and to learn from her mistakes since they gave up on keeping her from her abuser.

The only person who Kenda could truly call a friend was Roslyn. She knew she could count on her girl to stick it out with her. Though Roslyn never stopped insinuating that Kenda should let Jerome go, she never ridiculed Kenda's decision to stay with him.

Kenda was sure that she'd made the right decision. She could see Jerome changing already. They had scheduled an appointment with a counselor and were supposed to be meeting with her next week. Jerome had told Kenda that if she didn't feel comfortable being around him, he wouldn't be upset if they took a break from each other. But the look in his eyes contradicted his words and her heart went out to him. Declining his offer for space, Kenda stood by her man, despite the strain it was putting on her other relationships.

"Kenda, you ready?" Aundrey stuck his head inside her room.

Kenda took one last look in the mirror, finger-combed her hair, and straightened out her outfit before turning to her brother with a smile. "Yep." She grabbed her skates before heading out of the room.

Ever since he'd found out about her being abused, Aundrey had been trying to spend more time with his big sister and Kenda didn't mind. She enjoyed being around her brother because no matter what she was going through, he managed to keep her smiling.

"Dad said we can use the car as long as we're careful," Aundrey said as they locked up the house and headed toward the Lexus convertible.

Aundrey handed Kenda the keys and she shook her head. "No, you drive." She laughed as his eyes practically popped out of their sockets. She knew what he was thinking. He'd just gotten his license and didn't want it to be taken because he'd wrecked their dad's car. She smiled and said, "Drey, you're a much better driver than I am. Plus, I just feel like chillin' while the wind blows through my hair." She posed as she ran her fingers through her natural curls.

Aundrey rolled his eyes and got into the driver's seat as Kenda walked around the car and hopped into the passenger's side. Although December had arrived, the sun hadn't stopped shining and the temperatures were those of a cool fall day. Aundrey let the top down as he backed out of the garage.

Kenda groaned as her brother inserted his Tupac Shakur CD into the disk player and turned up the volume. She'd heard him play the CD so many times that she knew many of the words to some of the rap songs, and caught herself when she began to join in on the parts she knew. Her brother looked at her and smiled.

"So you do like Pac," Aundrey observed as he stopped at a red light.

Kenda shrugged. "He a'ight."

They shared a laugh that was interrupted by the constant

sound of a blaring horn. Kenda turned her head slightly to her right to see Jerome's Mercedes in the next lane. She smiled as he rolled down his window.

"Where you goin', sweet thang?" Jerome grinned. Aundrey rolled his eyes.

"We're just going to the skating rink," Kenda said.

"Mind if I join you?" he asked.

Aundrey was ready to end this conversation. "Actually, today it's just me and my big sis. Sorry," he said, though his tone was unapologetic. "Maybe next time."

Aundrey smiled at the disgusted look on Jerome's face and was satisfied when the light turned green. Kenda waved as her brother sped under the traffic light. Aundrey looked in his rearview mirror and was glad that Jerome had made a right turn.

"Why were you so rude?" Kenda asked as they made a left.

"Was I rude? I thought I was being polite by not jumping out of this car and whippin' his—"

"Don't even go there, Drey." Kenda put her hand in his face. "Now if we are gonna hang today, you're gonna have to not even bring that mess up. For real."

Aundrey shrugged. "Fine."

He pulled into the parking lot of the skating rink and they both hopped out. After paying a standard fee, they walked into the crowded building. Kenda put on her skates and immediately went out onto the rink. She let the music fill her body as she turned around and skated backward. She waved as she passed her brother who, struggling not to trip over his own feet, looked as if he hadn't skated a day in his life. When Kenda routed the rink for a second time, she grabbed Aundrey's hands to guide him, laughing when he barely missed running over a child who was obviously better at the sport than he was. She continued to skate backward as she held his hands, singing along with the music that played over the loudspeakers. She laughed when Aundrey fell over his own feet, then helped him up and continued to snicker as he struggled to stand.

"I think I'm going to sit this one out," Aundrey said when a new song began to play.

"Okay." Kenda smiled as she continued around the rink.

She let the music take over her body as she swayed back and forth, keeping her feet in sync with the rest of her bodily movements. She bounced as her favorite Alicia Key's song came through the speakers, singing the lyrics of "No One" as she closed her eyes and thought about Jerome. Even with all that he'd put her through, Kenda was still in love with him, and nothing or *no one* could change that. She could see herself with him for the rest of her life, especially once he was rehabilitated from his abusive habits.

But something wasn't right. Jerome was on Kenda's mind, but Raymond's face was what she saw in the darkness behind her eyelids. She quickly opened her eyes as a woman skated past her. Kenda momentarily lost her balance and tried to steady herself before she fell.

Why was Raymond always intruding in on her thoughts about Jerome? Every time Kenda tried to get him out of her head, he'd find some way to sneak back in. Since her conversation with Roslyn about their unspoken feelings for each other, it had gotten worse. Kenda had been having dreams. In the beginning of the fantasy, she would be with Jerome, but as the dream played out, Jerome would evolve into Raymond, and it seemed as if the dream would end with her being in a happier relationship with her ex. Even when she saw Raymond at school, she'd find herself longing for his attention.

Kenda quickly wiped the tears that had somehow found their way to her eyes, though she'd tried fighting them. She didn't even understand why she was crying. Sure, she missed talking to Raymond and having him by her side when she needed someone to be there for her. And yes, she missed their relationship, but she had Jerome now. Someone who could take care of her like she needed to be cared for, both physically *and* financially.

But that's not what I have in store for you.

Kenda tripped over her feet and fell bottom first onto the hard rink. She watched as several skaters passed her by without a second glance. She slowly got up and looked around to see who'd spoken the words. The voice sounded like a thunderous whisper and it had scared her half to death. She continued to skate, figuring that it was all a part of her imagination.

"All right, folks. These next few songs are for couples only," the DJ said over the loud speakers. "Couples only on the rink," he said again as he began playing slow jams.

Kenda made her way to the area where she and her brother had placed their things. She smiled as Aundrey waved her over, but her smile faded when she saw the guy sitting at their table. Kenda thought her mind was playing tricks on her, but not even her imagination could conjure up the perfect shade of dark eyes she saw before her. Those were definitely the penetrating eyes of Raymond Shepherd, and Kenda wished that she had someone to skate with because she didn't want to go near the table where he and her brother were sitting.

She smiled as she stepped off of the rink and onto the carpeted floor. She skated to the table, all the while, trying to suppress the butterflies that had suddenly filled her stomach. Kenda almost tripped when she saw him look into her eyes and slightly smile in her direction. She tried her best to keep her composure as she sat down at the table.

"H . . . hi," Kenda stammered. It seemed as if not talking to him for so long had some kind of adverse effect on her speech.

Raymond smiled, causing more butterflies to join the bundle already in her stomach. "Hey," he greeted as he tied the laces on his skates.

Kenda turned toward Aundrey and gave him a suspicious glance. He shrugged and she turned her attention back to Raymond. "So, what brings you here today?"

Raymond smiled again and she was sure if any more butter-flies joined the group, her stomach would burst . . . or she'd become airborne. "I come here all the time, or don't you re-member?" His eyes bore into hers.

Kenda did remember. Fondly. Raymond would bring her here at least twice a month when they were dating. In fact, he was the one who taught her how to skate backward. She remembered falling multiple times before being able to keep her balance. Seeing the couples out on the rink now made her think about the many times they had been one of the couples that were skating in each other's arms.

"I promise, I won't let you fall," Kenda remembered Ray-mond saying the very first time they'd came to the skating rink. She smiled at the memories, but swiftly put them out of her mind when she reminded herself that he was the past.

An unfamiliar surge of jealousy swept over her body when a female came over to their table wearing a too-tight, too-short skirt. Kenda was known to wear her skirts well into the fall months, as long as the weather permitted, but they usually went past her knees, and once December hit, she'd pack them away until the spring weather came around again. She didn't even know how the girl could skate. As tight as her skirt hugged her thighs, it would seem as if she'd be unable to move her legs. As the girl skated over to their table, Kenda knew she was in for a fight, and she was pre-pared for the battle. Whether the girl was coming for her brother or her ex-boyfriend, Kenda put on her game face as if the girl was treading in on her territory.

"Hi," the girl said once she reached the table.

Kenda watched as both Raymond and Aundrey let their

eyes travel from her hot pink inline skates, all the way up her legs, to her slim hips, past her two-sizes-too-small t-shirt, and then finally on her face.

" 'Sup," Aundrey said with Raymond nodding in her direction.

Kenda held a tight-lipped smile as the girl's big doe-like eyes landed on Raymond.

"Wanna skate?" she asked him with her hands on her hips.

Raymond looked back at Aundrey, and then his eyes rested on Kenda. Kenda glanced in his direction before averting her gaze. She was sure he was wondering if she'd be upset if he joined the scantily clad girl out onto the rink. She didn't know why he was even trying to consider her feelings, though. It wasn't as if they were together.

"Sorry," Raymond replied. "I already have a partner." He stretched his hand out toward Kenda with a lopsided smile on his face, revealing one of his irresistible dimples.

Kenda turned toward him and was sure she was close to tears, but this time she knew it was out of pure happiness. She took his hand and they stood. She smiled as the girl looked on in defeat as she and Raymond got onto the rink. Kenda was sure her brother was just as shocked as the girl was, but neither of them was on her mind right now.

As the soft melody radiated throughout the building, Raymond turned around so that he was facing Kenda. She smiled as he skated backward, holding her hands as she skated forward. Their movements were so in sync that anyone watching would have thought that they'd practiced at home and came to the skating rink just to show off. It was as if their separation had had very little affect on the connection they'd always shared.

Raymond grinned as Kenda began to sing along with the song playing over the loud speakers. When she caught him smiling, she quickly silenced. He pouted. "See, that's not fair."

"What?" Kenda smiled.

"You never sing in front of me anymore. You used to do it all the time when we were dating."

Kenda shrugged. "I don't sing in front of anyone," she said, avoiding his last statement. "You practically have to catch me off guard when I'm not really paying attention." She laughed as Raymond continued to pout.

As another slow ballad began to play, Raymond turned around and began to skate forward along with Kenda. She smiled when she felt his right hand on her waist and his left one holding her left hand as Jordin Sparks's "No Air" rang out through the speakers. She took in everything she could so she'd be able to savor this moment forever—the smell of Raymond's cologne, the feel of his touch, and the warmth that enveloped her as they skated around the rink.

Kenda could feel the muscles in Raymond's arm tighten as he turned her around and began to lead her in a backward skate. She laid her head on his chest and smiled at the feel of his beating heart. As they skated, Kenda put the fact that she belonged to someone else out of her mind. She forgot about Jerome and his order for her not to interact with Raymond. As they skated, Raymond's arms around her made her feel safe from the harm and danger that she knew would come if Jerome ever found out about this. Feeling as if Raymond deserved it, Kenda closed her eyes and began to softly sing the lyrics to the song.

Raymond smiled as Kenda's soft soprano voice caressed his ears. He felt as if the song was an anthem to their dissolved, but still simmering relationship. There had been many days when he felt as if he could hardly breathe without Kenda in some aspect of his life. Now with her in his arms, he could perform the innate task without worry. He tightened his arms around her waist and inhaled her perfume. He relished in the feel of her soft skin touching his.

Raymond hadn't felt like this in a long time, and he

wished it would last forever. He didn't know what was going on in Kenda and Jerome's relationship right now, but he knew that Jerome could never treat her with the respect and care that she deserved. Jerome couldn't love Kenda like he could . . . like he *did*. Raymond wished he could reveal his heart to her, but a negative response might be too much for him to take in right now. He knew that there was a chance that she still had feelings for him. The fact that she was in his arms right now proved that. But he didn't know for sure if her feelings for him were even close to what she felt, or what she thought she felt for Jerome.

Raymond wished he could make Kenda see that she wasn't making the right choices for herself, but he didn't know how to do that without causing her to get upset and losing her for good. He took time out to pray for her every day, hoping that his prayers were being heard by God, and would soon be answered before it was too late. He didn't want to see Kenda end up in a hospital, or even worse, a casket. Just the thought of something like that happening caused his grip around her waist to tighten as if she would somehow slip through his fingers.

They were so caught up in their moment that they hadn't realized the DJ had ended the intimate songs, opening the rink up to all skaters once again. A small girl made it out onto the rink and clumsily skated near Raymond and Kenda. Trying to keep her balance, the child pushed herself into Raymond's leg, knocking him out of the trance that Kenda's voice had placed him in. Raymond lost his footing and his leg slipped from under him, causing him to fall onto the floor near a corner in the rink. Kenda laughed so hard that the reddening of her face could be seen even in the dimly lit building.

"Oh you think that's funny, huh?" Raymond reached up for her to help him stand.

Kenda accepted his hand, but instead of pulling himself

up to a standing position, Raymond pulled her down to the floor with him. She landed on his leg and continued to laugh.

"I can't believe you just did that," she said.

Raymond's melodious laughter rang throughout Kenda's ears and captivated her soul. She felt a mixture of emotions as she looked at his dark, handsome face. She lost herself in his mysterious eyes, falling into the deepness of his dimples as he smiled down upon her. Her eyes rested on his full lips and she wondered if his kiss was still as sweet as it was almost a year ago. She didn't have to wonder long as Raymond claimed her lips as his own.

As they kissed, they didn't notice that there were children, skating past them, wondering what they were doing in the dark corner. They didn't notice the adults who looked at them in disgust, or the ones that looked at them and saw the young love that was blossoming between them. Neither did they notice the young man coming toward them with the most livid expression of all.

"Kenda!" the familiar voice boomed throughout the skating rink, breaking the connection that their lips had shared.

Kenda's eyes shot upward and opened wide at the sight of Jerome standing in front of her with the angriest look on his face, and she wondered if she'd make it home tonight.

Chapter 16

The frightened look in Kenda's eyes did little to diminish Jerome's rage as he grabbed her by the arm and practically dragged her out of the skating rink into the cool evening air. Kenda looked back at Raymond. He struggled to get to his feet and chase after them, but his skates hindered him. He looked around for Aundrey and spotted him coming from the men's room.

"Hey, Aundrey!" Raymond yelled. "Aundrey, man, Jerome's got Kenda," Raymond said, finally kicking off his skates and racing to put on his tennis shoes.

"What are you talkin' 'bout?" Aundrey looked around the area and saw that many people nearby seemed to be looking in their direction.

"Man, just c'mon 'fore he kills her!" Raymond said, dashing out toward the parking lot.

Jerome was trying to force Kenda into his car, but she refused to get in, only escalating his anger.

"Kenda, get in the car!" Jerome yelled.

"No, Jerome!" Kenda screamed back at him.

He raised his hand to hit her and was temporarily caught off guard when someone grabbed hold of his wrist. The grip was so tight that Jerome would have thought it was a body builder who'd come up behind him. He turned around to find himself, once again, face to face with the guy who hadn't tried hiding his feelings for his girlfriend since Jerome and Kenda started going out. Jerome was tired of Raymond trying to be the hero; it was time to end this now.

"Man, you might wanna step off," Jerome said, snatching his hand out of Raymond's grasp. "This ain't got nothin' to do with you."

"It has plenty to do with me." Raymond stepped closer to Jerome who was about three inches shorter than he. "That's my friend you've been putting your hands on for the last few months and I ain't been appreciatin' it."

"I don't care what you do or don't appreciate, this is *my* girlfriend and I can do as I please."

"I don't think so, playa," Aundrey said, stepping up. He'd been getting tired of Jerome treating his sister any kind of way, and if Kenda wouldn't do anything about it, he certainly would. "That is *my* sister and I don't like the way you been slangin' her around like she some kinda rag doll. It ends today."

"Man, what you gon' do?" Jerome was amused at the sixteen-year-old's courage. Although Aundrey was a couple of inches taller and slightly more built than Jerome, he wasn't any match for a nine-millimeter. Neither was Raymond and if they thought they were, Jerome would have to show them otherwise.

"You guys, will you please just stop it." Kenda was tired of the arguing, mainly because it was giving her a major headache. "Drey, let's just go," she said to her brother, who was all too eager to start a fight.

Jerome grabbed her arm, almost causing her to slip in the skates she was still wearing. "You ain't going nowhere. Not

until you tell me what you were doin', kissing this fool for."
He pointed in Raymond's direction.

"Jerome, I don't have to explain anything to you. I'm sick
of—"

Jerome's backhand cut off her statement and knocked her
off her feet onto the hard concrete. Instantly, Raymond's fist
met Jerome's right eye and Aundrey's punch to his stomach
sent spit flying out of Jerome's mouth. Jerome grabbed his
gun from his pants, stood upright, and pointed it toward
Raymond. He watched in satisfaction as both, Raymond and
Aundrey, simultaneously, took several steps back. He was in
control now, and if either of them thought they were going
to get away without a bullet wound, they were sadly mistaken.

"Now that everything's back in proper order," Jerome
smiled, "I would like to have a few words with *my lady* . . . if
that's all right with you two gentlemen."

Kenda got up and steadied herself on her skates. She
wondered how in the world she'd gotten herself in this
mess. Why had she gotten caught up in the moment that she
and Raymond had shared earlier? Why hadn't she just de-
clined his offer to skate? She looked at her boyfriend and
the pistol in his hand. She couldn't believe he was actually
holding them at gunpoint. He was clearly out of his mind.

"Jerome, please don't do this," she begged as she grabbed
his arm lightly.

Jerome looked over his shoulder at her. Kenda's eyes
pleaded for him to put the gun down, but in his mind he had
the perfect image of Raymond lying six feet underground.
He couldn't let go of that picture. Out of the corner of his
eye, he saw a few people come out of the skating rink. It was
just beginning to get dark outside, but because of his distance, the patrons wouldn't have been able to see him if it
weren't for the lights in the parking lot. With a deep grunt,

Jerome lowered the gun and stuck it back in his jeans, but the anger had not diminished from his face; neither had it disappeared from Raymond's or Aundrey's.

Kenda looked at her brother and Raymond. "Guys, can you give us a minute alone . . . please?"

For a moment, neither boy moved, but Kenda's glare forced them to leave. She waited until they had walked a reasonable distance away before looking back at Jerome who was leaning against his car with his arms crossed.

"Jerome . . . I . . . I really don't have an excuse for what you caught me doing in there," Kenda began. "I don't know what to say except that I'm sorry."

"Are you sorry you did it, or are you sorry because you got caught?" Jerome asked her. "'Cause Kenda, it looks like you're sorry you got caught."

Kenda was unprepared for his question. She didn't want to answer because, honestly, she had been sorry only because she'd gotten caught. For some strange reason, she hadn't felt guilty about kissing Raymond. It had actually, for a moment, sent peace into her heart; as if that was how things were supposed to be.

"Jerome, I've apologized. How you take that apology is on you." She placed her hands on her hips when she saw him ball up his hands into fists. She was unsure of where this sudden courage had come from, but she relished in it and stood her ground.

Jerome stood to his full height at the challenging look on Kenda's face. She was actually daring him to hit her, and if her boys hadn't been standing only a few feet away he would have taken on that challenge, but he wasn't about to go to jail because of a few dead bodies. He softened his eyes, hoping he could use his charm to get her back into the palms of his hands.

"Listen, baby," he said softly placing his hands on her hips, "I love you. For real, I do. I thought you loved me too, but I guess I was wrong." He glanced in Raymond's direction and stepped closer to her, just to annoy him.

"Jerome, I do love you," Kenda said as he smiled. Then she backed away from him. "But I can't handle the beat-downs anymore. I'm tired of being your punching bag every time you get mad. I'm tired of you using me to do your dirty work. I'm tired of you saying you're going to get help and that you want to change, but yet you're out here slapping me all over the place." She looked up at him and saw his jaw twitch, but it didn't faze her; she was going to walk away from this without a battered face.

"Let me ask you something, Jerome. Do you remember telling me about your parents and how your mother had to endure an abusive relationship for years because of your dad's anger problems?" She paused and he looked into her eyes. "I think that may be hereditary." Jerome tightened his grip on her waist. "You might wanna go get some help before you end up in a jail cell next to your father," she said force-fully, removing his hands before skating away.

"Kenda," Jerome called her name and she turned to face him once more. "What about the appointment?" he asked, his eyes beseeching for her to accompany him to the coun-selor's office.

"You told me that if I didn't feel comfortable around you that you wouldn't mind us taking a break." Kenda paused to make sure he remembered the words he'd said to her a week earlier. "Well, consider this a *permanent* break." She turned and made her way back toward the recreation build-ing with Raymond and Aundrey following close behind.

"I can't believe you kissed him," Aundrey continued to say as they drove home. He'd been in the restroom when every-thing had happened. The last thing he remembered was the girl, who'd asked Raymond to skate, storming off in defeat before he headed for the arcades.

"I wish you'd stop saying that." Kenda sighed.

"I'm sorry, but when a brotha misses something, he needs to be filled in on the details." Aundrey laughed. "So you said you and Ray were skating, and then y'all fell, and then y'all kissed . . . and then that's when Jerome showed up?"

"Yes! Now will you drop it?" she said, exasperated. "I'm tired of talking about it." She rubbed the side of her face that had been slapped earlier.

Aundrey glanced at his sister's cheek and noticed the red bruise already making its presence known. He was glad that she finally cut Jerome loose. He still couldn't believe that Jerome had the nerve to slap her in front of him and Raymond. If he wouldn't have pulled out that gun, Aundrey would have stomped him into the ground, but he was content with the blow he gave Jerome's stomach. Maybe now he'd think twice about beating up his sister or any other female again.

"Drey, promise me that you won't tell Mama and Daddy about this." Kenda's words cut into his thoughts.

Aundrey scowled. "You're kidding me."

"I mean it, Drey.

Shaking his head, Aundrey said, "Why are you protecting him, Kenda? You ain't with him no more, remember? You finally broke up with him, so why you still covering for him? That fool clearly needs to be locked up."

"He doesn't need to be in jail, Drey. Whether I'm with him or not, he still needs help. Jerome needs help and he's not gonna get it behind prison walls. Just don't tell; okay? Please, Drey. Please promise me that you won't tell Daddy and Mama what happened tonight."

Aundrey heaved a sigh of utter disbelief. "Fine," he agreed grudgingly. "I won't tell this time, Kenda. But I swear on a stack of Bibles; if he ever does anything like that again, I'm not only gonna tell our parents, I'm gonna tell the cops. He can rot in jail as far as I'm concerned. Help or no help; that psychopath can rot in jail."

Her brother was angry enough, and Kenda didn't want to say anything more that would sound like another excuse for Jerome's behavior. So she left it alone; grateful that Aundrey had agreed to keep the confrontation a secret. She knew it wouldn't be a problem to get Raymond to do the same. He'd do it just to make her happy.

Once they got home, they noticed a bouquet of red roses in a crystal clear vase on their porch. "I wonder who those are for?" she said aloud as Aundrey parked the car.

Kenda got out and ran up to the porch to read the card.

Baby, I'm so sorry. I didn't mean to hurt you. Please forgive me. I need you beside me if I'm gonna make it. Please.
I love you,
Jerome

The words were heartfelt, but they only caused Kenda to frown.

"So who are they from?" Aundrey asked.

"Jerome," she mumbled as she unlocked the door and walked inside the house. She moved into the kitchen and threw away the card, but set the roses on the kitchen table. "He must've already had these in his car in order for him to get them here before we made it home." Kenda spoke as if talking to herself. Jerome had so many things to apologize for that it was certainly a realistic possibility.

Aundrey curled his top lip in disgust and watched as his sister stared at the flowers for a moment. He wondered if she were contemplating taking Jerome back. He prayed to God that the thought wasn't even crossing her mind.

"Don't worry, I'm not going to let this change my mind," Kenda said, knowing exactly what her brother was thinking.

"Good," he said as he walked up the staircase. "I'm going to take a shower."

Kenda followed him up the stairs after making sure all the doors were locked and that the security system was activated. She walked into her room and fell back on her bed. Letting out a heavy sigh, she rolled over and buried her head in her pillow. Praying that her headache would soon go away, she closed her eyes and drifted into a deep sleep.

Once again, Kenda was in an unfamiliar building, crouching low in a corner with her body in fetal position, as the man above her continuously punched her in her face, stomach, and anywhere else his fists would land. She kept crying out for help, but no one came to her rescue. Suddenly, no longer worried about her own safety, she placed her hands over her stomach to protect the little life hiding inside.

"It's gonna be okay, baby," she whispered as the man continued to punch her. "Mama's got you."

Kenda woke up in a cold sweat. Holding her chest, she tried to catch her breath. She couldn't figure out why she kept having the same dream over and over. Ever since she had come from Jerome's apartment weekends ago, she continuously had the same dream. She could never figure out where she was nor could she figure out who was hitting her. She had a good feeling it could be Jerome, but all she saw in her dream was a shadowy figure. And why did she always protect her stomach as if something . . . or *someone* was inside of it? She cried and wondered what the dreams meant. Whatever was the reason behind them, she hoped she'd find out soon, so she'd be able to sleep through the night.

Chapter 17

Kenda looked in the mirror once more before heading out to Chantal's car. She had called her friend Sunday night, telling her all that had happened on Saturday and was happy she didn't have to beg for a ride to school. Kenda was sure that despite what had happened over the weekend, Jerome would pretend as if everything were normal and would come to pick her up for school this morning. She didn't want to have to go through telling him that she no longer needed him to transport her to and from school, so she'd asked Chantal to come and pick her up a little earlier so she wouldn't have to confront him. If push had come to shove, and she didn't have a ride, Kenda was fully prepared to take the bus.

She ran out of the house and locked the door, then hopped in the backseat of the convertible before Chantal pulled out of the driveway. It felt good to be back in the car with her friends. They chatted as if their friendship hadn't been strained in the weeks before.

"So Kenda," Roslyn said from the passenger seat, "are you and Ray hookin' back up?"

Kenda smiled as she reminisced on Saturday night's events. She hadn't heard from Raymond all weekend, but she hadn't worried over it. She knew that they both needed time to sort out what had happened and where their relationship was headed. Though Kenda wasn't ready to jump into another relationship, she did wish to be with Raymond. But she also knew that she would need to change her own ways before she could even get Raymond to ask her out. She was well aware of the fact that he wasn't going to put up with her trying to spend all of his money like she'd done in the past. But she wasn't overly concerned with that. After dating Jerome, she knew gold digging came with a price that she didn't want to pay. After being slapped around by Jerome, Kenda was going to take precautions in her relationships from now on. Now that she knew that money did not classify a guy as being a great catch, she was going to judge from personality.

Kenda looked at Roslyn and smiled. "Nah, I don't think so. At least not right now. I think we're gonna try to just be friends for now."

Chantal smiled. "Is that *just* friends or friends with benefits?"

Kenda rolled her eyes. "Girl, you know Raymond's not like that."

"I'm not talking about Ray. I'm talking about you. I mean, after losing your virginity to Jerome and seeing how good it was, are you just not going to have sex now?"

Kenda thought about what Chantal was saying. She knew for a fact that if she and Raymond did start dating, there wasn't going to be any sexual activity going on. Raymond, and all of his desire to please God, would see to that. But after the experience she'd shared with Jerome, Kenda didn't know if she wanted to be celibate. She knew it would be hard, especially after experiencing how it felt to be loved physically, but if that was what it would take for her to be with Raymond, there was definitely no harm in trying. She shrugged her shoulders and left her thoughts to herself.

As they pulled up to the school, Kenda saw Raymond getting out of his car. He'd begun walking toward the building, but was stopped in his tracks when Chantal whipped into her parking space and shut off her engine.

"Girl, you bet' not hit my ride, drivin' like a maniac," Raymond said as Chantal climbed out of the car.

"Well, everybody can't drive as slow as you, Grandpa Ray." Chantal laughed.

When Kenda stepped out of the car, Raymond's eyes rested on her as he assessed her apparel. She'd chosen to wear a pair of jeans that smoothly hugged her curves, and a fitted sweater that covered her completely, but still showed off her assets. And her hair was in its natural form, but swooped up into a chic style, complimenting her unique facial structure. She could read his expression and it revealed that he liked what he saw. Kenda's face flushed and turned a deep red in response to his gawking.

Chantal and Roslyn exchanged glances as they watched Kenda and Raymond look at each other like they were the only two people in the world. Both girls cleared their throats noisily, gaining the couple's attention.

"It's kinda chilly out here," Chantal said. "So I'm going inside." She and Roslyn began walking toward the building.

Kenda looked at Raymond who made a sweeping motion with his hand, suggesting she go first. She smiled as he followed her into the building full of students who were waiting for the start of the school day.

The day was progressing far too fast for Kenda. It was already lunchtime and it seemed as if the minutes were becoming seconds as the clock's hands seemed to move at the speed of light. She'd been enjoying her day, especially the classes she had with Raymond. During class, she would periodically glance in his direction only to catch him looking right back at her. There was no denying it; their feelings for each other were beyond obvious, and Kenda hoped that they could make their bond official very soon.

After purchasing her salad, she sat down at her usual table. Her eyes roamed around the cafeteria, but she didn't see Raymond anywhere, so she began to eat, letting millions of thoughts consume her mind—thoughts of Raymond, thoughts of Jerome, and thoughts of how she was going to stop using guys just to get the finer things in life.

Last night, Kenda had gone through all the things Jerome had bought for her. She had a box full of jewelry: bracelets, rings, earrings, necklaces, and a couple of watches. she'd even packed up the few pieces of lingerie he'd purchased for their stupid little fashion show. She'd closed them all up in the box, but didn't know when or if she were even going to give them back. Kenda never usually returned the items given to her by her ex-boyfriends, but she felt the need to rid herself of anything that would remind her of her abusive relationship with Jerome.

She looked around the cafeteria again and wondered where Raymond could be. She'd been anticipating spending the lunch period with him and hoped he'd join her soon. She had so much that she wanted to say to him, but knew that she'd most likely keep her resurfaced feelings secret and simply enjoy being in her friend's presence.

"Looking for me?"

Kenda smiled at the familiar voice. "Nope, I wasn't looking for anyone," she lied and kept her eyes on her meal as Raymond sat next to her. She got a whiff of his cologne and the smell brought back memories of Saturday afternoon.

"Sure." He smiled mischievously.

She watched him pray over his food before biting into the greasy pizza. "Ray, do you do that all the time?" she asked him.

Raymond swallowed his food before replying, "Do what?"

"Pray. Do you always pray over your food before you eat it?"

He nodded. "All the time. You never know what might be in it; especially this school food." He chuckled. "I make sure I ask God to take anything that may harm me out of it before I eat."

Kenda smiled, and then continued to eat her salad. They sat in silence for a moment and then a thought popped into Kenda's head. She looked at Raymond. "Ray," she said, getting his attention once again, "I just wanted you to know that I appreciate everything you've done for me over the last few months."

"Huh?" he asked, obviously confused. "What did I do?"

Kenda smiled. "You prayed for me. You were concerned, although you tried not to let me see it, and you talked to Chantal and Roslyn to see how I was doing." Kenda cocked her head to the side. "You know they tell me everything."

"Everything?" Raymond swallowed. He remembered telling Roslyn that he loved Kenda and he should have known she would go and tell Kenda what he had said.

Kenda's smile revealed what she knew. "Everything."

Raymond decided that since he'd never tried hiding it before, he wasn't going to start now; he was happy she knew how he felt. "Well then, you're welcome. I'm just glad that you're okay."

"And about Saturday," Kenda started.

"Please, don't bring it up. I shouldn't have done that. I wasn't even thinking." He looked at her. "I'm sorry."

She laughed. "Why are you apologizing? It wasn't like you jumped on me or something." She looked into his dark eyes. "It . . . it was actually . . . nice." Kenda was surprised to see a bit of red show though Raymond's dark skin.

He rubbed his chin. "Really? You thought so?" He smiled as he looked back at her. His eyes were looking right through her. "So does it mean anything, Ms. Tyson?"

Kenda was sure her face was as red as the sweater she was wearing. "It could, Mr. Shepherd," she flirted. "But for now let's leave things how they are. I don't wanna move too fast. Besides, I need to work on myself before I can be with anyone else."

Raymond nodded. "I understand." He touched her bruised cheek. "I hope this is the last time I'll ever see a scar on this beautiful face."

"It will be." She smiled as he lightly rubbed her cheek with the back of his hand and then touched her chin, sending chills throughout her body.

Minutes later, the bell rang that signaled the end to their lunch period and they walked back to their class.

The last bell sounded, and students rushed from their classrooms and out into the halls. The end of the day had come much too quickly. As she walked out of her class, a strange feeling washed over Kenda and she knew, without any type of visible proof, that Jerome was waiting outside to take her home. She stopped at her locker as Chantal and Roslyn walked toward her.

"You ready to go?" Chantal asked.

Kenda cringed. "Yeah, but I think I may have to handle some business first."

Roslyn looked confused. "What's wrong?"

"I think Jerome is here."

Chantal said, "Did you see him?"

Kenda shook her head. "But I have this feeling that he is. I never told him not to pick me up, but I would think he'd realize that would end right along with our relationship."

"Kenda, you should have told him straight out," Roslyn said.

Kenda sighed as they walked outside. Sure enough, Jerome's Mercedes was parked in its usual spot, and in his usual stance, he waited for Kenda to exit the building. She took slow steps and hoped that in the midst of all the students exiting the school, he wouldn't be able to see her.

She jumped when she felt a pair of hands over her eyes, but relaxed and smiled when she noticed the familiar scent mixing with the atmosphere around her. Kenda turned around to see Raymond grinning down at her.

"Guess what?" he said, excitedly.

She smiled. "What?"

"I have two tickets to Friday night's Falcons game." He pulled the tickets out of his pocket. "Do you wanna go?"

Kenda looked at Roslyn and Chantal with a huge grin on her face. She'd missed the game that her friends had gone to because of Jerome's selfishness, but this time he wasn't standing in her way. Then she thought about her promise not to use guys just to get things she wanted.

"Ray, I don't know. I don't want you to—"

"Kenda, I didn't buy these tickets," he said as if he knew what she was thinking. "You know my boy, Qwanell? Well, his dad knows the head coach and he hooked me up. I don't have anyone else to take and I know how much you love the Falcons, so I thought I'd take you. You know . . . as a friend."

"Well, I don't know how good they are without my baby, Vick." Kenda smiled. "But I'd love to go," she said, and then remembered that Jerome was standing only a few yards away, probably watching her every move. She thought about showing Raymond her appreciation with a hug, just to make Jerome upset, but something inside made her think twice.

She turned around and looked Jerome directly in his eyes before turning back to her friends. "You guys, I have to take care of something before we leave."

"Kenda, don't fall for his mess," Chantal warned, "or I swear I'm leaving your behind right here."

Kenda laughed. "I'm not. I'm just going to tell him that I'm riding with you guys," she assured as she began to walk toward the luxury car. "Just don't leave me," she yelled back.

"All right," Chantal said as they all watched her approach Jerome.

"Hey." Jerome greeted Kenda with a hug that was a little too friendly.

Kenda pulled away from him and noticed the black eye that Raymond had given him on Saturday and struggled not to sarcastically point it out to him. She looked around before asking, "What are you doing here?"

His laugh made her uncomfortable. He looked down at her. "Did you get the flowers?" he asked, ignoring the question.

"Yes. Thank you," she said. "But you didn't have to get them for me."

"But I did." He looked at her intently. "Doesn't that count for something?"

Kenda rolled her eyes. "Jerome, I don't have time for this. I have to go. I just came over here to tell you that you don't have to pick me up anymore because Chantal is my ride now." She tried to walk away, but he gripped her arm tightly, pulling her back to him.

"Kenda, why are you trippin'? You act like we can't be friends or something?" Jerome looked up and saw Kenda's friends looking at him, waiting for him to make a wrong move. His eyes rested on Raymond, and then he locked his gaze back onto Kenda. "Is he your new man now? That's why we can't chill no more? Kenda, he can't take care of you like I can, baby. That punk over there," he nodded in Raymond's direction, "he ain't no real man. He doesn't love you like I do. For real, remember?" He smiled. "Remember that weekend *and* Thanksgiving . . . how good we were?"

Kenda tried to pull away from him, but his grip was too strong. With angry tears brimming in her eyes, she glared at him and said, "Yeah, Jerome, I remember *everything*. I remember how you made me sell your drugs, and how you beat the crap out of me because I wouldn't. Then I remember you threatening me. I remember everything and, frankly, Raymond is more of a man than you will ever be." Kenda's anger rose with each statement. "And that's because he does know how to treat me. Never has he put his hands on me in the past year that I've known him. He's always shown his love through kindness and gentleness. I have never had to wake up and look in the mirror at a scar that appeared overnight because he got angry about me talking to another guy.

"Jerome, you're not a real man. A real man would face the facts and realize that a diamond like me can never be replaced, no matter how beat up it is." She tried walking away again, but his grip had tightened during her speech. "Jerome, let me go!" she said through clenched teeth as she tried her best not to draw attention toward them. Still his grip hadn't loosened and tears began to stream out of her eyes as fear arose in her at the look in his eyes.

Jerome's gaze was filled with fire. "Girl, how dare you stand in my face talkin' all that mess? Do you know how much time and effort *and* money it took me to take care of your gold diggin' behind? Do you know I went out of my way to make you happy?"

"Jerome, *nobody* asked you to do those things for me!" Kenda spat in his face, having no choice but to draw the attention of the students that were closest to them. Ignoring the stares, she continued, "I *never* asked you to buy or give me anything. You did it on your own. And if you're looking for your payment, then you might as well look somewhere else because the last time I checked, my debt was paid in full the *first* time the back of your hand flew across my face!"

Jerome looked around and saw several students staring at him. "Kenda, you are causing a scene," he whispered harshly.

"Well good!" she yelled even louder. "The world needs to know how much of a disrespectful, abusive dog you are!"

Jerome grabbed her other arm and jerked her closer to him, but before he could react even further, he looked up to find Chantal, Roslyn, and Raymond standing behind Kenda.

"Let her go, man," Raymond instructed in a low, even tone, "before your left eye becomes the mirror image of your right." He saw the tightness in Jerome's jaw and smirked. "And don't even think about trying to hold me up again. Campus police got this place on lock."

Kenda looked at Jerome, who only hesitated slightly before he finally loosened his grip on her arm. She wiped her tears. "You need to go to that counselor or else you're always going to be alone," she said, massaging her arm as she turned and walked away with her friends.

Chapter 18

Raymond rang the doorbell and took a few steps back. He straightened out his Falcons jersey and waited for an answer. Seconds later, Aundrey appeared at the door, grinning from ear to ear. Raymond could tell that Aundrey was extremely excited that he and Kenda were going out tonight and though Raymond's outward appearance seemed cool and collected, his insides were a jumble of nerves and excitement.

"Wassup, man?" Aundrey greeted Raymond with a friendly handshake and hug. "Come on in. Kenda should be down in a sec. You know how long it takes her to get ready." He motioned for Raymond to sit on one of the leather sofas. Aundrey walked toward the stairs and yelled, "Kenda, Ray's here, so hurry up!"

"Okay!" Kenda yelled back.

Aundrey sat on the sofa opposite Raymond. "So where are y'all going after the game?" he asked.

"We'll probably go get something to eat and just chill," Raymond said, settling against the cushions.

Aundrey nodded as if he were giving his approval to Raymond's plans. When Kenda came down the stairs, Raymond stood and admired the short red mesh Falcons jersey dress she was sporting over a pair of flared jeans complemented by a pair of red and black Air Forces. She held a Falcons fleece jacket in her hand and her hair was flowing free. Casual, but sexy, Raymond thought. Just like he liked it.

"Hi," Kenda said as she entered the living room.

Raymond smiled. "Hey. Are you ready to go?"

"Yep," she replied as he took her hand and they walked toward the door.

"You two kids have a good time." Aundrey deepened his voice as if he were trying to sound like their father. "And have her back by twelve-thirty, young man."

"Bye, Drey." Kenda laughed along with Raymond as they walked out of the house.

Raymond helped Kenda into the car before getting in himself. It had been a while since someone had opened the car door for her, and she relished in the feeling.

After Raymond had gotten situated in the driver's seat, he noticed that Kenda had settled back in her seat with a wide grin on her face. "What are you smiling about?" he asked.

She looked at him with her smile still in place. "Nothing," she replied, though in her heart, she knew the small gesture had meant everything to her.

The drive was quiet as they rode into downtown Atlanta toward the Georgia Dome. Raymond was glad that he'd thought to pick up Kenda nearly two hours before kickoff. Interstate traffic was horrible. It always was when there was a home game scheduled. He turned on the radio to try to cover the silence that lingered as they sat in the midst of the heavy, bumper-to-bumper traffic.

Kenda smiled as Alicia Keys's voice streamed through the speakers. Raymond knew this was her favorite singer and he definitely racked up more points by playing the CD now.

She began to hum softly as "Like You'll Never See Me Again" played. Without realizing it, she began to quietly sing along. Her eyes were closed, so she couldn't see Raymond staring at her beautiful side profile. He watched as she quietly sang from the depths of her soul. Raymond smiled. Kenda had the voice of an angel and she didn't even know it. He was going to have to find a way to help her acknowledge her God-given talent. Help her acknowledge God.

When the song ended, Kenda opened her eyes and her face flushed when she noticed Raymond staring at her in awe. She turned away from his gaze, but could feel him still staring at her. Her heartbeat quickened and she was glad when traffic began to flow more steadily, causing him to break his eyes away from her.

"You know," Raymond said in a tone just above a whisper, "you have a gift, Kenda."

Kenda kept her eyes focused on the license plate of the car in front of them. "Ray, please don't start on that again. I don't sing in public."

"Why not?" Traffic stopped once more, allowing him to focus on her again. "You could change a lot of lives with that voice of yours. It's not by accident that you've been blessed with a voice like that. God gave it to you for a reason."

She turned to face him. "And exactly what would that reason be?"

He smiled. "I can't tell you that. The answer to that question can only come from the man upstairs." He pointed upward.

Traffic began to move again and nearly thirty minutes later, they were parking and heading toward the entrance. It took a few moments, but they finally located their seats, which were surprisingly close to the indoor field. Raymond excused himself and returned several minutes later with two soft drinks in his hands. He handed one to Kenda and she thanked him before focusing her attention toward the field. Kickoff was just a few minutes away. She screamed in excitement as the players lined the field.

Raymond looked at her as if she had lost her mind. "Kenda, calm down. You act like Mike Vick is on the field and he just waved at you or somethin'."

"Please." Kenda rolled her eyes. "If that was the case, I'd be doin' a lot more than screaming." She looked down onto the field. "I'd be jumpin' over these seats trying to get to him."

Raymond shook his head and slouched down in his seat as she laughed.

"Raymond, do I sense a little jealousy here?" she teased.

"No. What I got to be jealous about?" He didn't sound convincing.

Kenda smiled and looped her arm with his. "Don't worry; you have my attention for the rest of the night."

Raymond returned the smile and took her hand.

Her grin became sly as she rubbed the back of his hand with her free palm. "When I say the rest of the night, I mean *after* the game." She laughed. "During the game, only the men wearing tight uniforms and got the bird on their helmets have my attention."

She laughed when Raymond sucked his teeth and released her hand, only to resume the slouching position in his seat. He continued to playfully sulk in jealousy as the game kicked into gear.

As the couple exited the arena, hand-in-hand, Kenda was full of excitement; the Falcons had won by seven points and their leading quarterback had scored the game-winning touchdown.

"Thanks, for bringing me to the game tonight, Ray" she said with a smile as they walked toward the parking garage. "I had so much fun."

"You're welcome. I'm surprised you're not hoarse after all of that yelling you did, especially after they scored that last touchdown." Raymond laughed. "I've never known a girl who actually knew what was going on during the game."

Kenda took his statement as a compliment. "Me and Drey watch football together sometimes. I used to have no clue as to what the players were doing. All I saw was them jumping on each other and knocking each other down, but then Drey started explaining things to me and I grew to really like the game." She looked up at him. "When we were in middle school, I used to play street ball with some of his friends, but my dad made me stop 'cause he said they were playing too rough." When Raymond laughed, she asked, "What's so funny?"

"*You,*" he said. "The Kenda Tyson I know wouldn't be caught dead playing street football. You're too . . . too girly for that."

Kenda stopped walking and placed her hands on her hips. "What is that supposed to mean?"

"Kenda, look at you." He gave her the once over. "You get your nails and your hair done on a regular basis. It takes you two hours just to get ready for school. You wear those little thin high heels that look like a weapon to stab somebody in the eye with if they messed with you." He laughed. "You even wear them to school when you know you're gonna be walking from class to class to class *all day.* You care about your looks too much. I can't even imagine you tussling in the dirt with a bunch of boys."

She crossed her arms and arched one eyebrow. "Really? You think so?"

"I do." He laughed. "Now stop looking all mad and come on," he said as he began to walk off.

Kenda waited until he was a few feet away before she ran full speed and pounced on his back. She caught him off guard, but he quickly steadied himself, keeping them both from falling onto the pavement below. She laughed as she wrapped her arms around his neck and locked her legs around his waist.

"Girl, are you insane?" Raymond laughed with her as he held onto her legs.

She smiled. "Yep, I'm a maniac, maniac," she sang.

Raymond continued laughing as he carried her toward the car. Kenda rested her chin on his shoulder and inhaled his scent. Closing her eyes, she wished it could be like this forever—just the two of them without any hindrances.

After making sure Kenda was settled in the car, Raymond got in and pulled out of the garage. Traffic was even worse leaving. They should have left before the end of the game, but if they had, they would have missed the final score. As the cars in front of him crept along like snails, Raymond and Kenda sat in silence.

Every so often, he'd look at her and catch her staring right back. There was something different about her, something he hadn't seen during the last few weeks of her relationship with Jerome, but he could clearly see it now. Kenda was happy . . . genuinely happy. Raymond smiled, knowing her contentment had something to do with him. He was surprised when she reached over and grabbed his right hand that had been resting on the armrest between the seats. He gazed at her as he intertwined their fingers and gently rubbed his thumb across the back of her hand. The rest of the drive was spent listening to the jazz station as they simply enjoyed each other's presence.

After creeping through the traffic, Raymond was finally able to increase his speed. He pulled into the parking lot of TGI Friday's and helped Kenda out of the car, before leading her into the crowded restaurant.

"Ray, it's packed in here," Kenda observed. "We can go somewhere else."

He looked down at her. "No. They have your favorite here, so we're staying."

Kenda smiled. She couldn't believe that he remembered one of her most favorite dishes was from this particular restaurant. Raymond's tendency to remember the small things made Kenda feel special. She liked that he opened the door for her and that when he looked at her, she only saw admiration and love, instead of a lustful gaze. And she loved to hear him compliment her; it made her feel cherished and she wanted to feel that way for as long as she could.

After several minutes, the host finally led the couple to a table. He placed two menus in front of them and said, "Your waiter should be here momentarily," before walking away.

Kenda only looked at her menu long enough to make sure that her dish of choice was still listed, then she set it aside and watched as Raymond looked over the food choices. She studied his movements and watched his dark eyes as they moved left to right while he continued to scan the menu. She dropped her eyes when he looked up so that he wouldn't catch her staring at him.

When the waitress approached their table, she first took their drink orders. Then she asked, "Can I offer you an appetizer for starters?"

Raymond took charge. "We'll take the Three-For-All." He smiled as the girl wrote down the order before leaving.

Kenda looked at her date incredulously. "Ray, I can't believe you just ordered that. That's a platter of potato skins, fried mozzarella sticks, *and* Buffalo wings," she said looking at her menu. "That's like a meal in itself. How are you going to eat all of that *and* your food?"

He smiled. "I have a big appetite."

She shook her head as the waitress came back with their drinks. "Your appetizer should be out in a couple of minutes."

Once the appetizer arrived, the waitress asked if they were ready to order their entrees.

"Yes. May I please have the Cajun Shrimp & Chicken

pasta," Kenda said from memory as the woman scribbled on her pad.

"And I would like the New York Strip & Shrimp," Raymond said, and then gave both menus to the waitress before she walked away.

Kenda looked on as Raymond first said his grace, and then dove into the food as if he'd die before he got a chance to finish eating it.

He looked up with a mozzarella stick in his hand. "Want some?"

Kenda looked at the platter. "No thanks. Unlike *some* people, I want to have room for my food." She laughed as he rolled his eyes and continued to eat.

The platter had been devoured ten minutes before the entrees arrived. Kenda used her fork to pick up a shrimp, but before she could stick it into her mouth, Raymond cleared his throat for her attention.

"Yes?" Kenda asked with her fork up in midair.

"You're not gonna bless your food first?" Raymond asked as she looked at him, dumbfounded. "Did you not see all those homeless people asking for money after the game? They don't have food to eat, but you do. It's only fair that you thank God that you're not in their position." He watched as she lowered her fork and her eyes as if in shame. Raymond shrugged. "There could also be something in your food that could make you sick and you wouldn't know it." Nodding toward her plate, he added, "You might wanna asked God to cleanse that before you stick it in your mouth."

Kenda sighed and awkwardly placed her hands together. "God . . . thank you for this meal and, uh . . . please take anything unclean off of my plate. Amen." She looked up. "Happy?"

Raymond smiled. "Very much so." He watched as she began to eat. It wasn't his intent to force her into praying over her food and he could tell it was very uncomfortable for her to do so. "Kenda, you don't pray very often do you?"

She looked up at him and answered honestly. "No, not really."

He shook his head. "We're gonna have to do something about that." He cut a piece of steak and stuck it in his mouth.

Kenda looked at him and hoped that he was not going to try to turn her into the type of person who did nothing other than talk about God 24/7. It wasn't that she didn't believe in God, she just never felt as if she needed to speak of Him every time she was in a bind, or even if something good happened in her life. Nor did she think she should walk around telling everyone else about Him, especially when she knew so little about Him herself. With the path her life had been taking, Kenda wasn't sure if believing in someone she couldn't see was worth the hassle if she were just going to end up disappointed every time.

After their dinner, Raymond ordered dessert and Kenda began to fuss at him as if her were her son who was irresponsibly wasting his money on a meal, eating as if it would be his last.

"A Brownie Obsession?" Kenda stared at the dessert in disbelief. "Ray, you do realize that you just had a steak, one of the most expensive meats you could ever get at a restaurant? How are you going to pay for all of this?"

Raymond laughed as he ate a piece of the brownie topped with vanilla ice cream, caramel, chocolate sauce, and pecans. "Don't worry about it," he simply stated.

"But—"

"Kenda, if you don't want any, then I'll eat it all by myself." He ate another spoonful of the dessert.

Kenda looked at him as if he'd gone mad. She was sure this meal was going to cost well over his budget, and she hoped that he wasn't trying to impress her by spending all of his money on this dinner. It wasn't necessary. She'd spend her time with Raymond even if he refused to spend a dime on her.

"Ray, you don't have to do this," Kenda decided to tell him.

"Do what?"

"Spend all this money on this meal. I'm not all about financial security anymore," she confessed.

Raymond looked at her with raised eyebrows. "Kenda, I'm not splurging for this food because I'm trying to impress you, if that's what you think." He laughed. "I'm just hungry. I haven't enjoyed a decent meal in the last couple of months because I've been so worried about you."

Kenda smiled in surprise and watched as he picked up her spoon to scoop up a mouthful of the brownie. She laughed as he waved it in front of her face.

"What's wrong? The baby no want dessert?" Raymond mocked in his best child-like voice.

"I'm not a baby," she replied in playful defense.

He leaned forward with the utensil still in his hand. "Then stop acting like one," he said in a flirtatious whisper.

Kenda opened her mouth and Raymond fed her the dessert. The soft, moist brownie was so sweet and the ice cream melted in her mouth as she chewed. The chocolate and caramel only added to the irresistible flavor. She smiled in satisfaction as she licked the remnants off of her lips.

Raymond looked at her for a response and her grin said it all. He handed her the spoon and they enjoyed the remainder of the dessert together.

It was a quarter 'til one when they finally made it back to her home. They'd spent quite some time at the restaurant talking and enjoying each other's company. They stood under the porch light, neither wanting the night to end, but both knowing it had to.

Raymond took Kenda's hand in his as he looked down into her light brown eyes.

"I had a good time tonight," he said in all sincerity.

Kenda smiled. "Me too. Maybe we can do it again soon."

"Most definitely," he responded.

She closed her eyes as he leaned down to place a soft kiss against her cheek. "Goodnight," she said as she unlocked the door.

"Goodnight." He smiled as he waited for her to step inside before leaving the porch.

Kenda closed the door and sighed in satisfaction as she went upstairs. Her brother opened his room door with a grim look on his face.

"You were out past your curfew tonight, young lady." He pretended to scold her, but then broke into a huge grin.

She rolled her eyes and smiled. "Where are Mama and Daddy?"

"They turned in for the night. I told them you went out with Ray; they were happy. Did you have a good time?"

Kenda's smile widened. "The best," she said as she walked into her room.

She floated around as she changed into an oversized T-shirt and a pair of shorts. Raymond's smiling face was on her mind as she got into bed. As her eyes began to get heavy, she hoped she'd dream of him tonight.

Chapter 19

Chantal smiled when she spotted Kenda and Raymond walking down the hall hand in hand during their locker break. Both had wide grins on their faces and seemed to light up the entire hallway as they strolled. Chantal looked up at her boyfriend, Wesley, who noticed the couple's happiness as well. She didn't even have to ask Kenda and Raymond why they were so content, the answer was undeniably clear by the gleam in their eyes. They'd been going out since Monday and hadn't stopped smiling since. *Kenda must have gotten herself together real quick.*

"Look at 'em, baby," Wesley said as the couple neared them. "Look at my boy's face. He done got his girl."

"I know," Chantal said. "Look at her cheesin' like she just won Miss America."

"Are y'all talking about us?" Kenda asked once they stood in front of their friends.

Chantal looked at Wesley and they laughed. "Yeah, we talkin' 'bout them stupid lookin' smiles y'all got on y'all faces," Wesley confessed.

Kenda looked up at Raymond, who now had his arm possessively around her waist. "Well, we have a lot to smile about," Raymond replied.

"Uh-huh," Chantal looked them up and down. "I'm sure you do. It's about time y'all stopped frontin' and finally hooked up."

Kenda rolled her eyes. "Whatever."

Raymond leaned against the lockers and pulled Kenda toward him. She smiled and knew that this was how things were supposed to be. They'd had a long talk over the weekend, and Raymond let Kenda know that he'd wait for her for however long he had to, but he could tell she'd made a complete turnaround and was ready to begin anew with him. Not being able to suppress her feelings any longer, Kenda asked Raymond to be her boyfriend, much to his surprise and pleasure, during their lunch period on Monday.

Chantal elbowed Wesley and they held back laughter as their friends looked at each other with lovesick eyes.

"Mr. Shepherd. Ms. Tyson."

Raymond and Kenda jumped at the sound of a familiar voice. They turned and found their Calculus teacher standing firm with her hands on her hips and a slight smile on her face.

"Don't you two think that it is more important for you to get to my class on time than for you to be out here cuddled up against the lockers?"

Kenda's face flushed and she smiled back at her teacher. "We were just going, Ms. Hanson. Weren't we, Ray?" She looked up at her boyfriend.

"Uh . . . yeah," Raymond said as he opened his locker and took out his Calculus materials. "See, we're right behind you." He laughed as he took Kenda's hand and headed toward Ms. Hanson's class.

Chantal and Wesley shook their heads as they watched their friends walk away with Ms. Hanson behind them.

* * *

"Kenda, what's wrong?" Roslyn asked as her friend dragged her and Chantal into the nearest restroom.

Kenda checked the stalls to make sure no one was in the girls' room except her and her two friends. Then she rushed to the sink and splashed cold water on her face to calm herself. It didn't work.

Chantal grabbed some paper towels and handed them to her. "Girl, what's so important that you had us all come to the bathroom at the same time? We're gonna miss our midterm. You know Mr. Langston knows we didn't all have to use it."

Kenda looked in the mirror and held onto the sink as she inhaled and exhaled in order to ease her anxiety. She turned toward her friends and whispered, "I'm late."

"Late for what?" Chantal asked.

Roslyn's eyes opened wide. "You mean late, as in *late, late*?"

Kenda nodded.

Chantal froze. "You missed your period?"

Kenda nodded again, afraid to speak.

"When was the last time it came on?" Roslyn asked.

Kenda looked down at her feet. "October."

"October!" her friends yelled and then lowered their voices. "October?" they asked.

"Girl, it's the middle of December. Why are you just telling us this now?" Chantal paced with her hands on her hips. "We should have had this conversation a month ago."

"I didn't really think about it. I've missed it before, but it always came on the next month. I've never missed it twice."

Chantal stopped pacing and looked at Kenda. "You also weren't sexually active the times before, so you still should have said something."

"Chantal, please calm down," Roslyn said, softly. "We have to be positive about this, okay? Let's not blow this out of proportion here." She was trying her best to calm all of their nerves. "Maybe . . . maybe it's just stress. When you're stressed out it can affect your bodily functions."

"Yeah, Lyn's right," Chantal jumped in. "Maybe all the stuff that happened with Jerome has had you stressed out."

Kenda shook her head in disagreement. "Yeah, that's what I thought at first when I missed it in November, but I broke up with Jerome almost two weeks ago. I've been happy ever since, especially since me and Ray started going out. I was praying that I'd just missed last month, but I was supposed to come on some time around last Tuesday and I'm still waiting for some signs of PMS. No headaches, no bloating, no cramps. It's not coming," she said as tears began to stream down her face.

Roslyn pulled Kenda into a hug and Chantal encircled them in her arms. They tried to calm her down, but their own emotions got in the way of their mission. They couldn't believe that Kenda could be pregnant. Her life was just starting to get back on track. She'd gotten out of an abusive relationship, started a new, healthy one, and she'd been extremely happy. Now this. What were they going to do? What was *she* going to do?

Kenda pulled back and wiped her tears. "How am I supposed to take care of a baby? I can't have Jerome's baby. How am I going to tell Raymond?" More tears trailed down her face.

"Kenda, please calm down." Roslyn wiped her own tears. "First we need to get you a home pregnancy test. Then we need to get you to a doctor because it never hurts to get a professional to check things out. Then, you can decide what you're gonna do."

"Oh I know what I'm going to do," Kenda stated assertively, like she hadn't just been stressing over the situation a second before. "If I'm pregnant, I'm going straight to the clinic."

"My thoughts exactly," Chantal agreed.

Roslyn looked at her friends in dismay. "You can't be seriously thinking about getting an abortion."

"Lyn, she's too young to have this baby," Chantal stressed. "We still have five months left of school after we come back from this break, and then college after that. She doesn't have the time."

Roslyn placed her hands on her hips and faced off with her friend. "She wasn't too young to lay down with that boy and make this baby. She had plenty of time when she was sleepin' with him. This baby *didn't* ask to be brought into this world, but you can't just take it out like it's no big deal either."

"Lyn, have you ever had a child? Do you know what it's like to be an unwed teen mother?" Chantal asked. When Roslyn didn't answer, she concluded with a firm, "I didn't think so."

"Kenda has to face responsibilities," Roslyn spoke up. "If she's pregnant she needs to take care of this child."

"Roslyn, Kenda *is* a child. How is she going to take care of one?"

"Stop it!" Kenda screamed at them. "Just please stop it! I don't need this right now." More tears were clouding her vision. "I can make my own decisions. If I am pregnant, whether I choose to keep it or get rid of it, it'll be my choice." She wiped her eyes and massaged her temples. It had been a while since she'd had a headache like this one. "We don't even know if I'm pregnant yet." She tried to smile. "We could be wasting our breaths talking about all of this mess."

Chantal and Roslyn tried their best to smile also. "Yeah, you might be right," Chantal said. "It could be something else that's making you miss your period."

Roslyn pulled several paper towels from the dispenser and gave some to Kenda and Chantal, and then used the rest to wipe her own face. "Let's not talk about this anymore until we get the test."

"Speaking of test," Chantal said, "we better get back to class before we miss ours."

Kenda finished wiping her face before walking with her friends out of the restroom. She sighed and prayed to God, hoping that she was not pregnant.

"Kenda, why are you so quiet?" Raymond asked as they worked together in their Family Consumer Science class.

Kenda shifted her feet. "No reason." She couldn't possibly tell him that she may be pregnant, especially since the man who might have impregnated her was his worst enemy. She lowered her eyes and continued to cut out the pieces needed for the collage.

Raymond lifted her head using his index finger and gazed into her eyes. "Are you sure nothing's wrong?"

The concerned look in his eyes caused Kenda's eyes to well up. If she started crying, he'd definitely try to pry for information. So she willed the tears away, shook his finger from under her chin, lowered her gaze, and nodded her silent answer.

Raymond stared at her a while longer before resuming the task of gluing the cutouts onto the construction paper. Kenda had been acting extremely strange since third period, and here they were in sixth period and her mood had not changed. He wished he could read her mind so he'd know what was going on. Or better yet, he wished she'd just talk to him about whatever was bothering her. Today would be the beginning of their Christmas break and he didn't want her to start the holiday season feeling down, but there was nothing he'd be able to do about it if she refused to talk to him.

He decided to try again. "Kenda." He received her attention. "Baby, are you sure everything's okay," he whispered.

Kenda rolled her eyes playfully, mainly to keep the tears from spilling out of them, and smiled when she said, "Ray, you worry too much. Sometimes I just like to chill, you know what I mean? Just shut my mouth and think about different things." She grabbed his hand. "Nothing's wrong." She paused and then added, "I promise."

Raymond's gaze frightened her and she felt as if he could see right through the lie she'd just told him. But when he smiled and kissed the back of her hand, she breathed a sigh of relief. She didn't want to tell him anything until she knew for sure.

Kenda's mood had finally brightened. It seemed as if she had never even been upset earlier as she now stood outside with Raymond, waiting for Chantal and Roslyn.

"Mmm, I'm gonna miss you," Kenda said against Raymond's chest.

He smiled. "I'ma miss you too." He looked down into her eyes. "What if I take you out on Christmas Eve?"

She smiled. "Okay, but on one condition."

"What?"

"You have to let *me* treat *you* to dinner on New Year's Eve."

He groaned. "Baby, I wish I could, but I can't. My church has this service every New Year's Eve. We call it Watch Night and we stay in church until New Year's Day comes. I'm sorry." His eyes agreed with his words.

Kenda looked away. She really wanted to spend time with Raymond over the break, but because of his work schedule, she'd only have the opportunity to see him during Christmas and New Year's.

She remembered the offer he had made months earlier. ". . . *whenever you're free, you should come to a service.*" Kenda contemplated the option of attending church with Raymond. The thought scared her because she hadn't been in a church in easily seven years. Before her parents began their business, they'd been worshippers at a well established, predominately white church outside of Atlanta. But their busy schedules took the place of their time with God, and their religion was moved down a few slots on their priority list. But looking into his dark eyes and realizing that she could lose Raymond over this whole pregnancy issue made her want to be with him every second of every day that she may have left with him.

"What if I come to church with you?"

Raymond's eyes opened wide at the suggestion. "You wanna come to church . . . with me?"

Kenda nodded. "Yeah, is there something wrong with that?"

His grin was as wide as his dimples were deep. "No, there's nothing wrong with that. I'm glad you wanna come. I mean . . . it's great." His words couldn't even express how happy he was. He'd be praying that Kenda would come and worship with him so she could experience what it was like to be surrounded by the Holy Spirit. He couldn't wait until New Years Eve.

Raymond looked down into Kenda's brown eyes and wondered what the future held for them. He wondered if, fifty years from now, he'd still be able to hold her like he was now. Would he be able to tell her, ten years from now, that he loved her more than he did the day they met? He didn't want to have to wonder. Something inside of him made him want to tell her, now, how he'd feel tomorrow and the days after.

"Kenda, I love you," Raymond told her softly. "I love you so much that it seems unreal. The feelings I have for you are so unexplainable. I love everything about you. From the way you walk to the way you talk to the way you now carry yourself. You make me want to live every day just so I can see your beautiful face." He smiled as he used his fingertips to trace her jaw line. "You make me so happy and I feel so complete when I am with you. I want to love you today. I want to

love you more tomorrow. And even more in the days after
that. I want to love you forever, but even if we don't last forever, I will always love you." He wiped the happy tears as
they trailed down her face before leaning down to kiss her
tenderly.

Kenda wanted to feel like this until the day she died . . .
for eternity. She had been saying all along that no one loved
or cared about her. She thought that Jerome's love was the
real deal. She thought that his love was genuine, but today,
Raymond had showed her differently. The same love he'd
just expressed with his words was the love that she'd been
experiencing inside of her. But the whole while, that love
that she had been feeling—the love she thought she had for
Jerome—had been for Raymond. She'd just opened up her
heart to the wrong person.

When Kenda pulled away from Raymond's lips, she looked
up into his midnight eyes and knew that his love for her was
real. It was true, and perhaps, most importantly, it was pain-
less. "I love you too," she whispered.

"Umm, excuse me, but I just had my car washed. I don't
need all this love *oozing* onto it." Chantal laughed as she interrupted their moment.

"Sorry," Raymond grinned as he backed away from Kenda
and she stepped away from the car.

"You ready to go?" Chantal asked Kenda, and then looked
at Raymond. "Unless you wanna take her home with you."
She smiled.

Raymond laughed. "Naw, I gotta get to work," he said, and
then pulled Kenda toward him. "But I will see you on December twenty-fourth at seven P.M. sharp. Don't have me
waitin' on you, woman," he added playfully.

"Yes, sir," Kenda whispered, kissing him lightly on the
lips. "I'll miss you."

"Oh please," Roslyn spoke up, surprising them all. "Y'all
will see each other in a few days."

"So," Raymond retorted defensively as he looked down at Kenda with love-filled eyes. "I'll miss you too, baby."

Kenda smiled, and then laughed when Chantal pulled her into the car. She dramatically blew kisses at Raymond as they drove away.

"You know, y'all are ridiculous," Chantal said.

"Shoot, y'all are worse than ridiculous." Roslyn laughed. "Y'all are straight up in love."

Kenda smiled as she thought about her friends' words. *Straight up in love.* Roslyn was right, she was in love, for real this time; and it felt so good.

Chapter 20

"What does this one say?" Kenda asked Roslyn.

Roslyn read the instructions on the box. "It says that if the blue horizontal line appears, it's positive."

"And this one?"

Roslyn glanced at the second pregnancy test lying on her dresser. "Positive."

Kenda moved to the next one. "What about this one?"

"Kenda, it's a plus sign," Roslyn sighed. "It's positive."

Kenda's eyes filled with tears, but she wasn't giving up. "Wh . . . what about this one?"

Chantal got up from her place on the bed. "Kenda, the word is spelled out . . . P-R-E-G-N-A-N-T. They all say the same thing: baby, baby, baby, and baby. You're having a B-A-B-Y, baby," she said, frustrated with the situation.

Kenda fell onto the bed in tears. She couldn't believe it. She didn't want to believe it. She couldn't have a baby; she was too young. How was she going to take care of it? How was she going to tell her parents? How was she going to tell Raymond? How was she going to tell Jerome? She didn't want to have his baby. She didn't want anything that would keep her tied to him, period. Kenda wanted to get rid of any-thing that would cause her to relive any moment she'd spent with Jerome. She had already decided to give him back all of the things he'd bought for her. She'd chosen to get rid of it all, and that's what she'd have to do with this baby. She didn't want it any more than she wanted any of his other *gifts*.

"Kenda, everything is going to be okay," Roslyn said as she sat down next to her on the bed.

"No it's not," Kenda said, her words muffled by the pillow her head was buried in. She sat up and looked at her friends. "What am I going to do? I can't have a baby."

"Girl, we'll figure something out," Roslyn promised. "We still have to go to the doctor to make sure these tests are right."

"Please." Kenda smacked her lips. "These are four of the most accurate tests on the market. One of them even spelled out the truth." She sighed. "I don't need a doctor to make everything worse by telling me what I already know."

Chantal sat on Roslyn's bed next to Kenda. "What are you going to do?"

Kenda heaved a loud sigh and fell back on the bed. "I want to get rid of it."

"Kenda, please, don't do that," Roslyn urged. "You don't know what it's like after an abortion. It's emotionally drain-ing. It's heartrending. It's . . . it's . . . just not the best deci-sion."

Chantal rolled her eyes. "Lyn, how do *you* know? How are you going to tell her what to do if you've never even been in a situation like this? You could cause her to make the biggest mistake of her life by telling her not to get rid of this baby. Who are you to tell her not to do this?"

"*I* am somebody who's been through this before, Chantal. That's *who* I am to tell her not to have an abortion." Roslyn's tearful words shocked both her friends. "I've been through it, and it was horrible. I had nightmares for months. There were days that I could hear my baby crying, calling for me and asking me why I did it. I had dreams of it coming after me, trying to kill me because it wanted me to feel what it felt when I killed it. I was depressed, I was lonely; I was miserable. So don't you tell me what I haven't been through, Chantal, because you don't know *anything* about what I've been through!"

Chantal and Kenda looked at Roslyn in disbelief. Her words were foreign to them. Roslyn had never told them that she'd been pregnant before, let alone that she'd aborted a child. All this while, they'd been assuming that she was still a virgin. To hear this revelation was a shock.

"I'm sorry, Lyn," Chantal said as she got up to hug her emotional friend. "I didn't know. I'm so sorry."

"It's okay. I know you didn't know." Roslyn dried her eyes with tissue that Kenda handed her. "I never wanted you to know."

"Why not?" Kenda asked. "We're your best friends."

"Yeah, but you guys see me as the quiet one. The one who always does the right thing and makes sure everyone else does the same. I didn't want to let go of that."

"You thought this would change our opinion of you?" Chantal asked. "Girl, you must not know us at all."

Kenda looked at Roslyn. "When did all of this happen?"

Roslyn looked depleted as she sat in the chair at her computer desk. "Tenth grade. Right before I moved here from Valdosta. I'd been dating this guy for about a year and a half and we'd been having sex all throughout our relationship. Most of the time we'd use protection, but other times we'd get caught up and just forget about it. Well, one of those times we got caught up caused me to get knocked up. When I first told him, he denied being the father. But when I reminded him that he had been my first and only, he wanted me to abort it. We were only fifteen and I didn't want to take care of any baby, especially if he wasn't going to help; so I had no problems going to the clinic. Of course, we didn't have the money for an abortion, so I had to tell my parents that I was pregnant. They were so disappointed in me." She shook her head like the memories still shamed her. "Knowing I'd hurt them made me feel even worse. When I told them that I was planning to get an abortion, they agreed that it was best. So I got my half from my parents and he got his from his parents." Roslyn released a short, dry laugh. "Believe me when I tell you that his folks were all too eager to give him whatever he needed to help him avoid teenage fatherhood.

"I remember the day as if it had happened last night. It was raining really hard that day and that made the situation seem more dreadful. My parents dropped my boyfriend and me off at the clinic because we wanted to do this alone, and he stayed with me the whole time. At one point, I just felt like it was the wrong thing to do, but he assured me it was going to be okay. So I went through with it. I don't even remember what the doctors did because I just blocked it all out. When it was over, my boyfriend was there waiting with open arms.

"After that, everything went back to normal. We kept seeing each other and still had sex, making sure we used protection *every* time. But I'd have these dreams almost every night. My baby would be crying. Sometimes it'd be lost and looking for me. Sometimes it'd be angry, trying to kill me for what I had done." She wiped more tears. "Then to top off the dreams, I found out that my boyfriend got this other girl pregnant while he and I were still dating. She refused to have an abortion, so we ended up breaking up and he is now working part-time to take care of their daughter.

"I went into this awful state of depression. I wouldn't talk to anybody. Not my parents, none of my friends, nobody. I had to go to school every day and see the guy I thought loved me with this other girl who wasn't ashamed of being pregnant at all. I'd come home crying every day, and I'd still have to endure the dreams at night. At the end of my sophomore year, my parents thought we needed a change, so we moved up here." Roslyn gave them a small smile. "That's when I met you guys.

"When I first saw y'all in my class, I envied you. Y'all had style, sophistication, and most of all, self-confidence. I wanted that and I thought if I hung out with y'all, it would rub off on me. I just knew you'd never talk to me, though, and since I was still feeling down, I really didn't care. But being in this new environment and not having any friends was even more depressing. I eventually sought counseling from the youth pastor at a church my parents and I began to attend, and as my depression began to wane, the nightmares decreased and my confidence level began to rise. Even though you didn't know it, you guys were a big help just by being my friends. You always had me laughing, and that kept me from dwelling on my problems.

"But there were times when I still felt like I was being weighed down and like something was missing from my life. So a few months ago, I gave my life to Christ so that He'd be able to take away this burden that I'd been carrying for almost two years. I haven't had a nightmare since, and I've been happy and content." Roslyn stood up and walked over to the bed. "I just don't want you to have to go through the same thing that I did, Kenda. It's like an emotional rollercoaster with far more downs than ups, and that's hard to deal with."

Kenda was seeing her friend through different eyes. Here she was, thinking that Roslyn was the introvert, the one that never spoke up because she was so inexperienced. But now Kenda saw someone who'd basically been through much more than she could have ever imagined going through at such a young age. Kenda saw Roslyn as a survivor of trials. But that still didn't ease her anxiety or make her choice easier to make.

"Lyn, I'm so sorry about everything you've been through,"

Kenda started. "I know I definitely don't want to go through the same thing, but I just don't know if I'll be able to take care of this baby on my own. I don't want to have to deal with the stress. I won't be able to do anything for me anymore. It'll be all about the baby."

"Girl, who said you had to go through this alone?" Chantal jumped in. "All that money Jerome has. Shoot, you better make him pay some child support or something."

"I don't want to have *anything* to do with Jerome," Kenda emphasized. "I don't want his drug money or support, and I don't want to have his baby. I don't want anything that will keep me attached to him." Tears rose again as she continued. "I already know that I'm going to lose Ray over this. He's gonna be so angry with me. He still thinks I'm a virgin."

"You mean you never told him that you and Jerome slept together?" Roslyn asked in total shock.

Kenda shook her head. "We just started dating Monday. It never really came up. We haven't really talked about Jerome at all. We've just been focusing on us and our relationship, trying to get the past out of our minds and work on the future, you know?"

Roslyn sighed. "Kenda, you should have told him."

"Why?" Chantal asked. "It really ain't his business."

Roslyn faced Chantal with her hands on her hips. "Actually it is. It's a part of honesty, and honesty is essential in a relationship."

Kenda stood. "But it's not like he asked me. And honestly, I never really thought about it. If I weren't pregnant, he'd probably never find out."

"So what are you gonna do?" Chantal asked.

"Good question," Kenda sighed. "I just don't have a good answer yet."

Roslyn stirred in her sleep as the melodic sounds of Brian McKnight filled her room. Her eyes opened slowly as she reached over and turned off the alarm clock on her night-stand.

"You guys," she called out to her friends. "C'mon, you guys. We have to get up or we're going to miss the appointment."

Kenda groaned from her position beside Roslyn, then pushed Chantal's feet away from her face. "What time is it?" she asked, her face buried in her pillow.

"It's seven-thirty." Roslyn frowned when Chantal spread her legs across her lap. She immediately pushed them away.

Kenda groaned again. "Why'd you tell him we'd come this early?"

"Because it was the only time he could take us," Roslyn responded, looking down toward the foot of her bed.

Chantal was lying in a slanted position with her head near Kenda's feet, and with her legs opened wide as if she were the only one in the bed. Roslyn pulled the covers off of Chantal and slapped her on her behind, causing Chantal's head to pop up with a start.

"Girl, are you crazy?" Chantal hollered, massaging the pain. "That mess hurt."

"Whoa!" Kenda gasped when she saw the fullness of Chantal's tousled appearance. "Girl, you look like *How The Grinch Stole Christmas*."

"Oh shut up." Chantal's early morning voice sounded like a growl.

Roslyn laughed. "That's the name of the whole book, Kenda. Don't you mean she looks like the Grinch?"

"No. That's not what I meant," Kenda said. "I mean . . . look at her." She pointed at Chantal. "She looks like the *whole* book."

"You wouldn't look like a goddess this early either," Chantal said over her friends' laughter.

"Actually . . ." Kenda flashed a glamorous smile. Chantal rolled her eyes in response.

"But for real, Chantal. Why do you sleep so wild?" Roslyn asked.

"And snore like a grown man?" Kenda added.

Chantal sat up and ran her fingers through her short, mangled hair. "I don't know what you guys are talking about." She yawned and scratched her armpit at the same time.

"Yeah, right." Roslyn laughed at the sight of it. "Girl, your feet were over here," she pointed to the side of the bed she sat on, "and your big head was over there," she said, pointing to the opposite side.

Chantal laughed. "Yeah, I know. Once I almost fell on the floor 'cause I was so far to the edge."

They laughed together as they got out of bed and began to prepare for Kenda's nine o'clock appointment. It took a little over an hour for them to get ready. Once they were dressed and had eaten a light breakfast, they got into Chantal's car and headed to Roslyn's gynecologist's office.

"Are you nervous?" Chantal asked as she drove.

Kenda wrung her hands, but replied, "I'm fine."

They drove into downtown Atlanta and arrived at the doctor's office just in time for the appointment. Walking into the diminutive waiting area, they checked in with the receptionist at the front desk, who gave Kenda a clipboard of forms to be completed before she could be seen. Kenda was glad that, unlike most teens, she either knew or had all of the information the forms were requesting. Once she finished, she returned the clipboard to the receptionist.

Minutes later, a tall, handsome, youthful-looking man dressed in a white lab coat came from the back and into the waiting room. He walked up to the receptionist, who handed him Kenda's information. Kenda looked up and almost fell out of her chair. The man was beautiful. His tall, muscular, football physique made him seem more massive than the average male. His dark chocolate skin looked as smooth as a baby's bottom, and the dreadlocks that covered his head were pulled into a neat ponytail.

"Is that your doctor?" Kenda whispered to Roslyn.

Roslyn looked up from the magazine she'd been reading and nodded. "Yeah." She got up. "Hi, Dr. Akeem."

"My, my, my," Chantal said under her breath. She smiled when Kenda nudged her in the side.

"Hello, Ms. Roslyn. How are you today?" He had a very distinct Jamaican accent.

"I'm just fine," Roslyn answered as she led him toward her friends. "These are my best friends, Kenda Tyson and Chantal Black."

"How are you ladies?" he asked while shaking both of their hands.

"Fine," they sang together, smiling like two third graders experiencing their first crush.

Dr. Akeem turned toward Roslyn and said, "When you called me last night I was afraid that you'd gotten yourself into some trouble," he said, looking down at the clipboard in his hand. "But I see it's your friend who's here to see me."

"Yeah, I'm . . . we're here because my friend, Kenda, has, as you put it, gotten herself into some trouble," Roslyn explained.

Dr. Akeem looked at Kenda for confirmation and she nodded solemnly. He shook his head. "When are you young girls going to learn that—"

"Look, don't start on her." Roslyn hit his arm. "It was her first time. She made a mistake."

He shrugged his shoulders and beckoned to Kenda. "Well, come on back." He sighed as if he dreaded what he was about to do. "Would you like for them to come with you?"

"Sure." Suddenly, Kenda's palms were sweaty, and her body felt chilly, as if she'd just been outside in the cold winter air without proper gear.

The girls followed the doctor into a room that was unexpectedly bright. A mural of several families enjoying a day at the park covered the walls. Usually, all of the hospitals that Kenda visited were completely bland and made the appointment more dreadful, but this room warmed up her body and relaxed all of her muscles that had tightened up during the walk.

"Please sit here," Dr. Akeem said, pointing to the examination bed that was situated against the wall.

Chantal and Roslyn sat in chairs against an adjacent wall, and the doctor sat on a stool next to the examination bed.

"So what is that you need me to do?" he asked.

"I need for you to confirm my pregnancy," Kenda said.

"But I thought you said—" Chantal quickly closed her mouth when Kenda tossed an annoyed look her way.

Kenda returned her eyes to the doctor. "I took four pregnancy tests yesterday." She lowered her head. "They all came back positive, but I just really, really want to be sure."

Dr. Akeem's smile offered very little comfort. "There's nothing wrong with wanting to be sure," he said. "I can give you an ultrasound just to see if there anything growing in there."

"Okay." Kenda's voice was barely audible.

Dr. Akeem discussed whether or not her insurance would cover the cost of the ultrasound. Kenda immediately worried that her parents would find out, but she needed to have this done in order to figure out her next step. Once she was sure she would be paying very little out of her pocket, Dr. Akeem set up the ultrasound machine. Kenda's heart rate increased as she lay back on the bed and lifted her shirt, exposing her abdomen. Her belly was as flat as it had always been, but as Dr. Akeem rubbed a cold, clear, gel substance on it, and proceeded with the procedure, a strange rhythmic sound could be heard throughout the room.

"Well," Dr. Akeem spoke as he studied the picture on the monitor. "There's not much movement, and at this early stage, that's not unusual. But what we're hearing is definitely a heartbeat."

Chantal and Roslyn moved closer to take a look at the small, distorted image on the screen.

"Wow," Chantal mumbled in awe.

"Kenda, you have to see this." Roslyn spoke as Dr. Akeem pointed toward the image.

Kenda glanced at the machine out of the corners of her eyes, and caught a glimpse. She inhaled deeply as tears flooded her eyes. Her heart was immediately filled with love, but it also ached from the knowledge that her life would be completely altered if she were to have this baby. She closed her eyes and turned away from the machine. "My life is completely over." She sniffed.

Dr. Akeem wiped the gel off of her stomach and shut off the machine. Then he pulled up his stool and sat down in front of her. "Now Kenda, before you start thinking about yourself here, let's think about this baby." He helped her shift to an upright seated position, then handed her a few sheets of Kleenex from a nearby box.

Kenda wiped her face in silence. Thinking about this baby was all she'd been able to do ever since she realized how late she was. The baby was no bigger than a lima bean, and it was already taking over her life.

"We need to find out how far along you are." He picked up her chart. "But first, let's examine your basic health. We'll start by checking your weight. Step on the scale for me."

Kenda did as she was instructed. After charting her weight, height, blood pressure, and other basic health statuses, Dr. Akeem asked Kenda for her date of conception.

She hunched her shoulders. Just thinking about it made her ill. "I don't know. Some day in November, I think."

The doctor raised his eyebrows. "Now Kenda, I need a more precise date if I'm going to be able to help you."

"Well, the first time and last time I did it was in November."

"When was your last cycle?"

"October tenth," she responded as she tried to do the math in her head.

"Okay." He made more notes. "And you say that you lost your virginity in November? Do you remember a date?"

"The fourth," Kenda replied. "But it doesn't add up. I still should have started on time."

"Not necessarily," Dr. Akeem said. "Not to get too personal, but was this a one night thing?"

Kenda looked at her friends nervously, and then focused her attention back on the doctor. "It was a full weekend: Friday, Saturday, and Sunday."

"Okay, you could have conceived on either one of those days," he informed her. "A lot of young people are ignorant of this, but a woman's eggs are susceptible to fertilization fourteen days before her period begins," he explained. "You probably engaged in sexual activity days before you thought your cycle was to began, but in reality, you were already ovulating and your eggs were available for fertilization." He looked at her for a moment, before asking, "Did you use any form of protection?"

Kenda let her mind travel back to that weekend. She'd made sure Jerome protected himself. Didn't she? She strained to remember. Then it came to her. *That day he beat the mess out of me.* When Kenda came back to the apartment after delivering the package, she'd gotten in the shower, only to have him join her minutes later, completely exposed with *no* protection.

"Except for one time," Kenda answered. Her head dropped as quiet tears began to roll down her face. She quickly wiped them away.

"Do you know which day it was?" Dr. Akeem asked while

handing her more tissue. It was easy to guess that he was used to the scene that was unfolding before him.

"It was a Saturday," she responded.

He smiled slightly. "Now we've gotten somewhere. That Saturday was November fifth, so according to your date of conception, but relying more on the measurements of the fetus," he looked down at his calculations, "you are approximately six weeks pregnant. Your due date would be around July seventeenth of next year."

Kenda couldn't even imagine carrying a baby until next year. By July of next year, she would be only weeks away from enrolling into the college of her choice. But if she decided to have this baby, she'd be lying in a hospital bed screaming for some kind of drugs that would help ease the pain. She shook her head. Why couldn't she have just waited? Why on earth had she given her virginity to Jerome?

I asked you to wait, my child. Didn't you hear me whispering to your heart?

Kenda flinched and nearly fell off the examination bed.

"Are you okay?" Dr. Akeem asked as her friends looked on with concerned eyes.

"I . . . I'm fine," she mumbled. Where had that voice come from? It sounded oddly memorable; she knew she'd heard it before.

"So now that you have the information you need," the doctor said, "here are some pamphlets that may help you during your pregnancy." He looked down into her frightened eyes. "You are planning to have this baby, right?"

Kenda looked up at him. Something about his eyes looked familiar. *Raymond*. That's what it was. Dr. Akeem had eyes like Raymond, and suddenly, Kenda felt as if she were looking into Raymond's dark eyes. She could see the look of disappointment that would show on his face once she told him about this baby.

"Kenda?" The doctor tried again. "Are you planning to have this baby?"

Tears threatened to resurface as she said, "I don't know."

The girls left the doctor's office, scheduling another appointment in a month. All the while, Kenda wondered if she'd be coming back to this clinic . . . or an abortion clinic.

Chapter 21

Aundrey opened the door to his sister's room to find her still crying as she had been doing, on and off, for the past three days. He'd asked her multiple times what was bothering her, but she refused to give him an answer.

As far as he knew, Kenda's relationship with Raymond was right on track. The only time Aundrey hadn't heard her crying or moaning was when Raymond called her after leaving work in the evenings. Aundrey hadn't seen his sister genuinely happy in a long time. But what could be wrong after just a week and a half of dating? He wanted to phone Raymond, but didn't so as not to cause his sister any more frustration. One way or another, he was going to get to the root of the problem.

Inviting himself into her room, he sat on the edge of her bed. "Kenda," Aundrey called her name softly. "Kenda, would you please talk to me? What's wrong?"

"Nothing, Drey," she moaned from underneath her covers.

Aundrey pulled back the covers. "Then why have you been crying for the past three days?"

Kenda didn't answer.

His determination didn't waver. "Kenda, please. Whatever it is, you shouldn't go through it alone; especially when you have someone like me around. You know I'm here when you need to talk."

She raised her head and revealed her puffy, red eyes and runny, red nose. From her appearance alone, Aundrey knew this was serious. He repositioned himself on her bed so that he'd be facing her. Kenda had a wad of tissue in her hand and he waited patiently while she wiped her face and blew her nose.

Kenda pushed back her hair and looked at her brother solemnly before saying, "I'm pregnant."

Aundrey chuckled at first, thinking that she was kidding. When he saw more tears stream down his sister's face, his laugh quickly faded and he realized she wasn't joking at all. "You're serious?"

She nodded. "I found out Friday. Me, Lyn, and Chantal bought a bunch of tests and they all came back positive."

Aundrey was so stunned, he could barely see clearly. He couldn't believe it. His big sister? Pregnant? Without asking, he knew that it was Jerome's baby she was carrying, and he hated it. Maybe it wouldn't seem so bad if it were someone else's child. Someone like Raymond. But it was Jerome's child that was developing inside of his sister's body and Aundrey couldn't stand it. He didn't want his sister to have anything to do with Jerome. It had taken her several months to rid herself of his verbal and physical abuse, now she was having his baby. This would only lead to her having to see him again and Aundrey didn't like that. He didn't like it one bit.

"You're not planning to have it, are you?" Aundrey was old enough and informed enough to know that aborting wasn't the best thing to do to someone who hadn't even asked to be brought into the world, but this was his sister, and she was not ready to take care of a child. Nowhere near ready.

Kenda shrugged. "I don't want to, but Lyn was telling me about how terrible it is after you have an abortion, and I don't think I want to go through that."

Aundrey frowned. "How would she know?"

"She got pregnant and had an abortion about two years ago, right before she moved here. She said the whole experience was horrible."

His eyes opened wide. "Roslyn?" He never would have guessed it. "She's so quiet, so goody-goody, you know?"

Kenda nodded. "Yeah, that's the same thing me and Chantal said, but it's true; she told us herself. And Lyn said she doesn't want me to have to go through the same ordeal she did."

Aundrey lay down next to her and propped himself on his elbows. "So what about Chantal? What did she say? I know she put in her two cents."

"She thinks I should get rid of it, but they both told me that whatever I decide, they'll still help me through it."

"How far along are you?" Aundrey glanced at her stomach. It didn't seem like she was pregnant at all.

"About six weeks." She looked at him. "It happened that weekend that I stayed with Jerome."

He shook his head. "I *told* you to use protection."

"I did," Kenda said, defensively. "Except for once when it just kinda happened."

"I don't even want to hear about it." Aundrey scowled. Just the thought of his sister being with that creep made him sick.

Kenda reached over to her nightstand and grabbed the pamphlets Dr. Akeem had given her. "I got these from Roslyn's doctor. He said—"

"*He*?" Aundrey cut her off. "You went to a male doctor?"

"Yeah. He's an OB/GYN. I don't have one, so Roslyn took me to hers. He was really cool." She smiled slightly. "And he was cute with nice dreads, and he had this Jamaican accent."

Aundrey sighed and shook his head. No matter what situation his sister went through, she always managed to be emotionally well enough to talk about a cute guy. "Okay, I ain't ask you all that. So what's in these brochures?"

Kenda flipped through the first one. "Well this one tells you about safe sex and the diseases you can get from not using protection. I read it and I've decided to get tested for some of them 'cause ain't no telling who Jerome might have been sleeping with before he met me . . . or even while he was with me." She glowered at the thought, then opened the next one. "And this one talks about motherhood. It gives information on the precautions that should be taken while carrying a baby, and it gives an outline on what the first few years of the baby's life might be like."

Aundrey took the second pamphlet and flipped through the pages. There were pictures of women who looked like they were going to deliver any day, and then there were other photos of women holding their newborns in their arms or holding the hands of their walking toddlers.

He looked at the last pamphlet that Kenda held in her hands. "What's in that one?" She handed it to him and he read the title aloud, *"Making a Decision."*

"That's the one I've been reading for the past few days," Kenda explained as he skimmed through the information. "I could probably recite it from memory by now." She released a half-hearted chuckled.

"It says here that having a baby before you're ready can have various affects on you emotionally, physically, and mentally," Aundrey read from the pamphlet. "But right here, they're warning you about the emotional setbacks that may occur if you decide to abort." He continued to scan the book. "And look. Right here it says that adoption would be the best choice for a mother who is not ready to take care of a baby, but not willing to abort." He looked at Kenda and tried to give her new hope. "You could put the baby up for adoption."

"I know. I read that part, but I still couldn't decide." Kenda had let the adoption alternative swirl around in her head for quite some time. It wasn't such a bad idea. She could have the baby, and then give it to a family who'd love it and take better care of it than she could.

"It even gives you a list of adoption agencies that you could check out. There's some right here in our area," Aundrey said as he looked over the information. "It says that some of the adoption agencies will even let you pick the parents you want your baby to live with. You can stay in touch with them throughout your pregnancy and once you have the baby, you hand it over to them and even set arrangements for you to see the child every once in a while. It's called an open adoption," he informed.

Kenda sat up on the bed and ran her fingers through her hair to remove several strands away from her face. "I don't know if I'd want to see it, though. He may grow up thinking I'm just a family friend, then one day, if the truth comes out, the kid will have all these questions for me. Stuff like, why I didn't want him, or why did I keep something like this from him for all this time. I don't want to have to answer those questions."

Aundrey nodded in agreement. "I understand that, but you need to make a decision pretty soon because it says here that after you enter your second trimester, which is your fourth month of pregnancy, it's not best to have an abortion." He kept reading. "Oh wait a minute. It says that there's another type of abortion. It's called partial-birth abortion, and you could have this done at anytime during your pregnancy, even at nine months. It's like they abort it while you're in labor."

Kenda cringed. "When I read that, I almost puked. It seems so cruel."

"Well, it does say that many doctors wouldn't advise this procedure, nor would they agree to perform it. So if you were to choose to abort," he looked at her, "you'd need to do it within the next six weeks."

Kenda sighed. "I don't know. I still have to tell Raymond."

"You mean you've talked to him every night this week and haven't told him anything?"

She shook her head and tried to hold back the tears by biting down hard on her quivering lip. But just thinking about losing Raymond over a mistake this stupid made them burst forth like water from a bursting dam.

"It's gonna be okay." Aundrey hugged her as he continued to try to reassure. "I'm sure everything will be fine."

"But, Drey, I just know he's gonna break up with me. He can't stand Jerome, and when he finds out I'm pregnant with his baby, he's gonna be furious with me."

"It's not like you cheated on him." He tried to calm her.

She sniffled. "But I lied, Drey. I'm *still* lying to him."

"What are you talking about?"

"Ray thinks I'm still a virgin," Kenda explained. "He has no idea that I lost my virginity to Jerome."

"Did he ask you about anything like that? Did he specifically ask you if you slept with Jerome or if you were still a virgin?

"No."

"Then you're not lying to him. You're just—"

"Hiding it from him," Kenda jumped in. "And that's basically the same thing. I don't want him to know that I gave up something that I should have kept to myself. I don't want him to know anything about it, but I don't have a choice. If I wasn't pregnant I could just keep it to myself. But I'm sure I'll start showing in a few weeks, and since me and him ain't never done nothing, he's gonna know that it's Jerome's."

Aundrey needed to find a way to calm his sister down. She was an emotional wreck and it was tearing him up inside.

He tried to keep his own reactions in tact, but it was no easy task as Kenda continued to cry like a little lost baby. He hated seeing his sister like this. He wanted to keep telling her that everything was going to be okay, but he was having a hard time trying to convince himself. Not knowing what else to do, Aundrey continued to hold her and rub her back as she cried.

Kenda eventually cried herself to sleep. When she did, he gently moved her so she would be lying down on her pillow, pulled the covers up around her neck, and kissed her cheek before leaving her room.

"Kenda, I love you; can't you see that?"

"Get off of me, Jerome!" Kenda screamed as he continued to try to kiss her.

"Why are you fighting me?" he asked in a voice that was calm, but eerie. Jerome pulled her closer and she continued to fight back, using all of her strength to try to get out of his arms.

"Let me go!" She writhed violently to free herself from his hold.

Apparently, tired of her rejection, Jerome grabbed Kenda and proceeded to slap her in the face. He pushed her toward the wall and punched her in the jaw. She could feel the blood inside of her mouth as she tried her best to shield herself from his fists. Punch after punch finally brought her to the floor and into a fetal position, praying that someone would hear her cries.

"Somebody, help me please!" Kenda screamed as his expensive leather shoes made repeated vicious contact with her body.

"Shut up!" Jerome yelled.

While he beat her nonstop, Kenda realized that her life was not the only one at stake. Her baby was in danger too. Trying to protect her unborn child, she wrapped her arms around her protruding belly. "Mama's got you," she whispered through Jerome's persistent abuse. Kenda continued to cry and cradle her stomach, hoping the torment would soon end. "I've got you, baby."

The dream was brutal. Kenda tossed and turned under the covers so much that her comforter had long ago fallen off the bed. Her body was soaked from the sweat that drained from her pores. She held her stomach tight as she continued to thrash about in the bed.

"Mama's got you," she said aloud. "Mama's got you."

The sound of her own voice frightened Kenda out of her chaotic sleep. Her eyes popped open and she looked around the room. Panting. Panting. Everything seemed to be moving in a circular motion. The room was spinning. Pushing the remaining bed sheets off of her body, Kenda sat up and wiped the hot sweat from her forehead. She needed a shower to calm her nerves. A cold one.

She stripped out of her clothes and stepped under the running water. It took a while, but her breathing returned to normal and she sighed. She thought the nightmares would end once she got rid of Jerome, but apparently she had been wrong.

When Kenda first had the dream, it had been a blur in her mind. She couldn't tell where she was or who was hitting her, but the dream she'd just had was much more vivid. She could clearly see that she was in the living room of Jerome's apartment and that he was the abuser. She just didn't know why her sleep was being haunted. Kenda hadn't had any contact with Jerome since that day in the school parking lot when she clearly told him she no longer wanted to see him. He'd called her a few times, but she never answered the phone, nor had she returned any of his messages. She had been planning to stop by his apartment so she could drop off the things he'd given her, but after that dream, Kenda didn't know if it was such a good idea.

All at once, the last part of her dream popped into her mind. Her stomach was swollen and she was fighting to protect her baby. Did that mean that she had decided to keep it? Was this dream some kind of indication of the future? Kenda knew for a fact that she wasn't psychic, and she did not believe in anything that dealt with the supernatural. She'd never even read a horoscope, let alone believed in one. Those unexplainable, supernatural things had never appealed to her. But what was the meaning of her dreams? Maybe she was being cautioned. Maybe the dreams were trying to advise her not to have this baby. If she kept it, maybe its life would be in constant danger. Maybe if she didn't get rid of it now, someone else would.

Kenda laughed aloud at her own stupidity. Why was she being analytical? It was just a dream. But something deep inside wouldn't let her forget a single detail of the reoccurring nightmares, and it frightened her to think that in some way, the dreams could actually come true.

Chapter 22

After showering, Kenda moisturized her body with her favorite scented lotion. It also happened to be the one Raymond preferred to smell on her skin. A few months after they began dating last year, he'd taken her out to the mall and caught her checking out the fragrance, and had later purchased it for Kenda as a surprise. After they broke up, she rarely used the moisturizer. But tonight, it was important that everything about her appearance was perfect.

Kenda walked into her closet and pulled out the long red halter dress that she'd decided to wear. Before putting it on, she slipped into her bathrobe to style her hair and apply her makeup, knowing her hair would take up a lot of her preparation time. First, she flat ironed her shoulder length tresses, and then she grabbed it section by section, wrapped it up, and pinned it into a chic, sophisticated style. On her face, Kenda only used a little loose powder, knowing that too much makeup would ruin the flawless natural look that Raymond loved so much. After adding a bit of eyeliner, mascara, and lip gloss, she went back into her room to get dressed.

Kenda stepped into her dress and fastened it around her

neck, and then pulled her arms into the matching jacket. She found the red spike heels that Chantal had let her borrow several weeks back, and slipped her feet inside. A pair of sparkling silver dangling earrings was chosen to adorn her ears, and a diamond tennis bracelet did the same for her wrist. Kenda left her neckline bare, deciding that the jewelry she had on was enough. She didn't want to overdo it.

She looked at the clock and sighed. Raymond wouldn't be ringing her doorbell for another ten minutes. She had just enough time to sit down and dwell on how she was going to break the news.

Kenda didn't want to just blurt out the shocker, but she didn't want to drag out the inevitable either. She'd thought about telling Raymond on the way to the restaurant, but then she realized that doing that would probably land her back on her front porch without even getting a chance to see where they were dining. She had also considered telling him over dinner, but when she imagined Raymond leaving her at the restaurant with no way to get home, Kenda scratched that one off the list too. Telling him at her front door when he brought her back home tonight sounded like a winner for a while, but she knew that would seem cowardly, like she didn't want to talk about it or explain herself, which she wanted to do.

Kenda wanted Raymond to know that she'd made a mistake and that if she could take it back, she would. She wanted to tell him that she didn't want to have this baby and that she did love him, and didn't want to do anything that would break his heart. But how was she going to tell him all of that if she couldn't even tell him the one thing that would lead up to her expressing those feelings?

Chantal and Roslyn had called with different ways to approach the conversation, but Kenda didn't know if she would be able to use either of their methods. Chantal's were too blunt and Roslyn's were too reserved. Kenda wanted a way to tell him that would fall somewhere in between the two extremes.

And another thing. Kenda had to find a way to keep her emotions in check tonight. She definitely didn't want to start crying in the restaurant. She would have to be cautious of serious water works. She didn't want to make her confession any harder than it had to be.

A deep inhale filled her lungs when she heard the doorbell ring. Kenda wished Aundrey wasn't out with his girlfriend tonight. She really needed someone else to answer the door, just so she'd have some extra time to calm her nerves. Since her parents were working late, yet again—this time so they *would* be able to spend the holidays with their kids—Kenda was home alone. She had no choice but to answer it herself. Grabbing her coat, she slowly made her way down the stairs. Another deep breath was taken before she opened the door.

"Hi," she greeted.

Raymond stood in front of her, dressed in a black double-breasted suit with a red vest and tie with a matching handkerchief in his suit jacket pocket. In his hand, he held a single red rose.

"Hi." He smiled as Kenda looked him up and down in approval. "You look fantastic," he said as he handed her the rose. His smile widened when she closed her eyes and inhaled its fragrance.

"Thank you," she said softly.

"Are you ready to go?" He offered her his arm.

"Yes," she responded as she linked her arm with his and paused to lock the front door behind their exit.

Raymond helped Kenda into the car and then rushed to the driver's side to get himself situated. As he pulled out of the driveway, Kenda prayed that Raymond had mistaken her trembling for chills brought on by the lower temperatures. She didn't want him to realize that she was about to ruin their special night.

They were seated just moments after walking into the restaurant and had been waited on promptly by their server. But something was wrong and Raymond couldn't figure out what it was. The food was great, the live jazz band added a romantic ambiance, and his date for the evening was beautiful. But she wasn't happy.

"Kenda, aren't you hungry?" Raymond asked as she played over the chicken and vegetables that sat on the plate in front of her.

Shaking her head, Kenda replied, "Not really."

He placed his hand over hers and gently massaged the back of her hand with his thumb. "Are you feeling all right?"

Tears threatened, but she blinked them back. "Yes, I'm okay."

She was talking to him, but she wasn't making any eye contact and it was starting to worry Raymond. Could something be wrong? Was she tired of their relationship already? Could there be someone else? Raymond's imagination got the best of him and he began to panic. Could Jerome be back in the picture? Raymond knew Kenda had loved Jerome, but she seemed to resent him last time he checked. Could there still be love for Jerome in her heart, pushing the love that she had for him out of the way?

Maybe he could cheer her up with the gift he'd bought for her. He reached into his pocket and pulled out the square container. "I have something for you." He held the box out for Kenda to see.

She looked up at him. "But I didn't get you anything," she barely whispered.

He shrugged. "To me, Christmas is about giving, and I want to give you this." He handed the box to her.

She slowly lifted the lid as Raymond smiled in anticipation of her reaction. But when she noticed the sparkling earrings, Kenda's lip began to quiver and her hands shook as she stared at the gift.

"Kenda, what's wrong?" Raymond asked in frustration.

"I'm okay," she repeated, though her tears were saying otherwise.

Raymond lifted her chin so she couldn't avoid his eyes when he asked, "Are *we* okay?"

Kenda didn't answer as her tears slowly streamed down her face and onto the table. When Raymond saw the pool of water, he released her chin and let her gaze lower. He took slow, steady breaths to calm his nerves. He didn't know why she was crying, and a part of him didn't want to find out. He gazed at her and wondered what he could have done. Or maybe it wasn't him. Had she done something to jeopardize their relationship? He watched as she took her napkin and dabbed away the tears. But they continued to come.

Raymond took the box of earrings and placed it back into his pocket. Then he motioned for the waiter to bring the check. Although they had barely finished eating, he thought it would be best for them to leave now. He took Kenda's hand and led her out of the restaurant after paying the check. The drive was quiet as Raymond drove in a direction opposite of Kenda's home. When he pulled up to a vacant park, he heard a soft sigh escape her lips.

The park was luminous and breathtaking under the stars. The lighting alone was all that was needed to make a couple fall in love on the spot. Raymond got out of the car, walked to the passenger side, and helped Kenda out. He knew that she had something to tell him, but he wanted to let her know that everything was going to be okay. With the car door still open, he turned up the volume of the radio as the slow jams played, and took her hand. He pulled Kenda close to him and began to sway back and forth to the beat of the rhythm.

Raymond didn't know it, but his gentleness wasn't making

it any easier for Kenda to tell him her secret. He could feel her heart beating unusually fast and he immediately began to worry about their future together, wondering if she were about to reveal something that would cause them to end it all tonight, leaving them both with broken hearts. Again.

Kenda pulled away from him, and the terrified look in her eyes erased any doubt from Raymond's mind that trouble was on the brink. He watched as she struggled with finding the words to tell him what was bothering her.

"Ray, I . . . I'm . . . I have something . . . something that I want . . . need to tell you." Kenda held onto his hands as if she were afraid that if she let go, she'd lose him forever. "I'm . . . pr . . . pregnant."

Raymond stood staring at Kenda like a deaf-mute who couldn't even read lips. Surely he couldn't have heard her right. This had to be a joke with a delayed punch line. But when she held her gaze into his eyes, looking like she was frightened by a response he hadn't given, Raymond realized that what he'd just heard come from her mouth was no prank. She was drop dead serious.

"You . . . you're . . . pregnant?" he asked in a hoarse whisper.

Kenda nodded as her eyes welled up and tears began to drop once again. Raymond could clearly see the fear in her eyes because of his lack of response. But he could hardly sympathize with her pain because he was in pain as well. He just wished this was a dream he would awake from, but there was no chance of that happening. And there was no chance he could continue to love Kenda when she continued to hurt him. He allowed his hands to fall from her grasp as his anger began to mount.

"You're pregnant?" Raymond said again, this time his voice level rose a bit higher.

"I'm sorry," Kenda said softly.

He looked down at her with sorrow-filled eyes. "It's Jerome's, isn't it?"

"I'm so sorry," was all she could muster past the lump in her throat.

Raymond turned away from her and rubbed both of his hands across his head and down his face. He punched his left palm with his right fist as if he were preparing for a fight. He sharply turned back around to face her. "You . . . you slept with him?" Angry tears were collecting in his eyes.

"I'm sorry," Kenda said for the third time, stepping closer to him.

"No!" he screamed. "Don't touch me! Just don't . . . touch me!" He turned his back toward her once again. "Ugh!" he hollered at the top of his lungs. The sound echoed in the empty lot, causing Kenda to wince in fear as tears continued to pour from her eyes.

Raymond couldn't even express how torn he was. He hadn't been expecting good news, but he hadn't been expecting news like this either. Actually, he hadn't known what to expect, but he definitely wasn't prepared to hear that the girl he loved was pregnant by her abusive ex-boyfriend. He just didn't want to believe it, but the more he thought about it, the more real the truth became. Raymond turned around, looked down at her tiny waist, and imagined the beautiful life developing inside of her and it tore him apart. She looked back up at him with a grief-stricken expression. Even with red eyes and tears flowing like a river down her face, Kenda still looked beautiful. Raymond hated that he loved her so much.

He wiped his face as he tried to regain his composure. "I think I better take you home." His voice was calm as he turned and walked toward his car.

"But Ray—"

Raymond stopped walking, but didn't bother to turn toward her. "Kenda, please . . . just get in the car."

She pulled her coat closer to her body and solemnly did as he asked. The drive back to her home was long and painfully quiet. The love songs that had been playing caused Raymond to feel sick to his stomach and he had long ago turned off the radio. He kept his eyes on the road as he listened to Kenda's soft sniffles. He wanted to hold her, but he refused to do so. He wasn't going to just let this slide without any consequences. Raymond wanted her to hurt like he was hurting. She had slept with someone who didn't even love her, regardless of his claim that he did. She had given herself to an abuser who'd probably been around the block more than a couple of times. She should have known better and he wasn't going to comfort her. Not this time.

When Raymond pulled up to her home, Kenda waited a few moments before moving. He knew she was trying to see if he would get out, open her door, and walk her to her porch as he usually did. But he refused to budge from the driver's seat. She looked at him, but he'd stopped acknowledging her presence a long time ago.

She sighed. "So this is it?"

Still glaring ahead, Raymond gravely answered, "Yeah . . . yeah, it is."

Kenda clutched her purse and opened the door, but before she climbed out of the vehicle, she turned back to him and said, "I still love you, Ray. I always will."

She got out, closed the door, and walked to her porch. Raymond closed his eyes as he waited for to get inside, struggling with trying not to run after her and assure her that he would always love her too. He opened his eyes and saw her still standing on the porch. She was probably hoping he'd still approach her, but he stood steadfast. As soon as she opened the door and stepped inside the house, he peeled out of the driveway without a second glace. And promised himself that he would never look back.

Chapter 23

Kenda reached over to her nightstand to pick up the phone that had noisily awakened her Christmas morning.

"Hello?" she answered groggily.

"Merry Christmas!" her best friends sang joyously.

Her lips tugged into a slight smile. "Merry Christmas, you guys."

Chantal laughed. "Girl, you sound like you have a hangover."

"That would feel better than having a heartache." Kenda chuckled dryly.

"What's wrong, Kenda?" Roslyn asked.

"Ray broke up with me last night." Kenda tried to keep the tears back. She'd cried all night as her brother comforted her and she didn't want to start up again.

"Oh, Kenda, I'm so sorry." Roslyn's tone was sincere.

"Me too," Chantal said.

A sad sigh escaped Kenda's lips. "It's okay."

"How are you?" was Roslyn's next question.

Kenda tried to smile, but couldn't. "I'll be fine." She hoped she was telling the truth, but it didn't feel like it.

The line was silent for a few moments, before Chantal said, "Well, I hope that the two of you will at least stay friends."

After seeing the look in Raymond's eyes last night, Kenda doubted it. "I don't know about that," she responded.

"Why not?" Roslyn asked. "Raymond has always been there for you."

Kenda wiped away the single tear the rolled down her cheek. She was so tired of crying. "He hates me."

"No he doesn't," Chantal said as if what her friend had just said was the most ridiculous thing in the world. "That boy loves you like somebody crazy."

"She's right," Roslyn interjected. "Raymond loves you like his life depends on it. Even if he's upset with you, he doesn't hate you. I'm sure of that."

Kenda shook her head like her friends could see her silent rebuttal. Then she said, "But you guys didn't see the look on his face, and you didn't hear him yell at me, and you didn't have to watch him cry."

"He yelled at you?" Roslyn asked.

"He cried?" Chantal added.

"Yes." Kenda answered both of their questions in a single word. "Not only that, but he didn't want me to touch him either. And then when he dropped me off, he wouldn't even look at me." Kenda paused and her voice level dropped. "When I told him that I still loved him, he acted like he didn't even hear me."

"You can't be serious," Chantal said. "I don't even believe that."

"Well, believe it."

"He was just upset, Kenda," Roslyn reminded her. "You can't blame him for being upset. Any guy would be under the same circumstances."

Kenda used her thumb and middle finger to rub her eyes. "I know that. I just feel so horrible."

"Well, you need to cheer up because today is Christmas, and I know that your parents have a lot of gifts under that tree for you." Chantal was trying to sound jovial.

"Girl, if only you knew," Kenda chuckled. There were so many gifts downstairs that Kenda had lost count just trying to calculate her own.

"Well, we were just calling to wish you a happy holiday," Roslyn said. "I have to go because we are about to have breakfast and my mom needs help with the biscuits."

"And me and my little sister are supposed to be cleaning up for our guests," Chantal announced. "My dad's side of the family is coming over, and they are supposed to be staying until New Years. Girl, I hope my bad lil' cousins don't wreck my nerves."

Kenda laughed. "Okay, y'all. Bye."

She hung up the phone, climbed out of bed, and headed into the bathroom to take a shower. Thirty minutes later, she came out wrapped in a towel, pondering what to wear. Something casual seemed befitting. After a short search through her dresser drawers, Kenda chose a yellow sweater and a long jean skirt.

She decided that she wasn't going to dwell on her breakup with Raymond. Today was Christmas, and she needed to be happy in spite of all of her problems. And she was determined to do so. Having her parents at home today would help keep her spirits up. She was almost giddy that they didn't have to work. Last Christmas, they chose to work overtime on a career-defining case, and Kenda ended up spending the holiday with her grandparents in Texas, along with her brother who'd been too grumpy to have even an ounce of Christmas cheer. As she went downstairs and found her mother in the kitchen cooking dinner, she hoped this year would be better.

"Hi, Mama," Kenda greeted, and then kissed her mother's cheek. "Merry Christmas."

Maxine was caught off guard by her daughter's display of affection. She smiled. "Merry Christmas to you too."

Kenda pulled a bowl out of the cabinet and grabbed a box of Frosted Flakes from the top cabinet. After preparing her breakfast, she sat at the table and bowed her head to bless her food.

"Kenda," her mother called once she'd finish praying, "did you just do what I think you did?"

Kenda smiled. "I know. It's Raymond's fault. He got me all freaked out. He kept saying that I didn't know what could be in my food, so I need to ask God to cleanse it before I start eating."

"That Raymond is something else," Maxine said.

Kenda released a quiet exhale. "He sure is," she mumbled in agreement. How could she have messed up so badly with such a great guy.

Maxine opened the oven to check on the turkey before looking at her daughter. Kenda had changed so much in just the past few weeks. Her attitude had improved and she seemed happier. Maxine had been so afraid for her daughter when she was dating Jerome, but she figured that if Kenda was going to make the mistake of staying with someone who abused her, she'd have to make it on her own. From what Maxine could tell, her daughter had made the right choice, even if she did take too long to make it.

"How are you and Raymond?" Maxine inquired.

Kenda didn't answer right away. Her mother had never really shown interest in her personal life before, except when she'd found out about Jerome's abuse. She didn't want to tell Maxine that she'd messed up with Raymond. The news would be devastating, but Kenda knew it had to be done.

"Me and Ray . . ." Kenda's voice trailed. "We broke up last night."

Maxine was visibly concerned. "Why? It's only been a couple of weeks. What could have happened so soon?"

Kenda fidgeted around in her seat. There was no way she could tell her mother she was pregnant. Maxine would be more than disappointed in her. Her parents had been working to build up a company that they could one day pass down to her. Kenda had been waiting for the day that she'd be able to take over the small, but prominent law firm. She couldn't tell them, at least not until she made a decision.

"Umm." Kenda fought with the truth. "We decided that we just want to be friends." The quiver in her voice threatened to give her away.

"Are you sure that's all it is?" Maxine questioned, walking over to the table. "You sound kind of upset."

"Yes, ma'am, I'm sure." Kenda lowered her head and pretended to be engrossed in the soggy cereal in her bowl. "We got caught up a little too fast and everything just kinda fell apart."

"Oh." Maxine still didn't sound too convinced. "Well, as long as everything is all right." Her statement sounded more like an inquiry, and Kenda was tempted to spill the beans. Maxine placed her hand on her daughter's shoulder and said, "Kenda, I love you, and I want you to know I'm always here if you need to talk."

Kenda looked up into her mother's eyes and smiled. It was the first time she'd heard her mother say those three words in years. Happy tears filled her eyes as she said, "I love you too, Mama."

Maxine wrapped her arms around her daughter and held her tight. It had been much too long since she'd done so, and she made a mental note to do it more often.

The sound of feet pounding the stairway signaled that Xavier and Aundrey had awakened and were ready to celebrate the holiday. Kenda finished her cereal and headed toward the living room where the Christmas tree was set up with endless gifts sitting beneath and around it.

"'Morning, Daddy," Kenda greeted him with a kiss.

"Good morning, princess." Xavier smiled.

Kenda looked at her brother and smiled. She noticed that he was fully dressed, having learned that Maxine wouldn't allow one gift to be opened until everyone was washed up and dressed. It had been a rule in their house since they were kids. " 'Morning, big head," she greeted her brother.

Aundrey smiled back at her when he realized Kenda hadn't called him "big head" in months. It was nice to see her smiling, especially after having to watch her cry herself to sleep the night before. He knew her happiness had everything to do with their parents being home with them today.

"Good morning to you too, snot face." Aundrey laughed.

"All right, you two." Maxine walked into the living room with two mugs of coffee. She handed one to her husband and then sat on the sofa. Looking at her children, she said, "What are you guys just sitting there for? Go ahead and open the gifts."

Aundrey ran toward the tree and grabbed the biggest box with his name on it, but before he could open it, his sister grabbed his arm.

"Wait," Kenda said.

"Man, what is it?" her brother groaned.

Kenda stood. "I would like to say something first, if you don't mind." She rolled her eyes at her brother. He groaned like waiting was torture. She turned toward her parents. "I know I haven't been the best person to be around in the last few months, but I'm thankful to have parents," she turned to her brother and added, "and a sometimes wonderful, but always annoying younger brother who stood by me through it all. And even though I complained about it, I'm also thankful for all the time you guys put in at work so we can have all these nice things. I just want you to know that I love you all." She smiled as she sat down on the sofa.

"Great speech," Aundrey mocked. "Now can we open the gifts?"

"Wait," Maxine said, laughing out loud when her son released an exasperated sigh. "I would like to add to the things that my beautiful daughter has just said. I appreciate all of you, especially my fine, fine husband, who has helped make both of our dreams come true by helping me build up this company that I hope we will one day be able to pass on to our daughter." She turned to her children. "And I'm thankful for both of you for bearing with me and your father. We know we don't spend much time at home, *but* all of that is about to change in the coming year because we've hired more workers who will help shorten the hours we spend at the office so that we can be at home with you more often." She smiled at Kenda whose expression revealed all of her happiness. "Despite what may have been said, done, or even thought about, your father and I love you both with all of our hearts and we hope that you know that."

"Thanks, Mom. We love you too," Aundrey said. "Now, about these gifts—"

"Hold on there, son," Xavier said.

Aundrey groaned and dropped his head in his hands.

"Boy, calm down." Xavier chuckled, like making his son wait was Christmas gift enough for him. "I've got something to say about my wonderful family as well, and you're gonna put that gift down and listen to me." He stifled a smiled as his son did as he was told. "I'm just happy to have such a great family. To my wife, who gets more beautiful every single day," he smiled at Maxine and winked, "I love you very much. To my son, who's starting to look and act more and more like me, I love you too." He chuckled as Aundrey popped the collar of his button-down shirt. "And to my wonderful daughter . . . you've been through a lot, and by the grace of God, you conquered the obstacles and survived the storm. Your mother and I love you no matter what you may believe." He stared deeper into her eyes. "It's the truth."

Kenda smiled at her father. Being with her family made her happy. She couldn't have asked for a better Christmas gift than the love she'd been receiving since she'd awakened this morning.

Aundrey got up off of the floor. "Well, I guess I gotta say something too." He glared at his sister. "Thanks a lot, Kenda."

Kenda laughed when he sighed as if he were being forced at gunpoint.

"Let's see. What can I say?" Aundrey began. "I have a pretty nice family. Well, sometimes." He tossed an evil look at his sister and she laughed again. "But for real. Most of the time, you guys are great. I'm just glad to be able to see *you* smiling," he told Kenda. "You don't look good when you be walking around here with that ugly, gorilla-looking frown on your face."

"Oh, whatever." Kenda tossed a pillow at him.

He laughed, catching the pillow in his hand and giving his best Heisman Trophy pose. Then he pitched it back to her. "I'm serious. You look much better with that stupid grin. Anyway, I love you guys and . . . that's about it." He sat back down on the floor. "Now it's time to open the gifts."

Aundrey gave Kenda a box and their parents watched as their son tore through the expensive wrapping paper, while their daughter took her time unwrapping hers, like she planned to save all the paper and use it to wrap gifts next year.

Kenda pulled so many clothes out of the boxes that she was sure she'd need a new closet. She loved the Louis Vuitton purse and small backpack her mother had gotten for her. The 24-karat gold, heart-shaped diamond necklace and matching bracelet her father had purchased was what she'd been hinting for since she saw it in the store a couple of months ago.

Aundrey admired the new stereo system he'd gotten. He

could finally make his own music on his computer with the new software his dad had gotten for him, and he couldn't wait to show off his new clothes as soon as school re-opened.

"Thank you, Mama and Daddy," Kenda said as she hugged both of her parents.

"Yeah, thanks." Aundrey followed her lead.

"We came up with some money and got you both some-thing," Kenda announced as she reached under the tree and pulled out two small boxes. She handed one to each of them. "Merry Christmas," she and her brother sang in unison.

Xavier and Maxine tore through the wrappers and opened their gifts. Xavier admired the two-tone stainless steel Seiko watch in astonishment.

"Turn it over, Dad," Aundrey said.

Xavier complied and flipped the watch over in his hands. He read the inscription out loud. "#1 Dad: We love you." He smiled up at his children. "Thank you so much. This must have cost you a pretty penny."

Kenda shrugged. "We used some of our allowance money that we had saved up."

"Yeah, and watches are cheaper if you get 'em online, so we got it off Amazon," Aundrey added to his father's amuse-ment.

Kenda rolled her eyes. Her brother had no tact at all.

Maxine pulled the handheld Blackberry PDA out of the box and gasped. "I love it. How'd you know I needed this?"

Aundrey laughed. "You were running 'round here like a mad woman a few months ago, talking about all the appoint-ments you had on your calendar, but couldn't keep up with." Aundrey pointed at the device in his mom's hand. "So we thought you could use this."

"You thought right. Thank you." Maxine smiled and then looked at her husband. "I'm sorry, Xavier. All the running around we did for the kids, and I didn't get you a thing."

Xavier wiped his brow as if sweat had begun gathering there. "Whew! That's good 'cause I didn't get a chance to get you anything either." They laughed together.

Maxine leaned over and kissed her husband. "Merry Christmas," she spoke against his lips.

"You *really* wanna make it a merry Christmas?" Xavier asked, rapidly raising and lowering his eyebrows.

Maxine grinned at her husband's proposition and grabbed his hand. They ran out of the living room and up the stairs, giggling like two little kindergartners in a game of tag.

Kenda looked at her brother and pretended to gag. "They're just too old for that," she said while gathering the trash.

Aundrey laughed as he helped her clean up. He looked up at his sister and said, "I really am happy to see you smiling."

"Thank you. I guess I have to keep smiling so I won't be so sad. I'm happy that we spent Christmas with Mama and Daddy and all, but I have so much going on right now." She brought her voice to a whisper and added, "Ray broke up with me last night because of this stupid baby."

Aundrey didn't seem surprised. "I know. I kinda figured that when you couldn't stop crying long enough to tell me what was up. Have you decided what you're going to do?"

Kenda shook her head. "But that abortion is looking better and better every day."

"Keep thinking about it." Aundrey wanted her to be sure. "Don't make a rash decision just because of one person's reaction."

She smiled. "Thanks; I won't. But I only have a few more weeks left to decide."

The sound of the doorbell echoed throughout the house and Aundrey glanced at his sister. "Are you expecting someone?" he asked.

"No, but if it's for Mama or Daddy, you might as well tell whoever it is that they're unavailable." Kenda chuckled as her brother went to answer the door.

Seconds later, Aundrey returned with two boxes in his hands. One was long and rectangular, and the other was small and square. "It was some delivery guy who had me sign for these." He looked down at the boxes. "They're for you."

Kenda was taken aback as she took the boxes out of Aundrey's hands and placed them on the sofa. When she opened the long box and discovered two-dozen white roses inside, she couldn't help but hope the gifts were from Raymond.

"Oh my goodness," she gasped. "These are absolutely gorgeous." She inhaled their scent and then looked inside the box for a card. "Who are they from?"

Aundrey shrugged and handed her the other box. "Open this one."

Kenda took it and tore off the wrapping paper. She removed the top and gasped loudly. Inside were velvet pieces of cloth, protecting a sparkling diamond tiara. She picked it up delicately and fingered the diamonds. She looked inside the box and found a card underneath the velvet materials. She opened the envelope and read the handwritten letter silently.

To my precious Kenda,

I miss you something awful, and I just want you to know that I love you with all of my heart. You were right. I saw this diamond crown and realized that you were a diamond that could never be replaced. I wish you'd forgive me and reconsider your decision to move on without me. I want to get help, but I can't get it without you by my side. I love you so much that I'm hurting without you. I want you. I need you. I love you.

Forever yours,
Jerome

Kenda closed the card and threw it back into the box. She tossed the tiara into the box also. She knocked the roses onto the floor and let the angry tears roll down her cheeks. "Why can't he leave me alone!" she cried as her brother hugged her. "I'm trying to get over it, but he's making it so hard."

Kenda had been truly happy. It had been the best day she'd had in years with her family, and Jerome had to come and ruin it all. Why couldn't he just get the picture and move on like she had. There was nothing left to hold on to . . . except for the baby. But she would change that soon enough.

Chapter 24

"So what are you going to do now?" Roslyn asked Kenda over the phone.

"It's been four days and Ray hasn't even called," Kenda responded. "It's over."

"No, Kenda. I mean the pregnancy," Roslyn clarified. "You're almost eight weeks now. You need to make a decision."

Kenda sighed. She hadn't even thought about what she was going to do about the baby. All she'd been thinking about was Raymond and their broken relationship, especially since receiving Jerome's gifts. She wanted to call Raymond, but was afraid of him yelling at her again. She'd never seen him so livid before and it had scared her terribly. She just wished she could make all of her problems go away.

"Lyn, right now I don't even want to think about this stupid baby. I can't stand it for all the drama it's putting me through," she said. "Right about now, an abortion is sounding pretty good."

Roslyn's deep sigh almost brought Kenda to tears, but she was very close to making that her final decision. She didn't want to disappoint her friend, but this baby had caused her to lose the one person who truly cared for her. The one person who'd shown his love for her, not only with his words, but with his actions. Why would she want to keep something that would continue to ruin the relationships she'd been waiting so long to establish?

"I'm sorry, Lyn, but I can't do it."

Roslyn wasn't giving up that easy. "Have you thought about what Jerome might want?"

Kenda's head snapped back. Of course she hadn't thought about what Jerome might want. She didn't give a flying flip what he wanted. He wasn't going to tell her what she was or was not going to do with this baby. Kenda calmed herself before replying. "Why?" she asked. "It's not like he has a say-so."

"Actually, Kenda, he does," Roslyn replied. "He is the child's father."

Kenda's head jerked again. She didn't even want to think about the fact that he was her unborn baby's father. She could just imagine the type of father he'd be. If her child were a boy, he'd probably teach him how to deal drugs and beat on women. If she had a girl, he'd probably abuse her for no reason at all; just because she was female. Kenda could hardly stand to think about the horrible consequences Jerome's presence would have on her child.

"Number one," she told Roslyn, "just because he is the baby's father doesn't mean that he can be a father to the baby. Number two, I don't want to have *his* baby. It's not an option. I'm getting an abortion and I'm going to get Ray back."

"Fine, Kenda. Do what you want," Roslyn said, finally giving up the fight.

There was silence on the phone for a long moment. Kenda was happy that Roslyn was finally putting the issue to rest. She hated the discontent she heard in her friend's voice, but Kenda knew she was doing what was best for her.

"Kenda, how do you know that Ray wouldn't be against you getting an abortion?"

Kenda had almost forgotten that Chantal was on the phone. She'd been surprisingly quiet as Kenda and Roslyn argued. It wasn't like Chantal to just hold the phone and opt out of a conversation.

"Well, I'm sure he'd be happy that I don't want to have this baby. You know how much he can't stand Jerome," Kenda answered.

"But you know he's a Christian," Chantal responded.

"And?"

"Most Christians don't believe in abortions, Kenda."

Kenda was getting frustrated. Her friends were making it seem as if she were only thinking about herself while she struggled with the decision she had to make. And okay . . . maybe she was. Why shouldn't she only consider herself in this decision? *She* was the one who was going to get fat. *She* was the one who had lost the love of her life. *She* was the one who be tormenting in labor for hours. *She* was the one who would be sitting up late at night with a crying baby. *She* was the one who would be fixing bottles, changing stinky diapers, and cleaning up nasty vomit. *She* was the one whose whole life would be altered. No one was truly going to be affected by her choice except her . . . and her baby. The last part of Kenda's thought stabbed her, but when it all came down to it, what other choice did she really have if she were to have any hope of a normal life?

"If I want to get Ray back, I have to do this," Kenda said as a small white card lying on the floor next to her dresser caught her attention. She walked over and picked it up. *Greater Faith Tabernacle: Worshipping in Spirit and in Truth*, she read the words on the card and smiled. "But I want to talk to him first, so I'm going to his church this Saturday and I'm going to explain everything to him and tell him my decision. Then everything should go back to normal.

I'll have the abortion, get Ray back, and forget that this ever happened."

"You really think it's going to work like that?" Chantal asked.

Kenda's tone was confident when she said, "I know it will."

Chantal pulled up to Greater Faith Tabernacle almost an hour after the service had already begun. She watched Kenda take a deep breath before grabbing her coat and purse.

Chantal touched her shoulder. "Good luck, girl. Call me if you need a ride home. I should be up at somebody's party." She laughed softly.

"Thanks," Kenda responded as she got out of the car.

If Kenda had her way tonight, Chantal would be able to stay all night at whatever party she was planning to attend. She was praying that by some miracle, Raymond would allow her the chance to speak with him.

She walked into the building and looked around. She had no clue where to go. There were so many halls and doors that she'd be all night trying to find the sanctuary. She could hear music, though, and the sound became louder when someone walked from behind a door down the hallway that was directly to her left.

Kenda turned and smiled at the sight of the young lady who was apparently taking her son to the restroom. "Excuse me," she called, getting the young woman's attention. "Hi."

"Hello." The woman greeted her with a warm smile.

"Could you please tell me how to get to the . . . Watch Night service?" Kenda looked down at the young boy who seemed somewhat familiar to her.

"It's right through those doors." The woman pointed to the doors she'd just exited through.

"Thank you."

When Kenda walked into the sanctuary, the music became louder and swept through her body, welcoming her into the service. She looked around and sighed. This was going to be harder than she thought. There had to be at least a thousand people in the building.

A woman dressed in casual white and black attire greeted Kenda and showed her to a seat in the center section of the church. She waited as the woman asked several people to move down, then Kenda sat in the seat that had been vacated for her. She looked around the church, but couldn't spot Raymond anywhere. She watched as the people clapped and danced to the choir's upbeat songs. Kenda was glad she was near the back so she could stay seated without being noticed. She bobbed her head to the beat of the song, but her search for Raymond distracted her. When the music came to an end, Kenda's eyes focused on the middle-aged man who was now standing at the podium, adjusting the microphone.

"Somebody say amen," the man spoke into the microphone.

"Amen," many members replied.

"Amen ... amen ... amen," the man said, pronouncing each word as if each were a standalone sentence. "It is good to be in the house of the Lord one more time."

"Amen," the crowd said in response.

"Well, I'm glad to be here tonight. In less than an hour, we will be celebrating a new year that our gracious God has bestowed upon us. Many people won't live to cross that bridge with us, but if it's the Lord's will, I plan to be here tomorrow. What about you?"

"Amen!"

Apparently it was the standard response for everything.

"Before we begin, I'd like to welcome all of our visitors. Whether you're a first time visitor or a returning visitor, we are glad you've decided to join us tonight in bringing in New Year's Day." He opened his Bible. "Let us visit the book of Ephesians tonight. Ephesians, third chapter, beginning with verse fourteen. I'm reading from the New International Version," he informed before he began.

" *'For this reason I kneel before the Father, from whom His whole family in heaven and one earth derives its name. I pray that out of His glorious riches He may strengthen you with power through His Spirit in your inner being, so that Christ may dwell in your hearts and through faith. And I pray that you, being rooted and established in love, may have power, together with all the saints, to grasp how wide and long and high and deep is the love of Christ, and to know this love that surpasses knowledge—that you may be filled to the measure of all the fullness of God.'* " He paused and looked out into the congregation. "Today I want to talk about love," the preacher spoke with a smile.

His words instantly grabbed Kenda's attention. *Love.* It was the reason she'd walked through the church's front doors.

Murmurs swept throughout the sanctuary as the congregation voiced their approval to the topic.

"God's love, that is," he specified.

The murmuring died down. Kenda couldn't help but wonder if those around her had been thinking about natural love; just as she had.

"You see, at the first mention of the word love, many of you immediately thought of romance." He said it like there was no doubt in his mind that he was speaking the truth. "Maybe your thoughts gravitated to your significant other, your husband, your wife, or maybe even a secret lover." He eyed the members as they mumbled some more. "Some of you may have thought of your children, other family members, or friends. But how many of you thought of Jesus?"

The preacher gave them time to digest his words and then he continued. "In this pericope of text, Paul was praying that

God would reveal His wondrous love to the people of Ephesus. Paul wanted them to experience what was meant to be loved unconditionally. You see, the world has begun using the word love so carelessly that its meaning, in a worldly sense, has become nearly invaluable. It's so easy for us to say, 'I love you' without thinking about what that statement actually means. This is particularly true in the romantic context."

Kenda sat in the back of the church wringing her hands together nervously. She didn't know why, but the pastor's message was already gnawing at her conscience. She knew she had been guilty of misusing the phrase on more than one occasion, especially when she had been with Jerome. At the time she had actually thought she was in love with him; now, she wasn't sure if she knew what love meant. She listened as he continued.

"But the most perfect example of true love is God sending His only begotten Son, Jesus, to die on the cross for our sins," the pastor proclaimed. "Jesus willingly gave his life for you and me. How many people do you know that would give their lives up for you? Not many, I'm sure. This was done out of pure agape love. Love that is selfless, love that is unconditional and everlasting. Jesus shows us this love day in and day out because He wants what is best for His children. He loves us so much He gave up His life so that we can have an opportunity to live in victory; a life full of hope and purpose.

"God doesn't expect us to be perfect. We may fall, but God's love will pick us up. Without His love, we would be nothing!" he exclaimed.

"Amen!" was shouted from all angles of the building. Expressions of praise erupted as the congregation lifted up the name of God.

Kenda watched the people around her rise to their feet as the pastor continued his message. Her heart began racing and her legs trembled. She felt something inside of her that she'd never experienced before; it made her squirm in her seat.

"The thing we have to understand is that God's love is so strong that it is enough to sustain us in *whatever* situation we find ourselves in. God is so awesome that He knows our situation before we can even acknowledge what it is we've gotten into. And His love is there with us from beginning to end. He may allow us to swim in the flood of problems we have, but he won't let us drown!"

That brought a new eruption from the crowd. Kenda moved her foot so the big lady next to her wouldn't crush it as she leapt with her hands raised and her eyes closed.

"You may be experiencing debt and financial instability. Your lights or gas maybe in danger of being turned off. You might be in a detrimental relationship and can't seem to find your way out. Maybe you're strung out on drugs and have been to rehab so many times that you've decided to stop trying to quit. Your friends may be trying to get you to do things you know are against the will of God, but you've gotten so caught up with them, trying to be accepted by them. You may find yourself in a life-altering situation, and you think you've made the best decision, but you still have your doubts. You may be so stressed out that you're looking for direction in all the wrong places. But because of the love of *Jesus!*" The pastor had been strutting from one end of the pulpit to the other as he spat out scenarios, and it caused the congregation to kick their praise into a higher gear.

It seemed as if the man of God were talking to Kenda without actually putting her on the spot for everyone to see. Tears began to sting her eyes as she looked at the pastor who was steadily traveling the course of the pulpit and wiping his forehead. She felt the message throughout his words and her heart was heavy. All this time, she'd been searching for romance in order to fill the void she'd had in her heart when, according to the minister, all she had to do was turn to Jesus. He was the only one she needed. *Jesus*. He'd possessed everything she'd been longing for.

"Even though you are going through hard times, don't fail to notice that by some miracle, you are still holding on. Look around you, sisters and brothers. Look at what you've experienced. You should've been in some hospital. You should've been in some mental institution. You should've been in some jail cell. You should've been in your grave!" Sweat poured from the pastor's head and he skipped across the pulpit, apparently feeling the same anointing that many of the members of his congregation were feeling. "God's love is continuously pulling you through. Don't you see that? It's God's love that rescues you time and time again. Not the love of man, but it's the love of the Heaven Father that has allowed you to experience and overcome these trials. It's His love that has brought you out, every time you thought you were stuck. It is time you realize that this unconditional love is available whenever you need it. Stop believing that you're not worth it, or that you're undeserving. That's just the devil trying to bring you down, but the devil is a liar! Acknowledge the power of God's love, embrace His grace. He will pull you through!"

He stopped in front of the podium and looked out into the audience. One hand was on his hip and his heavy breaths echoed though the speakers by way of the cordless microphone he held in his hand. "If any of you doubters need more evidence that God cherishes each of us," he said with a smiled as he pointed to the clock on the back wall of the church, "He's proved it again by allowing us to see another year. You ought to give Him the highest praise."

As the people worshipped God, the musicians suddenly began an upbeat tune. In a matter of seconds, the floor was flooded with people, dancing all over the building. Kenda had never seen such behavior. People were running around the building with their hands up and shouting out words in some language she couldn't even identify. She looked around and saw others on their knees crying out with thanksgiving. She winced as the big sister next to her began to jerk so violently it moved the whole pew.

Kenda wanted to leave, but something wouldn't release her from her seat. She felt as if some magnetic force was keeping her bottom glued to the fabric beneath it, and she began to cry.

Kenda didn't know where the tears were coming from, nor did she understand why they were falling. She wasn't upset. She wasn't mad. She wasn't even happy. All Kenda had wanted to do was come to church to look for the guy who had her heart. She couldn't find him, and now that she wanted to leave, she couldn't do that either. She quickly wiped her face before someone could notice her tears.

The music began to slow down and the pastor took the microphone. "Tonight, someone heard God pleading with them to come home. Tonight, this message touched someone's heart. I'm opening the altar to anyone who wants to answer the call. Anyone who wishes to accept Jesus Christ as their personal Lord and Savior, please come. Come now, and suffer no more."

Soft music began to play and the woman that had shown Kenda toward the sanctuary stepped up onto the pulpit and took the microphone. She began to sing a song that Kenda had never heard before, but it was fairly simple. All she kept saying was "Come to Jesus."

Kenda felt her heart urging for her to go up to the altar, but she couldn't bring herself to her feet. It was as if the force that had kept her down before, so she wouldn't be able to leave, was now keeping her in her seat so she wouldn't make the walk. She watched as many people walked toward the front to accept Jesus' invitation, but she couldn't make herself do the same. Kenda didn't even know if she were ready for that type of commitment. She wanted to live life to the fullest before being tied down and not being able to do anything except go to church and talk about Jesus. Besides, she hadn't come here to find Jesus, she had come to find Raymond. And it was apparent that he wasn't here.

As the pastor instructed those who had come to the altar to follow a minister to a room where each individual would be counseled, Kenda could still feel her heart yearning for a change. She could hear her spirit telling her to go before it was too late, but she wouldn't move. By the time the service came to an end, Kenda was way past being ready to leave. She hadn't seen Raymond and she felt sick to her stomach. After the benediction, she grabbed her things and took out her cell phone to call Chantal.

As soon as she turned to walk out of the door, a familiar side profile at the far end of the sanctuary caught her attention. Because the gentleman was standing on the other side of the church, where dozens of people were pushing their way toward the exit, Kenda couldn't make out his face completely, but she knew it was Raymond. She smiled as she began to approach him, but her footsteps came to a halt when she saw him place his arm around the woman who'd greeted her upon arrival. When he kissed the woman, more tears sprang into Kenda's eyes. She couldn't believe it. Raymond was here with another woman. And one who had a son at that.

Kenda remembered the little boy who was holding the woman's hand tightly as she walked out into the foyer. When Kenda looked at him, she'd seen the dark eyes that smiled at her when she'd greeted his mother. She'd known those eyes looked familiar. They were Raymond's eyes. Kenda watched him now as he picked up the little boy and planted a kiss on his forehead. She was at a complete loss for words. Raymond had a son. She'd known him for nearly two years and the child couldn't be more than one. He'd been lying to her from the start. She shook her head and walked swiftly out of the sanctuary.

Chapter 25

The tears in Kenda's eyes blurred her vision. No matter how many times she reached up to wipe them away, they continued to flow. She quickened her steps, trying to get away from the building as fast as she could. She kept her eyes lowered as she swiftly walked toward the exit, bumping right into a man who was standing in the foyer. Startled, she took a few steps back.

"I'm sorry," Kenda said with her eyes still downcast as she tried to move past him and toward the exit.

"Kenda?"

She turned around and looked up, wiping her eyes to make sure they weren't playing tricks on her. "Ray? But you were ... I mean, I just saw ... Weren't you just ... ?" She knew she wasn't seeing double. She was sure that had been Raymond she had just seen inside of the sanctuary.

"What are you doing here?" Raymond asked her.

Kenda stood upright and wiped her eyes. "You invited me, remember?"

He stared into her eyes and noticed her tears. "Are you okay?"

"No," she said with her hands on her hips. "Where's your girlfriend?"

Raymond looked confused. "What girlfriend?"

"Don't even try ly—"

"Wassup, Ray Ray?"

Kenda quickly wiped her eyes again before turning around to see a tall, dark, handsome man coming their way. He looked a lot like Raymond, except his head was completely bald, his skin and his eyes were slightly darker than Raymond's, and surrounding his lips was a neat goatee that made him look a few years older. Beside him stood the woman who'd greeted Kenda earlier, and the little boy who'd been with her.

"Wassup, Ron?" Raymond greeted the man with a hug.

"How you doin', man?"

"Good, good," Raymond replied.

The man looked down at Kenda. "Who's this lovely young lady?" he asked Raymond.

Raymond looked at Kenda before saying, "This is my . . . I mean, this is Kenda Tyson. Kenda, this is my cousin, Ronald McAfee."

Ronald stuck out his hand. "Nice to meet you."

Kenda timidly took the man's hand and shook it gently. "You too." She felt like a fool. The man she'd thought was Raymond was actually his cousin. They looked more like brothers. Almost like twins.

"This is his wife, Nevaeh, and their son, Nicolas," Raymond continued.

Nevaeh smiled. "We've met," she said and surprised Kenda by pulling her into a friendly hug. When Nevaeh pulled back, she searched Kenda's eyes. "Are you all right?"

Kenda smiled, feeling better after receiving the warm embrace. "Yes, I'm fine."

"Well, I hope you enjoyed the service." Nevaeh returned her smile.

"I did."

Ronald spoke up. "Well, we have to get going if we plan to make the service later on this morning." He slipped his arm around Nevaeh and kissed her cheek.

Raymond smiled. "Yeah well, just make sure y'all are on time. Nevaeh has to lead praise and worship."

"Can't make any promises, cuz." Ronald shrugged and then looked down at Kenda. "Will you be visiting with us again?"

Kenda avoided looking up at Raymond as she replied, "I don't know."

Nevaeh picked up her son and said, "Well, I hope you do. It was really nice meeting you."

"You too," Kenda said as they walked off.

She watched as the family left and smiled slightly when she saw Ronald whispering something in Nevaeh's ear, causing her to giggle like a young teenager. She turned back toward Raymond and noticed that he had been looking at her as she watched his family.

"I'm sorry," Kenda said.

"For what?"

She sighed. "I thought your cousin was you and when I saw him with Nevaeh, I thought . . . well, you know."

Raymond surprised her with a subtle laugh. "We do look a lot alike. A lot of people think we're brothers." He looked down at her and his smile vanished. "But that doesn't explain why you're here."

Kenda fidgeted under his gaze. She could see that he was still angry with her and she desperately wanted to change that. "I . . . Well, I was . . . I mean . . ." She stopped and sighed. "Could we please just go somewhere and talk?" Noticing his hesitation, she added, "*Please?*"

Raymond shook his head, but motioned for her to lead the way out of the church. Once outside, he stepped in front of her and she followed. They stopped when they reached his car, and Kenda was pleased when he opened the door for her to get in. Once a gentleman, always a gentleman. The corners of her mouth tugged into a smile.

They drove to a nearby 24-hour coffee shop. The establishment was small and there was only one other couple there. Kenda walked up to the woman behind the counter and ordered a mocha espresso. It was much too late for caffeine, but right now she needed all the extra energy she could get.

"Do you want something?" Kenda asked Raymond as he patiently waited for her to receive her drink.

Raymond shook his head. "No, thanks."

Once the woman returned with Kenda's order, they found a table that offered the privacy they needed. Kenda took one sip of her drink, and then pushed it aside. She nervously placed her hands on the table, and then put them in her lap. Her eyes gazed out of the window as she watched speeding cars go by. Kenda had no clue as to where to start, but she had to say something. She looked up into Raymond's dark eyes so he'd know that she was being sincere when she said, "I'm really sorry, Ray. I'm sorry that I lied to you and I'm sorry that I didn't tell you sooner. I was just afraid that you would—"

"Leave you," Raymond finished her statement. "Kenda, what I don't understand is why you would sleep with him. That's your most valuable treasure, and he didn't deserve that in any way. Not with the way he was treating you. That gift that you gave him was supposed to be kept to yourself until you found the love that you would spend the rest of your life with." He looked into her wet brown eyes. "I'm talking about *me*, Kenda. That should have been your gift to me on *our wedding night*."

Kenda's eyes opened wide in surprise. "Raymond, how can you know that you want to spend the rest of your life with me? We're only seventeen. Still in high school. We're not mature enough to make those types of decisions yet. So how can you say that?"

"Because Kenda, I know what I feel and what I feel for you is stronger than anything I've ever felt for anyone else. Did you see how my cousin and his wife were interacting? My love for you is twice the love they have for each other, and trust me, they got plenty of love for each other. They've been together since they were freshmen in high school, and they knew back then that they wanted to be together for life," he paused. "Don't you feel the same way? Can you honestly look me in my eyes and tell me that you don't think you are meant to spend the rest of your life with me?"

Kenda wanted to challenge Raymond, but her heart wouldn't allow her to. Everything he'd just said was true. She could see herself with him for life and she wished she'd realized that before she'd met Jerome. "I can't tell you that," she replied, "and I won't even try because I *can* see us together forever. I was imagining that when I was watching your cousins," she admitted. Then she took a deep breath to build up her confidence before saying, "And it can still happen."

Raymond shook his head. "No, Kenda, it can't. You're pregnant and I'm not the father. I'm not gonna take care of someone else's child. I just can't do that."

"I'm not asking you to. I've decided to have an abortion," she announced assertively.

"What?" His eyes opened wide. "Why would you do something like that?"

"For us, Ray. I don't want to have Jerome's baby. I know you don't want me to either. I don't want to have to look into his face ever again. I don't want to have any ties with him."

Raymond was shaking his head in disagreement. "No, Kenda, I won't let you do that. You can't kill an innocent child just because you don't want it."

"But, Ray, it's causing me to lose you," Kenda said as tears began to run down her face. "I don't want to lose you, Ray. I love you so much and I don't want to lose you," she repeated.

Raymond blinked back the tears that were building up behind his own eyelids. "Kenda, you're not going to lose me. I'm always going to be right here when you need me. I'm only saying that a relationship for us is not going to work."

She continued to plead. "But we can make it work. If this baby is out of the picture, we can be together. Just you and me."

Raymond was getting frustrated, but he tried his best not to let it show on his face or in his movements. "Kenda," he sighed, "I'm trying to tell you that if you abort this baby, you *will* lose me. Not as a friend, but all the respect I have for you would go right out the window."

The serious look on his face scared her. Raymond was telling Kenda that he didn't want to be with her because she was pregnant, but he didn't want her to get rid of the baby so they could be together either. The confusion only caused more tears to free themselves from her eyes.

Raymond slowly wiped her tears away with his fingertips. "I'm not trying to hurt you, Kenda, but I just don't believe in abortions. As much as I can't stand Jerome, I wouldn't be able to stand myself if you aborted this child just to be with me." He took her hands. "I want us to be together, but if it's going to cost a child's life then it can't happen. I'm not saying that there will never be a future us. I'm telling you that there can't be a present us."

"Well, what am I supposed to do?" Kenda asked. "I'm too young to have this baby. I can't take care of it."

"There's always adoption."

"I know and I thought about that. But what if my child grows up and wants to find me. I don't want to have to answer all of its questions. It would just be too hard."

Raymond tilted his head to the side and looked at her. "Wouldn't it be better for the kid to ask you questions of why you gave it up for adoption instead of it haunting you in your dreams, asking you why you killed it?"

Raymond's tone was calm, but his question was meant to place fear in Kenda's heart. She thought about what Roslyn had said. *"I had nightmares for months. I could hear my baby crying, calling for me and asking me why I did it. I had dreams of it coming after me, trying to kill me because it wanted me to feel what it felt when I killed it."*

"Of course I don't, but—"

"Kenda, it's the only other option." He paused. "Adoption or keep it. If you keep the baby, I'm sure you'd be able to find someone who'd help you take care of it. Your parents . . . friends. That's what we're here for."

Kenda looked at him in disbelief. "Ray, you'd actually help me raise my baby?"

Raymond smiled. "Help you, yes. Raise it, no."

She managed a light laugh before saying, "Maybe I could look into adoption." She looked out of the window and sighed.

"You need to talk to Jerome first."

Her head snapped back and she looked at Raymond to make sure she hadn't heard the softly-spoken words come from his mouth.

"Yes, I said it," he assured her. "You have to talk to him. It is his baby."

"So!" Kenda was tired of her friends trying to make her include Jerome in this decision.

Raymond remained calm, although Kenda seemed to be on the verge of losing her cool. "So, he has a right to know that you're carrying his child."

"Why?" she snapped. "So that once I have it, he can abuse it too. Or maybe he'd just teach my baby how to make illegal money. That's why I should do it. So my baby can become a criminal just like its daddy."

"Kenda, calm down," Raymond said as the woman behind the counter looked in their direction. "I'm just saying that you should at least tell him you're pregnant. He does have a right to know," he stated.

Kenda began to relax and take in what Raymond was saying. "Fine. But not until after I find an adoption agency that will help me find a good home for my baby."

Raymond smiled at her.

"What?" she asked him. "Why are you looking at me like that?"

"For someone who is so determined to give this child up, you're sure using the phrase 'my baby' a lot."

Kenda hunched her shoulders. "Well, it's in *my* belly, so it's mine . . . until I give it up."

He shook his head with the smile still plastered across his face. "I want you to come to church with me tomorrow . . . I mean, today."

Kenda laughed. "Raymond it is already two o'clock in the morning. You're crazy if you think I'm going to get up to go to church after just leaving a service."

"And you're crazy if you think that I won't come knocking on your door at ten-thirty."

She sighed. Maybe it wouldn't be so bad. After all, she wouldn't only be spending time in church. She'd be spending time with Raymond. "Fine." She picked up her purse and drink as she stood to leave.

"I like the outfit," Raymond complimented as he stood with her.

Kenda smiled. The Baby Phat jean jacket and matching floor-length jean skirt had been one of the many outfits that her parents had gotten her for Christmas.

"Thank you," she responded.

Minutes later, when they stood on her front porch, Kenda hugged Raymond and thanked him for taking time to talk to her. He kissed her forehead and told her he'd always be there for her. She watched him as he walked down the stairs and back toward his car. Before she could get inside, he called her name.

"Remember," he said, "be ready by ten-thirty . . . *a.m.*"

She smiled. "Okay. Happy New Year, Ray," she said as she walked into the house.

"Happy New Year."

Kenda locked the front door before walking up the stairs. The hall light startled her when it suddenly came on, but she relaxed when she realized it was only her brother.

"What are you doing up so late?" She knew that he some-times stayed up well past midnight, creating music on his computer.

"I think the better question is what are you doing *out* so late?" Aundrey leaned against the wall.

"I went to church with Raymond."

He laughed. "Yeah right! I know that people stay in church for a long time, but I ain't never heard of somebody heading for church at eleven and not coming back until two-thirty in the morning."

Kenda shrugged her shoulders. "I don't care if you don't believe me, but that's where I was. So if you'll excuse me, I have to get some sleep because Raymond's picking me up for service in less than eight hours." She walked up to him and stood on the tips of her toes to kiss his cheek. "Good-night, little brother." She went into her room, leaving Aun-drey standing in the hallway, amazed.

Chapter 26

"So did you enjoy the service?" Raymond asked as he and Kenda exited the sanctuary.

She gave him her best smile. "Yes, it was really good."

"Did you get anything from Pastor McKinley's sermon?"

Kenda let her mind wander to what the pastor had said about being ambassadors for Christ. *"If you are an ambassador for Christ, you represent the kingdom of heaven. You're representing God ... God works through His ambassadors; He pleads to man through us. That means we are to go out and minister to others. Not only with our words, but with our actions. Let them know and see how wonderful God is, and what magnificent changes can occur in their lives if they were to accept Him into their hearts."*

"Yeah, I did. I think I'll even go home and read the rest of Corinthians 5," Kenda said to Raymond's satisfaction. They walked out into the foyer. "Ray, where are your parents?" She hadn't seen them in service.

"They come to the seven o'clock service. There's no way I can get up that early so I come to this one."

She nodded in understanding, and then said, "Your cousin's wife . . . Nevaeh . . . she can really sing."

Raymond smiled. "Yeah, she's talented, but I know someone who could give her a lil' competition."

"Who?" Kenda asked.

He looked down at her. "You."

She shook her head. "Please don't start with that again."

"You're always singing, but you never want to admit you have a gift."

Kenda laughed. She and Raymond were forever arguing over her not wanting to sing in public, and it was really starting to get old. "Hey, isn't that your cousin over there?" she asked, wanting to change the subject.

Raymond looked up. "Yeah," he said. "Hey, Ron," he called out.

Ronald turned to face the voice. "Hey, man, what's up?" he greeted, giving his cousin a brotherly hug.

"Hey, Nev." Raymond kissed her on the cheek and then picked up his baby cousin. "Wassup, lil' man?" Nicolas laughed as Raymond threw him up in the air and caught him in his arms.

"Hi, Kenda," Nevaeh greeted her with a hug.

Kenda welcomed the woman's friendliness and returned the embrace. "Hi. How are you?"

"I'm doing well," Nevaeh replied.

"Did you enjoy the service?" Ronald asked her as he took Nicolas from Raymond.

Kenda smiled. "Yes, I was just telling Ray that your wife is a great singer." She looked at Nevaeh.

Nevaeh downplayed the compliment with a wave of her hand. "I do it for Jesus."

"Well, *I* was just telling Kenda that she could give you a run for your money," Raymond interjected.

Ronald looked at Kenda. "You can sing?"

"I—"

"No," Raymond interrupted Kenda's response. "She can *sang*."

Nevaeh smiled. "Really? I'd like to hear you."

"Me, too," Ronald added.

"Well, I—"

"She doesn't sing in public," Raymond mocked.

Kenda pushed his arm.

"Why not?" Nevaeh asked. "If you have a gift you should use it."

Kenda shrugged. "I've just never really been comfortable singing in front of an audience."

"You sing for me." Raymond looked down at her.

Kenda looked up at him and noticed the enticing look in his dark eyes. She blushed as his eyes seemed to look right through to her heart. Ronald and Nevaeh noticed the exchange and smiled.

"Well, we could always work on your stage presence," Nevaeh interrupted their eye contact. "You'd just have to start off with a small audience . . . like us." She pointed to herself and then to her husband.

Kenda shook her head. "I don't know."

"Well, whenever you feel you're ready," Ronald stated, "we'd love to be your first . . . I mean, *second* audience." He smiled at his cousin.

"In the meantime, would you two like to join us for dinner?" Nevaeh offered.

Raymond looked down at Kenda, who nodded. "Sure," he replied.

Twenty minutes later, Kenda was being shown around the McAfees' home. Kenda loved the outside of the house. The redbrick, single-level home looked as if the young couple had it built from the ground up. The freshly manicured lawn looked great, but Kenda knew that in the spring, when the grass returned to its normal rich, green color, it would look even better.

There were a few rose bushes out front that she knew would look exquisite when the flowers bloomed.

The inside of the house was just as lovely as the outside. The cream-colored living room was the first thing that she saw upon walking through the front door. From the sofa, loveseat, and chairs, to the carpet and curtains, it was all cream. The kitchen was small, but certainly adequate, and the dining room looked rarely used. The table setting, high-lighted by gold plates and utensils, was elegant and looked as perfect as an oil painting.

"Your home is beautiful," Kenda remarked as Nevaeh showed her into the den where the big screen television sat in an entertainment center that had shelves that housed photos of family and friends.

"Thank you," Nevaeh replied. "It took a lot of work, but we got it done."

Kenda looked at the photos on the shelves. She noticed pictures of Ronald and Nevaeh as teenagers, and some of them at their wedding. She saw some of Nicolas as a small baby too. She looked at one picture and saw a young woman and a man with a smiling little girl, who looked to be about six or seven. Kenda felt as if she recognized the woman from somewhere, but couldn't remember. Then, it came to her. Kenda had seen her perform during the BET Awards just last year.

"That's my best friend, Shimone," Nevaeh said as she walked up behind Kenda.

"Shimone Calhoun?" Kenda asked. "You know her . . . like *for real* know her? I saw her on television a few months ago. She was on BET, performing. She was fantastic."

Nevaeh laughed at her star-stricken house guest. "Yeah, I've known her since I was ten. She's on the road right now, touring her new CD. She, her fiancé, Marques, and their daughter, Ebony, live here in Atlanta and were actually just over here for Christmas." Nevaeh picked up the photo and then placed it back down. "These days, it's hard to find Shimone not on the road or in a studio somewhere."

"Wow," Kenda said as she sat down on the sofa and looked around the room. "Where are Ray and Ronald?"

"I sent them down the hall to change Nicolas," Nevaeh said.

"Oh. He's not potty trained yet?" Kenda inquired, hoping she didn't sound accusing.

Nevaeh shrugged. "We've been trying to for the last few months and he's almost got the hang of it, but Nicky will tell us he has to use the potty *after* he's already wet his pants." She laughed. "That's what he did as soon as we got into the house. I'm sure the guys are having a hard time because Nicky hates the changing process."

Kenda smiled. "It seems like you have such a wonderful family. Nicolas is just adorable; he looks just like his daddy."

"And his cousin." Nevaeh laughed. "I still find it amazing that Ron and Ray look so much alike."

"I know," Kenda said remembering the mistake she'd made last night.

"So, are you and Ray . . . together?" Nevaeh asked her.

Nevaeh seemed like someone Kenda could talk to, but she wasn't sure just yet, so she simply answered, "No. We're just friends."

"Are you sure? Because you guys act like Ron and me used to act back in high school."

Kenda laughed. "Well, honestly, we used to date last year. Then we broke up for a long while. Then a couple of weeks ago, we got back together. But now we're broken up again."

It was Nevaeh's turn to laugh. "Yep, you guys sound *just* like me and Ron. We broke up several times during our relationship, especially while we were in high school. But somehow, we ended up right back together."

"How long have you two been married?"

"This coming May will mark three years," Nevaeh replied. "We got married a few weeks after I graduated from college." She giggled. "Nicky was Ron's wedding night gift to me. He'll be two next month."

"Really?" Kenda was probably far too old to allow something like a shared birth month excite her, but it did. "I'll be eighteen on February nineteenth."

Nevaeh laughed. "Nicky's birthday is the day after yours."

They laughed together and then the room turned silent. Kenda wondered if her baby would have someone to love it like Nevaeh seemed to love her son. She wanted a good home for her child, and she didn't want to regret her decision to give it up. She rubbed her stomach, which seemed pudgier than the last time she'd checked. An image of her baby's heartbeat entered her mind's eye, and she smiled unconsciously. There was actually life developing inside of her at this very moment.

"Why are you smiling?" Nevaeh broke her out of her trance.

Kenda's smile was still in place. "Just thinking." She sat up straight when she heard the men coming into the room.

"What took you guys so long?" Nevaeh asked as Nicolas ran, on wobbly legs, into her arms.

Ronald came into the den. "You know your son. He wouldn't let me take off the pull up. Then he cried and kicked while I tried to wipe him down. He got popped a few times. But he just doesn't listen." He sighed. "I think I'll leave this up to you next time."

Nevaeh smiled. "Well, I love you for trying." She kissed him lightly on the lips.

Kenda stood back and solemnly watched the couple's display of affection. Glancing at Raymond, she noticed that he was also watching them and wondered if he were thinking about his relationship with her. Kenda wanted so badly to ask him if there was even a small chance that they could reestablish their bond, but realized that everything that had happened to lead to their breakup was still painfully fresh on his mind. His response might be one she wouldn't be able to handle. Their eyes connected and Kenda allowed a small smile to stretch her lips.

"Dinner's waiting on us guys," Nevaeh asked. "Let's eat."

After sharing a meal of grilled chicken breast, rice, corn on the cob, and a dessert of lemon pound cake, Raymond and Ronald went outside to talk, leaving Kenda inside with Nevaeh and Nicolas. Kenda wanted so badly to talk to her, but she had no clue of how to begin such a touchy conversation.

"Kenda, can we talk?" It was if Nevaeh had read her mind.

After clearing her throat and shifting her sitting position, Kenda said, "Sure."

"I really don't want to get all into your business or anything," Nevaeh said, glancing at Nicolas who played on the floor nearby, "but it seems like there's something serious between you and Ray. I mean, at dinner you guys would look at each other and there'd be so much love in your eyes . . . I just don't understand." She shook her head. "Why are you all ignoring it?"

Kenda smiled, but pangs of guilt made her shift her position once more. "We're not really ignoring it," she admitted, somewhat glad that Nevaeh took the chance of getting *all into her business*. "We've just decided not to get involved."

Nevaeh was completely confused. "But it's so obvious that you guys were very serious about each other."

"We were . . . we still are, but some things happened and it just didn't work out the way we planned. But Ray knows that I still love him and I know the feeling is mutual."

Nevaeh chuckled softly. "I'm sorry, I just don't understand. You guys love each other, but you won't get together. What's stopping you?"

Kenda looked away and tried her best to keep the tears back. She touched her stomach and looked back at Nevaeh, who noticed that her mood had changed. "I'm pregnant." Kenda lowered her voice as if she were afraid the baby might hear it.

Nevaeh's eyes showed the shock her mouth didn't speak. "Oh," she replied. "And you broke up because he doesn't believe it's his?"

Kenda shook her head. "We broke up because he *knows* it's not his. We weren't sexually active during our relationship," she informed. "I got pregnant during the time Ray and I were broke up. I'm pregnant by an ex-boyfriend." She couldn't even bring herself to say his name.

Kenda went on to explain the horrible, tempestuous relationship she had endured for four months. She told Nevaeh everything. The drugs, the sex, the violence, the way she ignored the warnings of her friends and family members. All of it.

Then Kenda explained how she found out she was pregnant and how she told Raymond, which ultimately ended their relationship for good. By the time she was finished, she was in uncontrollable tears.

"I thought about abortion," Kenda said through heavy sniffles, "but Raymond said if I did it, I'd lose his respect. I don't want that to happen. I've been watching you with Nicky and part of me actually wants to keep my baby so I can have that kind of relationship, but the other part of me is ready to give this baby up the moment I give birth."

Nevaeh took the whole box of Kleenex that sat on her end table and placed it in Kenda's hand. "Sweetie, all you have to do is seek God. Ask Him to lead you in the right direction and He'll show you the way. You're trying to make this decision on your own and it's not going to work. You need to pray and ask God what His plan is for your life; what it is that He has for you to do. Only He can tell you that.

"I agree wholeheartedly with Raymond. You shouldn't abort and I know you're not even thinking about that as an option now because of Raymond's threat, but that shouldn't be the only reason you don't want to do it. You shouldn't want to do it because God wouldn't be pleased. The Bible says that God hates the hands that shed innocent blood. Every child born into this world—regardless of who his mother or father is—has a purpose." Nevaeh touched Kenda's stomach lightly. "This child inside of you has a purpose. God didn't create this baby to ruin your life. He created it because He has something for it to do in the future. Now what that purpose is, I wouldn't be able to tell you. Once again, you're going to have to get on your knees and pray about it.

"Even if you decide to give it up for adoption, don't make that decision based upon the ill-feelings that you have toward the baby's father. If you give the baby up, do it because you've prayed and heard God telling you that this child would be better off with someone else raising and nourishing it. God may want you to take responsibility for your actions and raise this child yourself, but He won't make you do it alone. He will place the right people in your life so that you will be able to do what He wants you to do. So don't cry." Nevaeh smiled as she watched Kenda wipe away more tears. "God knows exactly what He's doing. You just need to move out of His way and let Him do it. He'll work everything out."

Kenda smiled at the woman, feeling as if she'd known Nevaeh all her life. "Thank you." She paused before making a request that even shocked her. "Would you mind . . . praying for me?"

A wide smile spread across Nevaeh's face. "I was just about to ask if you'd mind me doing so." She took Kenda's hands and closed her eyes as she began. "Lord, I thank you for this day. I thank you for letting us see another year and I pray that we will grow stronger in you as each day goes by. I come to you right now, asking that you please place your loving arms around Kenda. She needs you right now, Lord, and you know exactly what to do. I pray that she will listen to your voice, and that she will hear you calling for her to join your family, so that one day she will be able to dwell with you in heaven." She loosed Kenda's hands and Nevaeh put her own hands on Kenda's stomach. "And I pray for her unborn child. Lord, protect it and help it to develop properly. Lord, although this child was conceived outside of your will, I know that you love it immensely and you have a purpose just waiting for it when it enters this world. Whether it's purpose is simply to bring joy to its mother, or to grow up and minister your gospel to a dying world, its purpose shall be fulfilled. Lord, I thank you once again for bringing us all together, and showing us that without your love, we wouldn't be able to survive. I love you and I praise your holy name. Amen."

Kenda dabbed her eyes with tissue. "Thank you so much." She wrapped her arms around Nevaeh and squeezed.

"You are so welcome," Nevaeh said as Kenda released her. "Anytime you need someone to talk to, I'm here."

Nicolas pushed himself up off of the floor and walked over to Kenda. She reached out and he allowed her to pick him up. Looking down into his dark eyes, Kenda wondered if she'd be better off keeping her child, or giving it up to a couple who could better care for it. Nevaeh's words came back to her. *"You're trying to make this decision on your own and it's not going to work. You need to pray and ask God what His plan is for your life . . ."*

And that was exactly what she was going to do. Kenda decided that she needed to have a long overdue talk with God.

Chapter 27

The first couple of weeks of the second semester made the holiday break seem as though it had never occurred. Students were loaded with so many assignments that they felt like they were being punished.

Kenda had a project in her Human Anatomy class, a written report due in her Economics class, and she had to give an oral report in her Psychology class. She had completed most of the Anatomy assignment, and she'd finished the research for her Economics report. Now she had to figure out how she was going to give an oral report on solutions to a teen's suicidal issues. Kenda never liked her Psychology class, but she'd registered for it hoping it would give her some extra practice in dealing with other people's dilemmas. She figured she could use that knowledge once she became a lawyer.

Even with all of the work from school, Kenda felt strangely peaceful, and she knew it was because of the recent change she'd made in her life. She smiled as she remembered walking up to the altar with Raymond on this past Sunday to accept Jesus into her heart. She'd cried a flood of tears as she was lead to the personal workers' room, where a seasoned minister led her through the Sinner's Prayer as she submitted to God. Raymond was by her side the entire time. After the prayer, he hugged her and let her continue to rest in his arms. After all the sad tears that she'd shed over the recent months, it felt good to be reintroduced to tears of joy.

Now she sat at home, taking a break from all the school work she'd had to deal with in the past week. It was a quiet Saturday afternoon, and it felt good to have the house all too herself. Her parents were at work and Aundrey was out with a few of his friends. Kenda sat cross-legged on her bed, reading through the adoption information she'd asked Dr. Akeem to send her.

She still hadn't revealed her pregnancy to her parents, only because she couldn't figure out the right way to come out and tell them. She figured that their reaction couldn't be any worse than Raymond's, but if it were, she knew that she could take it. Although they'd be disappointed, their anger would also be because they loved her and cared for her. Kenda would be able to find enough hope in that to get through it.

Xavier and Maxine had taken time out to spend a full day with her and Aundrey last Saturday, and they'd actually had fun. Kenda and her mother had gone to a day spa, and Xavier took his son to one of his famous client's recording studio where Aundrey recorded several musical compositions on the state-of-the-art equipment. Xavier and Maxine had become so involved in Aundrey and Kenda's lives in just the past few weeks that Kenda felt that her parents deserved to know about her pregnancy. Had it been a few months ago, she couldn't have cared less what they would have had to say, but she needed them to be there for her now more than ever; especially since she'd finally decided on what she wanted to do with the baby.

Kenda heard the garage door opening and wondered which of her parents were home. They weren't supposed to get off until seven-thirty that evening, and it was only four o'clock. But regardless of their reason for ending their shift early, Kenda was glad that she'd be able to finally relieve herself of the secret she'd been withholding.

"Hello? Is anybody home?"

It was her mother. Kenda unconsciously sighed with relief, knowing her mother would be easier to talk to. And she hoped that Maxine would then help her tell Xavier.

"I'm here, Mama," Kenda yelled from the top of the staircase.

Maxine smiled. "Hi, sweetie. Where's Aundrey?"

Kenda leaned over the banister. "Out with Patrice and some of their friends."

"Okay. I finished my work a little early and decided to come home."

"Well, how was your day?"

"Wonderful. We got the murder trial." Maxine beamed.

"Congratulations," Kenda said, remembering hearing her parents talking about the young female who'd been charged for murdering her boyfriend. Her parents strongly believed that the girl had reasonable cause for committing the crime, and they were determined to prove it was all in self-defense.

"What about you? How has your day been so far?"

"Good." Kenda shifted her feet nervously. "Umm . . . do you think we could talk?"

Maxine looked up at her daughter and searched Kenda's face. "Sure, we can talk in my room."

Maxine walked up the stairs, leading her daughter into the master bedroom. Kenda sat down on her parents' king-sized bed and waited for her mother to put away her things and join her.

"So what's up?" Maxine asked. When the tears fell, Maxine's face lined with worry. "Oh my goodness, Kenda," she said. "What is it?"

"Mama, I'm pregnant." She hadn't planned to just blurt out the truth, but she didn't have the energy to beat around the bush. Kenda expected her mother to yell, scream, or even cry, but when Maxine simply pulled her into her bosom and allowed her to cry on her chest, Kenda was surprised. Pleasantly surprised. She'd never thought that the most affection her mother would show her would be during a time when she'd be in trouble. It felt good to be comforted.

"I'm so sorry, Mama," Kenda bawled.

"It's okay, Kenda. Everything's gonna be all right."

Once Kenda calmed down, she told her mother everything that had happened between her and Jerome, in detail. By the time she'd finished, both she and her mother were pulling tissues from the box that Maxine had retrieved from the bathroom.

"Why didn't you tell us this sooner?" Maxine asked.

Kenda wiped her eyes. " 'Cause Mama, you and Daddy were always working and up until very recently, I didn't think you guys would have cared."

Maxine shook her head. She felt as if she'd failed at being a good parent. She'd always said her family would come first, but apparently, she had let her company take the forefront in her life. "I'm so sorry. I had no idea you felt that way." She looked into her daughter's brown eyes. "Kenda, your father and I love you and your brother. I know we haven't told you that as often as we should. You've probably heard it more in the last two weeks than you have in the last two years, and there's no excuse for that. So we're going to have to do better." She smiled slightly. "Now about this baby—"

"I'm having it," Kenda interjected.

Maxine nodded. "I want you to. Then you can decide if—"

"I want to keep it, Mama," Kenda interrupted again. "I was reading some information about adoption before you came home and I just don't think I'd want to give up my baby to complete strangers. I prayed about it too, and I know that this is what God wants me to do. It's time I take responsibility for my own actions."

Maxine smiled down at her daughter. "I'm proud of you." She kissed her forehead. "Now you know that your father and I will be here for you, but we're not going to raise this child. We'll help you financially until you can find a job and we'll even find a sitter or some other daycare provider that can take care of him or her while you're in school. I want you to know that this is *your* decision, and I'm praying that you've actually listened to what God has said and you're ready to do what He's instructed."

Kenda nodded. "I know this is it, Mama. I just know it."

Maxine stood from the bed. Her sigh sounded a bit burdened, but she smiled anyway. "Your father will be here in a few hours and we need to have this house spotless and his favorite meal ready so that he'll be in a good mood when you . . . we tell him this news."

Kenda smiled and hugged her mother. "Thank you. I love you so much, Mama."

"I love you too, baby." Maxine returned the embrace.

"So how did your parents take the news?" Raymond asked as they dined in a restaurant after church on Sunday.

Kenda smiled slightly as the scene at home replayed in her memory. "My mother actually hugged me. I mean like a *real* hug, and she told me that everything was gonna be all right." She laughed softly at the newest recollection. "My dad . . . well, he was another story. He yelled and screamed until his voice was hoarse and his face was red. I cried until my eyes wouldn't even give up no more tears," Kenda told him. "But when Daddy was finished saying all he had to say, and when he finally calmed down, he hugged me too."

Raymond smiled and nodded his head. "I told you. I knew everything was going to be okay." He looked at her from across the table. "So are you going to start looking for a family that will adopt the baby after it's born?"

Kenda shook her head. "I've decided to keep it."

His smile faded a bit. "You have?"

She nodded. She could tell that he was sort of disappointed, but she just couldn't do it. "Nevaeh told me to pray about it and I did. I know this is the best thing to do."

"You prayed?" Some of his smile returned.

She rolled her eyes. "You act like I've never prayed before. I mean, it wasn't easy," she admitted, "but once I got going I didn't stop until I received an answer."

Raymond's face was glowing and Kenda was happy that he was happy. They both knew that she was growing more and more in the Lord.

"So your parents are gonna help you, right?"

Kenda drank from her glass of water. "Yes. They're going to help me find a daycare or a sitter so someone will be able to watch the little one while I'm in school. I've decided to go to Emory University so that I can be closer to home if I need someone to help me with the baby."

"Someone like me?" Raymond asked.

Kenda smiled. "Maybe," she responded. "But I'm not saying I'm going to be calling you every day asking you to do things for me, I just would like for a few trustworthy people to be there if I need a little help from time to time."

He reached across the table and grabbed her hand. "Kenda, I'm always here for you." He intertwined his fingers with hers, his words sending a surge of love and warmth through her body.

Kenda's head tilted slightly to the side as an inquisitive expression clouded her face. "Ray, do you think we'll ever be able to go back to having a relationship beyond just friendship?"

He hunched his shoulders in a carefree manner. "Anything's possible."

Kenda hoped that one day it would happen. "There's one more thing that I have to do," she spoke after a brief silence.

"What's that?"

"I have to go see Jerome," she replied. "I don't have a choice. God is telling me that if I don't go see him, His plan is not going to be fulfilled. I have no clue as to what His plan is, but I do know that I want it to happen, so I have to do this." She sighed. "I'm just so scared."

"Why?"

Kenda told Raymond about her reoccurring dream. She didn't know if it had some type of connection to real life or not, but the images had been haunting her thoughts almost every night and she was becoming more and more fearful.

"I just don't know what might happen. I'm afraid that the dream will become reality," she confessed.

Raymond looked at her and said, "Kenda, you're not the same person you were weeks ago. You're more protected now than you ever were before because you have God on your side and He's walking with you every step of the way. So even if that dream does happen, you're going to come out victorious."

Kenda smiled. "Thanks, Ray. You know, you've been a really good friend."

"So have you."

"Ray," Kenda started and then paused. "Will you take me?"

"To Jerome's?"

She nodded. Even though he told her God would protect her, Kenda still feared going alone.

"Sure, if you really want me to."

Her eyes showed her gratitude.

Chapter 28

Kenda placed the tiara that Jerome had sent her for Christmas inside of the box. She picked up the huge teddy bear and the bracelet that he'd sent her for her eighteenth birthday, almost two weeks ago, and placed them into the box also. She had been avoiding this day for over a month. It was time to stop running. Raymond would be by to pick her up in a few minutes and she couldn't change her mind now. She was doing this for herself and for her baby.

Kenda smiled. *Her baby.* The ultrasound she had last week showed she was eighteen weeks pregnant and was most likely having a girl. She had been confused when Dr. Akeem used the phrase "most likely," but he explained that while he could see the genitals of the child, the image wasn't as clear as it could be. So the early detection of a little girl could very well change in the coming weeks as the baby continued to develop. Kenda was holding on to the hope of having a daughter. But regardless of her child's gender, she prayed that the baby would be healthy, and that she wouldn't carry any of her father's features. She didn't want to have to look into her baby's eyes and see Jerome staring back. She wanted to put everything that they'd ever shared behind her. Raymond ringing the doorbell signaled that it was time to do that now.

"Mama, Daddy, Ray's here," Kenda called out as she grabbed the box and walked out of her room. She wasn't surprised when her whole family came out into the hallway. Her parents had been hesitant to allow her to go to Jerome's house without them, but Kenda had convinced them that she was mature enough to handle the situation. She also told them that this was something she needed to handle on her own and promised that she would be extremely cautious. Her declaration that Raymond would be accompanying her seemed to slightly ease their worries.

"You be careful," her mother said, hugging her tight.

"If Jerome even *tries* to touch you, let me know." Aundrey cracked his knuckles as if he were ready for a fight.

Kenda smiled and shoved the box into her brother's hands before offering him a one-armed hug. "Thanks, Drey."

"And make sure you're back here within two hours," Xavier instructed. "Traffic's not that heavy today, but I know it takes a while to get out to his place. I'm giving you some extra time to hang out with Ray, since he's such a good *friend*."

She laughed. "Thank you, Daddy."

Kenda walked down the stairs, with Aundrey following behind her, and opened the front door.

"Hi," Raymond said. "Are you ready?"

Kenda nodded as she motioned for Aundrey to hand the box to Raymond. After assuring her bother for the fifth time that she was going to be okay without him, Kenda followed Raymond to the car. He placed the box in the backseat before opening the passenger side door for her. Before she climbed in, he grabbed her arm and looked her up and down with a wide grin pasted across his face.

"What?" Kenda was pleased with his intense gaze.

Raymond folded his arms across his chest. "You look beautiful."

Kenda blushed, but shrugged as she looked down at her clothes. "Ray, I'm wearing an oversized sweat suit to hide my weight gain, my hair's a wild mess because I'm too tired to do anything with it, I'm wearing no makeup, and—"

"And that can't be beautiful to me?"

Kenda shrugged again. "Well, I—"

Raymond moved so that his face was only inches from hers. "Just say thank you."

She stared into his eyes and whispered, "Thank you," before getting into the car.

As they drove toward Jerome's apartment, Kenda sat nervously in the passenger's seat. She continued to practice in her head what she wanted to say to Jerome. She didn't want to send him the wrong signals, nor did she want him to see her protruding belly, so she had purposefully dressed in baggy clothes. She wore no makeup, not even the eyeliner that usually highlighted her eyes, and she had done nothing to tame her naturally curly hair. Jerome had always liked it better when it was straightened to its full length. She had already prepared herself for his unwanted affection and she was determined not to let him think she was coming back to reunite with him. This was strictly a business visit and nothing he could say or do would change that.

When they reached the gated community, Kenda told Raymond the code and they entered the complex with no problems. Kenda noticed that Raymond's Honda looked extremely out of place among the luxury cars that decorated the parking lot, but he shamelessly pulled into an empty space and shut off the engine.

"Are you sure he's home?" Raymond asked Kenda who sat with her back stiff as if she weren't planning to get out of the car.

She nodded. "His car is here."

Raymond looked around and saw the Mercedes Benz parked a few cars down. He looked back at Kenda. "Do you want me to go in with you?"

She shook her head. "No, I have to do this alone." She looked at him. "But if I'm not back down here in fifteen minutes, call the police." She figured she would need a little extra time to explain to Jerome that she was going to have his baby and that she had every intention to raise the child without any form of assistance from him. "It's apartment 206."

He nodded, knowing she was serious, and watched her get out of the car and retrieve the box from the backseat. "Be careful, Kenda."

"I will," she replied before shutting the car door and walking toward the entrance.

"I love you," Raymond whispered, hoping that somehow she'd heard him. Immediately, he began to pray.

As Kenda walked into the building, her stomach began to get queasy. With each step she took, the feeling got worse. She stood in the elevator, praying that God would be with her. She got off at the second floor—still praying—and walked down the hall. When she stood in front of Jerome's door, she paused and took a deep breath.

"God, I can't do this," Kenda said aloud. "I'm so scared."

Yes, you can. My arms are around you, protecting you.

"Okay, Lord." She took another deep breath. "I trust you."

Kenda knocked on the door and took a few steps back. When the door opened, she rolled her eyes toward heaven. God had jokes. Not only did she have to confront Jerome, but she'd have to do in front of an audience.

"Well, well, well," G-Dawg said as he leaned against the doorpost. "If it ain't lil' Miss J-Man."

Kenda inhaled and exhaled slowly. She could hear

Jerome's friends hollering, probably in response to something playing on the television in the den.

"You know you done had my boy all down and out." He looked her up and down. "But I guess that's 'bout to change now."

Kenda rolled her eyes and sighed. "Is Jerome here?"

"Yeah, he here," G-Dawg replied. "Come on in."

She could feel the heat of his eyes burning through the back of her clothes as she walked past him and into the apartment, placing the box on the floor in the living room.

"Hey, fellas," G-Dawg yelled to the guys in the den. "We got ourselves a visitor. This here is lil' Miss J-Man."

Kenda walked into the den and looked around the house. She didn't see Jerome anywhere, only the thugged-out guys sitting in the den, looking at her as if she were a prime rib dinner. Fear arose in her, and she wanted to run out of the front door.

Be calm, my child. I've got this.

She relaxed at the sound of her Father's voice and turned toward G-Dawg. "I thought you said Jerome was here."

G-Dawg looked at her and licked his lips. "He is."

Kenda placed her hands on her hips. "Well, would you get him please?"

G-Dawg exaggeratedly mocked her stance. "Sure," he said as the guys laughed in blatant ignorance. He walked down the hall. "Yo, J-Man. Ya girl's out here lookin' for ya!"

Kenda stood in the den as the guys resumed watching a sports game on ESPN. She continuously prayed that God would keep her and let no harm come to her. When she felt her stomach begin to settle, she knew everything was in His hands.

"What girl, man?" Kenda heard Jerome ask as he came from the back of the apartment. "Kenda?" he whispered her name as if he weren't sure it was her standing there.

Kenda turned to face him with an impassive expression

on her face. She now knew she was completely over him. None of those feelings arose that she used to have at the sight of him. There was no giddiness, no excitement. no jitters, no butterflies. Nothing. Kenda had to admit to herself that he still looked good though. He hadn't let their breakup affect his appearance much and she figured that was because he still had to be presentable in dealing with his business.

Although she had it together, the look in Jerome's eyes showed that his insides were torn into pieces. But Kenda didn't feel any regrets, and her heart held only the love of Christ for him.

"Hi, Jerome," she greeted firmly.

Jerome walked over to her and gazed at her as if she were only a figment of his imagination. He reached up to caress her face, but she dodged his hand.

G-Dawg burst into laughter. "Dang, man, she won't even let you touch her."

Kenda turned a cold stare to G-Dawg, and then looked back at Jerome. "Do you think we could get some privacy?"

Jerome smiled slightly, obviously misreading her desire to be alone with him as some offer that would come with benefits. He kept his eyes on Kenda. "Fellas," he called to his friends, "be out."

The guys looked at him as if he were crazy.

"Man, how you gon' let her come up in here after she been gone for months and let her tell you to just throw us out like we some trash?" G-Dawg asked, insulted.

Jerome glared at him with warning in his eyes. "I said, be out," he repeated, his jaw tight.

Quickly, his friends got up, gathering their cans of beer and bags of chips, and left the apartment. Kenda and Jerome stood alone in the living room.

Kenda shifted her position to put a bit of distance between them. "I just came by to give you your things back."

"I've missed you," Jerome said.

She sighed. Apparently this was going to be harder than she'd thought. "Jerome, I don't have the time." She walked toward the sofa and picked up the box off of the floor. "I just came to give you all of this stuff back."

He glanced down at the open box and then looked back up at her. "Why? I gave all of this to you."

"I no longer want it," she declared.

"Why?"

"I just don't, okay?" she snapped. "I need to rid myself of everything that happened. Of our entire relationship. The only way I can do that is by giving you all of this junk back."

Jerome looked at her with regretful eyes. "Kenda, I'm sorry about everything that happened. I'm so sorry. I love you, baby. Please just give us another chance."

Kenda could tell he'd been drinking and the beer bottles lying on the table in the den weren't her first clue. "Jerome, I don't have time for this. My ride is waiting downstairs and I need to go." She dropped the box onto the floor and prepared herself to leave, deciding against telling him about the baby because of the state he was in. When she tried to walk away, he grabbed her arm and she felt herself immediately regressing back to the days of their relationship.

"Kenda, please," he begged.

She winced. "Jerome, you're hurting my arm. Please, let me go."

"Kenda, I'm practically begging you. Please, baby, don't leave me." He pulled her closer to him.

Kenda couldn't break free of Jerome's grip and she was so close to him that she could smell the liquor on his breath. Tears burned her eyes as she realized that Raymond would have to call the police before she would be able to leave this apartment.

"Jerome, please let go of me," she said, trying not to show her fear.

"Kenda, I love you," Jerome responded. "Don't you still love me?"

Kenda held a smirk on her face. "Yeah Jerome, I just *love* the way you beat the crap out of me." Her smirk disappeared when his grip tightened. *Be calm*, she told herself. *Don't do anything to set him off.*

"I said I was sorry," he said tightly. "I do love you, Kenda. You're not like other girls. You're the only one that was real."

"Jerome, please let me go."

Jerome pulled her closer. "Why you fighting me?" His voice was a little too steady and it frightened her even more. He pulled her as close to him as he could possibly get her. Her body became tense as he touched her face and wiped the tears that were escaping her eyes. "Don't be scared." His voice was calm. "I'm not going to hurt you, Kenda."

Kenda closed her eyes and prayed for a rescue. She felt Jerome slide his hands up her sweatshirt and caress the small of her back; she trembled. "Jerome, *please*—"

He cut her off by pressing his lips against hers. She pushed against him, trying with all of her strength to get him to stop.

"Jerome, get off of me!" Kenda demanded as she pushed him back and slapped him across his face. "Oh God," she whispered when she realized that what she'd just done. "Oh God." She prayed that it would only be a matter of seconds before the police would arrive. It seemed as if Raymond should have called them by now, but she knew it had only been a few minutes.

Kenda saw the surprise that flashed in Jerome's eyes, but the reaction was quickly replaced with anger. His face was turning red from the smack she'd just given him, but mostly from the rage that had arisen inside of him. She wanted to run, but couldn't move because fright held her frozen in place. Kenda watched as Jerome drew his hand back, and as if she were watching it in slow motion, it gradually came closer and closer until it landed across her face. Following it was a right jab into her jaw that knocked her to the floor. She immediately felt the blood in her mouth. She couldn't believe that this was happening. Her dream was becoming reality and it was her own fault. Jerome got down on the floor and slapped and punched Kenda repeatedly.

"Oh God," Kenda cried as Jerome's fist landed across her face. "God, please help me." She could feel him straddling her and she prayed that he wasn't about to do what she thought he was about to do. She cried out for help. "Please, somebody!" she screamed. "Please help me!"

"Shut up!" Jerome yelled, slapping her once more.

Kenda now wished that she had allowed Jerome's friends to stay while she handled their unfinished business. She wondered if any of them could hear her crying. Were any of them going to get help or were they just listening as their friend continued to abuse her.

Protect her and I will protect you.

Suddenly, anxiety concerning her own safety was pushed aside as she thought of her daughter. She instantly placed her arms around her stomach, praying that it was enough to keep her baby unharmed.

"Mama's got you," Kenda murmured through barely moving lips. "Mama's got you. God's got us."

She could feel Jerome's punches, but they were no longer hurting her. She could feel the backs of his hands flying across her face, but they were no longer painful. It was as if a barrier were between them—sort of like a shield—protecting her from the pain.

Kenda began to hum softly as the tears continued to flood her closed eyes. She'd heard the song last Sunday at church with Raymond. Nevaeh had sung it so beautifully. It was a song she hadn't heard since she was a little girl, when her grandmother used to sing it when she felt troubled. Kenda tried to remember the words. When she did, they poured from her soul.

"Amazing grace, how sweet the sound . . ." Kenda sang as Jerome yelled for her to shut up.

He still straddled her and she could hear him undoing the zipper on his jeans, but she couldn't move, so she continued to sing her heart out as she cried and prayed that someone would come soon.

"I once was lost . . ." she bellowed as she held her stomach as tight as she could, hoping and praying that she'd pull through this just so her baby would.

Kenda heard Jerome muttering curses as he tried to spread her legs apart, but if he were going to rape her, she wasn't going to assist him willingly. She stiffened her legs and continued to sing the song, wondering how much time had passed. Had it been fifteen minutes yet?

" 'Twas grace that taught—"

The front door burst open. "Kenda!"

It was Raymond, but she couldn't stop singing and her eyes wouldn't open. She kept crying and bellowing out the song that had become her anthem of praise. She could hear Jerome yelling obscenities at Raymond, but she still felt him sitting on top of her.

"Get off her!" Raymond yelled.

Kenda could feel Jerome struggling and Raymond's presence was near. Finally, she felt Jerome being pulled off of her, but still she didn't move.

"How precious did that grace appear . . ." Kenda could hear Jerome and Raymond fighting. Someone had been punched and had fallen to the floor nearby. She was surprised that Jerome had not yet pulled out his gun. She heard the continuous tussle, though, and knew that both guys were throwing punches rivaling those in a heavyweight boxing match. Although Kenda knew Raymond could take Jerome on any day and win hands down, Jerome's heavy-handedness could possibly make Raymond work a little harder to keep standing.

"Freeze!" an authoritative voice yelled from the doorway.

Kenda started singing a new song. "Yes, Lord . . ." She could hear the click of more than one pair of handcuffs and an agonizing scream from one of the guys. She wished she could tell them that Raymond was not guilty of any crime. She could hear him trying to explain himself, but apparently not being heard. Someone was searching through the apartment as if they'd come looking for something other than her.

"Kenda . . . Ouch!" She heard Raymond coming toward her. "Kenda, are you okay?"

Kenda didn't answer him, but continued to sing. She heard him struggle as he was being pulled away from her side.

Someone else was standing over her now, telling another person to call an ambulance, but she kept singing. Even when Kenda heard someone declare her delirious, but lucid, she didn't stop singing.

Kenda continued to hold her stomach as tight as she could; praying that her baby girl was okay. She was still singing when the ambulance arrived, and she continued as the medics strapped her to a gurney and loaded her onto the vehicle.

"My soul says yes."

Chapter 29

Someone was touching her forehead as if checking to see if she had a fever. Kenda opened her eyes slightly, and then closed them tight, shielding her pupils from the overhead lights, and the agony that seared through her body. She tried once more, but couldn't open them fully without causing herself pain.

"Mama?" Kenda could barely move her swollen lips.

Maxine placed her index finger against her lips, signaling for her daughter to not try to talk. She wiped tears from her own eyes. "Yes, it's me, baby. We're all here."

Kenda looked around as much as her half-shut eyes would allow, and saw her brother and father standing on the other side of her bed. She tried to figure out where she was, but she couldn't move because of the neck brace she was wearing.

"You're at Emory Hospital," Xavier told her as if he could sense her thoughts. "They brought you in yesterday and stitched you up."

She could see her brother crying silently behind their father. His emotional pain brought tears to her eyes as she remembered all that had happened.

"I'm . . . sorry," Kenda said as the first tear fell.

"Sweetheart, don't talk," Maxine stressed. "You don't have to be sorry. None of this is your fault."

"R . . . Ray . . ." Kenda refused to listen to her mother's request.

"Raymond's here," Maxine replied, "He has a fractured arm and his face is a little swollen, but he's okay."

Kenda's tears began to flow. It was all her fault. She shouldn't have gone to that apartment. She should have just thrown the things away and tried to avoid Jerome, but she couldn't do that. She had to go and see him.

"Kenda, it's not your fault," her father assured her. "You did what you knew God wanted to you do. Somehow, things just got messed up."

Kenda didn't want to tell her father that she was responsible for that, too. Had she not slapped Jerome, none of this would have happened. She looked at her brother again and figured that she must look pretty bad because he was crying like a baby.

"Dr . . . Drey," Kenda called him and he came closer to her. "N . . . no . . . tears."

"I'm sorry." Aundrey tried to wipe his face, but the tears kept coming. He touched her face lightly and pulled back when he noticed her wince.

Kenda looked at her parents with worry. "M . . . my baby."

Maxine smiled. "Your baby is fine. Apparently, you saved her life."

"Me?"

Xavier nodded. "The doctors are saying that because you kept your arms secured around your stomach, she was able to survive."

Kenda tried to smile, but the pain of her swollen face prevented it.

"Sweetie, Chantal and Roslyn are here to see you, so we're going to leave, okay?" Maxine leaned over and gently kissed the top of Kenda's head.

"Drey," Kenda called as her brother was about to leave along with her parents. "Stay."

There was a chair near the window and Aundrey pulled it closer to his sister's bed and sat down. He used the backs of his hands to dry the remaining moisture from his eyes.

Within seconds of Kenda's parents' departure, her best friends came rushing in. Chantal stood on one side of the bed and Roslyn on the other. Red eyes gave away that they'd both been crying.

"Do . . . I . . . look . . . th . . . that . . . bad?" Kenda mumbled, trying to smile again.

Chantal smiled slightly. "Yeah, girl, you do."

"Raymond's been asking for you," Roslyn informed. "The doctor won't let him leave his room. He's fine though. He's right down the hall and he's still the same old Ray." Roslyn tried to smile, but Kenda could still see her sadness.

Chantal attempted to lighten the mood by changing the subject. "Did you see Raymond's cousin? Girl, they look just alike. I thought they were brothers, except cuz looks better." She laughed softly.

Kenda's smile was getting a little better. Chantal and Roslyn chatted about various things, trying hard to avoid talking about the reason Kenda was there.

"Visiting hours are almost over, so we can't stay," Roslyn explained after they had spent just fifteen minutes in the room.

"But we'll be back tomorrow," Chantal promised.

They both kissed her head and walked out of the room. Aundrey still sat in the chair next to his sister's bed. The side rails didn't stop him from holding her hand.

"I'll kill him," Aundrey vowed, breaking the quietness in the room.

Kenda turned her eyes so she could see him. "N . . . no. Drey, no," she said.

"Why not? He tried to kill you . . . and Ray. He doesn't deserve to live."

She tried to shake her head, but to no avail. Her words continued to pour from her mouth with the speed of cane syrup. "God . . . spared . . . us. He . . . was . . . with us."

Aundrey seemed to calm, but she could still sense his anger. "So, you're saying that God saved you?" Her eyes answered yes. "But Kenda, your face is all bruised and Ray's out here stuck in a cast because of that jerk."

"But . . . we're . . . not . . . d . . . dead."

Kenda's mother came back into the room. "Aundrey, we have to go." She looked at Kenda. "We'll be back tomorrow, sweetheart."

Aundrey gave his sister's hand a tender squeeze. "I love you." He kissed her forehead.

Kenda smiled. "I love . . . you."

He walked out of the room with his arms around his mother and Kenda was left alone.

She looked up toward heaven and cracked a smile. "Thank you . . . Jesus." She closed her eyes and fell into a peaceful sleep.

Forty-eight hours later, Kenda felt much better than she had the nights before. The doctors had taken the brace off of her neck and she could finally fully open her eyes and look around her room. She smiled. There were so many flowers that their combined fragrances took away the usual sick hospital smell. She also had several cards, balloons, and fruit baskets. Many of her classmates had dropped by to visit her yesterday, even people she didn't really know, but recognized. Her teachers had excused her from all work until she got better and they assured her that her grades wouldn't suffer because of her absence.

Kenda was able to touch her stomach and she almost laughed aloud. She was nearly four months pregnant and her stomach was growing every day. She was happy that her daughter was okay. She didn't know what she would have done had something happened to her.

"Mommy is so . . . happy," Kenda said to her daughter as she rubbed her stomach. Her lips were still swollen, but she was able to speak a little better now.

She'd read somewhere that if a mother talked to her baby during pregnancy, the child could somehow actually hear her. She didn't know if it were true, but it wouldn't hurt to try. "I love you so much. I'm gonna . . . take . . . good care of you. You're going . . . to be the most loved, most spoiled baby girl . . . in the world."

"Talking to the baby?" A female nurse, pushing a breakfast cart, came in the room to check on her.

Kenda smiled. "Nev-aeh? I didn't know you . . . worked here."

"Every day from seven to seven," she said "I was off Saturday, Sunday, and Monday. My sister had an important dance recital and begged me to fly up to Howard to see it. But when Ron called me and told me what was going on, I made sure that they assigned you to my station because we have the best nurses over here." She checked the heart monitor. "How are you feeling?"

"Much better," Kenda responded. "I can move my . . . lips a lot better. Sunday, it sounded as if I hadn't talked . . . in years."

Nevaeh laughed. "Well, you're actually healing much quicker than the doctors expected." She checked the fluids that were being fed into Kenda's arms. "The swelling has gone down a great deal since you came in and your bruises are healing also." She looked down at Kenda. "God was with you, Kenda."

"I know. I was praying so . . . hard and I just kept on . . .

singing." She tried to laugh. "I heard the medics saying that I was out . . . of my mind, but I wasn't. I was just praising God."

Nevaeh smiled. "I heard. They seriously thought that you were on drugs or something, but once they found out the whole story, they just thought that you may have been in shock. I knew what it was though. It was God. It had to be God."

Kenda smiled. "It was. I know it because . . . when Jerome was . . . hitting me, I couldn't feel a thing. My . . . my only concerns were my baby and praying."

"Well, that surely got you through," Nevaeh said. "I have some other patients to check on, but I'll be back a little later. Raymond wants to see you, but I told him that he couldn't get up." She shrugged apologetically. "Doctor's orders."

Kenda nodded. "I understand."

Nevaeh walked out of the room and closed the door behind her. Kenda closed her eyes and once again thanked God for all He'd done. She looked at the breakfast cart that Nevaeh had left and frowned. She rubbed her growling stomach.

"I can't . . . wait to get you home, so I can feed you . . . some real food," Kenda told her baby as she pulled the cart toward the bed.

She nibbled on the soupy grits, unseasoned eggs, and cold sausage, and then finished it off with the orange juice that contained more pulp than juice. It was a horrible meal and she frowned as she pushed the tray away from the bed.

"You didn't like the food either, huh?"

Kenda smiled as Raymond came into the room. "I thought Nevaeh told you not to . . . get out of bed."

"I needed to see you." He seemed to be okay with the exception of the cast on his arm and the stitches below his right eye.

Kenda looked away. "I'm sorry."

He came closer to her bed and took her hand. "Kenda, you have *nothing* to be sorry about. If anything, I'm sorry for letting you go into that house by yourself."

Kenda shook her head. "You shouldn't . . . have even come up there. I told you to just call the police."

Raymond grinned sheepishly. "I was sitting in the car watching the clock, and as soon as it hit the fifteen minute mark, I called the cops. Then I let about another thirty seconds go by before I went up there myself." His smile disappeared. "I could hear him screaming at you from outside the door. I'd planned just to go up and see what was going on, maybe talk him out of doing whatever it was that he was about to do, but when I saw him sitting on top of you, I just lost it.

"It was like you were just lying there in some type of daze, and you were singing. I think that's what kept me focused." He smiled again. "That voice of yours is so powerful. It was like as long as you sang, I had enough strength to put Jerome's lights out." He laughed softly. "Wish you would have told me that the brotha had some hands though."

Kenda squeezed his hand affectionately. "You know, I was alert the . . . entire time. I just couldn't . . . move . . . I *wouldn't* move. I put everything in God's hands. I think . . . singing helped me to do that. Otherwise, I . . . would have been terrified."

Raymond looked down at her stomach, touched it lightly with their intertwined hands, and smiled. "I hear you're a *shero*."

Kenda laughed lightly. "No, I just did . . . what I had to do to . . . keep my baby here."

Silence occupied the space for a few moments, and then Raymond said, "Kenda, I love you."

Kenda gazed into his eyes. "I love . . . you too, Ray." She could tell there was more on his mind.

"I want you to know that I will always love you," he continued. "And . . . and I want us to be together."

"But . . . but what about the baby?" She was confused. "I thought . . . I thought you didn't want—"

He shook his head. "When I saw you in that apartment, I thought I was gonna lose you for good. It made me realize that none of us have as much time as we think we have on this earth. If I die tomorrow, I want to die happy, knowing that you were with me." He smiled down at her. "Besides, baby girl is going to need a father figure. Now, I'm not saying that I'm gonna sign the birth certificate or nothing like that. But I would like to help you . . . you know."

"Raise her?" Kenda asked. "Ray, I . . . can't let you do that."

"I'm not asking you to." He smiled. "I'm telling you that I am going to be there for you and her. I could be like . . . her godfather or something, and if a few years from now that happens to change . . ." He stopped and shrugged, leaving the rest up to her imagination.

Kenda smiled. "Ray, are . . . you propos . . . ing?"

Raymond's facial expression turned serious when he said, "No . . . I'm promising." He leaned down and kissed her lips softly.

Kenda smiled. This was how she wanted it to be. She'd finally gotten her man . . . for good and this time she wasn't letting go.

Epilogue

Five months later . . .

The trial was almost over and Jerome was facing several years in prison. Kenda had been asked to testify against him, and she readily agreed. She revealed their entire relationship in front of a judge, jury, and a room full of strangers. She'd even been questioned about her unborn child's paternity and hesitantly admitted that she was carrying Jerome's child. The shocked expression that spread across Jerome's face at that revelation would forever be etched in Kenda's mind.

Now, Kenda closed her eyes as she held on tight to her mother's hand. Maxine seemed to be unfazed by her daughter's loud screaming and strong grip; she was too busy trying to keep Kenda focused on the task at hand. Kenda had asked for a natural birth and now she was regretting it. She was tired of her mother telling her to be calm and just breathe. How was she supposed to do that when she had seven pounds of human flesh coming out of her body?

"I need something!" she shouted. "Anything! Please. Oh, God, please!"

It was as if her mother, doctor, and nurse were ignoring her as she screamed for something that would help ease the pain she was being forced to endure. During the first two hours, Kenda hadn't wanted anything because she was determined to have her baby naturally, just like her mother had done with both her deliveries. Early on, contractions had been several minutes apart, causing her very little discomfort during the minutes in between them. But now, she would have taken a brick to the head if that would take her mind off the suffering she had been enduring for the past hour.

Kenda could just imagine her family and friends listening to her screams from the waiting room. Raymond, Chantal, and Roslyn would mostly likely be praying; her father was surely pacing, and Aundrey was probably sitting impatiently, wondering when they would be able to leave the place that housed the "sick and the shut-in," as he liked to call them.

"Dr. Akeem, *please*," Kenda begged. Nevaeh was the attending nurse. Kenda's eyes pleaded with her too. She was a mother. It wasn't that long ago when she was giving birth. She had to know how excruciating this experience was. Why was she standing there smiling instead of helping her? If Kenda had a blunt object, she'd hurl it at Nevaeh and knock that stupid grin right off her face.

"Kenda, you're too far in your dilation," Dr. Akeem explained. "It's time to push."

Kenda held on tighter to her mother's hand as Maxine continued to tell her to breathe. Kenda inhaled and exhaled as she'd been taught in the Lamaze classes that she had taken just for this occasion.

"Come on, Kenda," Maxine said as she wiped her daughter's forehead. "You can do this."

"Push!" Dr. Akeem told her.

Kenda took a deep breath and leaned forward, pushing with all her might. She prayed that her daughter would just pop out and that would be the end, but she knew that wouldn't happen so she continued to breathe, prepared herself for the next urge to push . . . .which was coming right now.

"Baby, you're doing great," her mother encouraged.

"You're doing excellent, Kenda," she heard Neveah say.

"Push!" Dr. Akeem said again.

Kenda pushed as if her life depended on it. All she wanted was for this to be over, but her daughter seemed to be taking her precious time.

"Ah, there's a head in the room," Dr. Akeem announced.

"Oh, honey, you're doing so well," Maxine rooted.

Kenda clinched her jaws. This wasn't some Atlanta Falcons game and she didn't need any dumb cheerleaders. She wondered what would happen if she just hauled off and told her mother to shut up. But Kenda wasn't in so much pain that she'd lost her common sense.

"Last one," Dr. Akeem said to her relief. "Make it good. Now, push!"

Kenda did as she was told and relaxed when she heard the loud cries of her baby girl. She lay back on the pillow and smiled through a flood of tears.

"Ten fingers, ten toes. She's beautiful," Dr. Akeem declared, his strong accent filling the room.

Kenda watched through blurred vision as Nevaeh helped clean off the baby before wrapping her in a pink blanket and handing her to Kenda. She was so happy, not only because her labor had finally ended after what she felt was a grueling three hours, but also because God had blessed her with a healthy baby girl. Kenda looked for signs of resemblance. The baby had Kenda's heart-shaped face, light brown skin, and dark brown hair. She had the nose that Xavier and Aundrey shared, and she had Maxine's perfectly pouted lips. Nothing on her baby's face even remotely looked like Jerome.

"Thank you, Jesus," Kenda whispered.

* * *

"So have you chosen a name?" Dr. Akeem asked Kenda, several minutes later, when the rest of her family and friends had been allowed inside the room.

Kenda had been looking through several baby name books over the past few weeks, and there were so many names that explained how she felt about her daughter that she'd had a hard time trying to choose. Her friends had tried offering their choices, but she was not going to name her child Ramona, Aundrea, LaKenda, or Chantal. She wanted something that would describe what she'd gone through to get to this point in her life. Something that would let everyone know that her daughter had been a gift from God. And just yesterday, she had finally found the name that fit those two qualifications.

Kenda looked up at her doctor and smiled. "Angel Janelle."

"What?" Aundrey asked. "What happened to Aundrea?"

Kenda looked at her brother and rolled her eyes. "*Angel Janelle*. Angel because that's what she is, and Janelle because that means God is gracious." She looked down at her daughter. "And He has been."

Nevaeh smiled. "I like it."

"Me too," Maxine said, with Xavier nodding his approval.

Kenda looked up at Raymond, wanting his opinion the most.

He smiled. "Angel Janelle?" He gazed down at the child in Kenda's arms. "I like it too."

Kenda smiled as she gazed down at her newborn baby girl. "Angel Janelle Tyson. I love it."

Me too.

Group Discussion Questions

1. What was your favorite part of this story? Why?

2. If there was one outcome of a scene or event in the book that you could change, which would it be, how would you change it, and why?

3. It was established early on that Kenda only dated men who could financially provide for her. What problems arise when women search for quantity instead of quality in men?

4. Despite Kenda's relationship with Jerome, Raymond's feelings for her were evident from beginning to end. If you were him, would you have put up with Kenda's attitude as her infatuation with Jerome grew?

5. Why do you believe Kenda refused to break up with Jerome after she found out he was a drug dealer? Do you think it was truly because she loved him?

6. After Kenda's first physical encounter with Jerome, she vented to her best friends in hopes of receiving comfort and advice. Would you have agreed with Roslyn's suggestion for Kenda to break up with Jerome before things got out of hand, or with Chantal, who told Kenda to give him one more chance?

7. Kenda's parents were so wrapped up in their work as lawyers that they didn't realize they were neglecting

their children. How important do you think it is for a child's parent to be involved in and knowledgeable about every aspect of the child's life? How different do you believe Kenda's attitude toward men and relationships would have been had her parents been more active in her life?

8. Jerome seemed to be genuine concerning his love for Kenda, but his actions always showed otherwise. Do you think his way of dealing with his anger was completely a result of his past?

9. Kenda's feelings for Raymond were suppressed for the majority of the novel, but came to consciousness later on. When Kenda claimed that it was impossible for her to love two people as she did Jerome and Raymond, do you think she was truly in love with both or only one of them? Is it possible to romantically love or *be in love* with more than one person?

10. Roslyn's story of her life before meeting Kenda and Chantal seemed to have some sort of impact on Kenda's decision concerning her pregnancy. If you were in Kenda's shoes, what decision would you have made?

11. For readers of *Living Consequences* and/or *Testing Relationships*: Were you surprised with Ronald and Nevaeh's appearance in this novel? Had they not been introduced to Kenda, and regardless of Raymond's continuous invitations, do you think she would have been as drawn toward the church as she had been?

12. Pastor McKinley's New Year's message caused Kenda to feel convicted and realize what true love really meant. Can you recall a time when you may have forgotten that

despite the worldly definitions of "love," God's love was always sufficient? If so, how did you come to realize this truth?

13. Do you think Kenda's last encounter with Jerome would have been the same even if she had handled the situation differently?

14. Periodically throughout the novel, Kenda heard the whispers of God in her heart. She was unfamiliar with the voice and was most times frightened when she heard it. What reactions do you experience when God speaks to you? How often do you find yourself *not* taking His advice or listening to what He has to say?

15. For anyone who finds themselves in a situation of domestic violence or in a relationship where you fear for your safety, please tell someone you can trust, whether it be a family member, friend, or a trusted person in authority, such as your pastor, teacher, counselor, or mentor. Also you may contact the National Domestic Violence hotline at 1-800-799-SAFE (7233) or 1-800-787-3224.

AUTHOR BIO

Brittney Holmes is the daughter of Jonathan Bellamy and national bestselling author, Kendra Norman-Bellamy. She currently resides on the campus of the University of Georgia where she is a freshman, majoring in Journalism. As an active and involved student, she is a member of UGA HEROs, an organization that focuses on improving the quality of life for children affected by and infected with HIV/AIDS; a member of the Community Service Committee, Political Action Committee (PAC), Social & Cultural Programming Committee (SCPC), Black Educational Support Team (BEST), the National Association of Black Journalists (NABJ), and she serves on the Freshman Advisory Board of the Black Affairs Council (BAC).

Blessed to find her passion early in life, Brittney became a published author at the age of sixteen, when her short story, *Holiday Healing*, appeared in the best selling self-published anthology, *The Midnight Clear*. Now nineteen years old, Brittney enjoys "living on purpose" as a traditionally published author under Urban Books's Urban Christian imprint. *Grace And Mercy* is Brittney's third full-length novel, preceded by her award-winning debut book, *Living Consequences*, and its sequel, *Testing Relationships*.

Readers may visit Brittney online at www.BrittneyHolmes. com, or connect with her via MySpace at www.myspace.com/ authorbrittneyholmes.